MIDNIGHT SOMEWHERE

A SHORT-STORY COLLECTION

BOOKS BY
JOHNNY COMPTON

The Spite House
Devils Kill Devils
Midnight Somewhere

MIDNIGHT SOMEWHERE

A SHORT-STORY COLLECTION

JOHNNY COMPTON

Midnight Somewhere

Cover illustration/design & interior design by Jeff Wong.
Author Photo by Luis Scott/Scott Photography/San Antonio, TX.

Published by *Weird Tales*® Presents and Blackstone Publishing.

www.WeirdTales.com
www.BlackstonePublishing.com

Blackstone Publishing
31 Mistletoe Road
Ashland, Oregon 97520

ISBN: 979-8-228-36479-0
Fiction/Science Fiction/General

Printed in the United States of America

First Edition: 2025

10 9 8 7 6 5 4 3 2 1

CONTENTS

XII
יב
12
١٢
十二

FFUNS

Originally aired on *PseudoPod* (March 6, 2020, Episode 692)

Holding the unlabeled black videocassette somehow reassured her of the legitimacy of its contents. With that reassurance came effervescent nausea, an ugly, unreal sensation befitting the place she was in and the sight that awaited her.

There were thousands of purported "ffuns flicks" online, some more believable than others. Some were made for a laugh with puppets or shoddy animation, some made with award-worthy care and effects by aspiring filmmakers. None, however, were authentic. "Mick"—the big man with a gravel-lined throat and a measured manner of speaking—had guaranteed her this.

"We do not tolerate leaks. Cannot afford to. Confidentiality is critical to us. As for our buyers, they are not likely to spend a fortune on a 'one-of-one' item just to share it freely with strangers. And our suppliers—even those who never make it past the prospective stage—know better than to share our business."

She nodded, confident in his truth and—as a prospective supplier—understanding the warning within said truth. One of Mick's colleagues had met her at the door, frisked her, and taken her phone before bringing her inside the building, a not-yet-gutted science center on an abandoned college campus. The man had escorted her to a first-floor classroom full of stained and weathered lab tables, empty or shattered glass beakers and vials, and overturned stools. The hand-smeared chalk scrawl on the blackboard appeared to be the remnants of an unfinished lesson.

At the front of the classroom was a television cart the likes of which she hadn't seen since elementary school, and on the second shelf of the cart, underneath a tube television set, was a VCR. Both the television and VCR were plugged into a portable power bank on the floor. Static played on the television screen. She stood in front of it, videocassette in hand, every type of stinging, winged insect in the world flying in her stomach.

"Whenever you are ready," Mick said. "If you are still not sure after what you see, we will part ways."

Again, she nodded. She put the tape into the VCR, pushed the Play button, and straightened her posture to steel herself for what she was about to see.

On-screen appeared two men in a dark room. One lay supine on the floor wearing only black boxer shorts, the bare minimum for modesty. The footage wasn't as noisy and opaque as she'd expected, and it was clear that the man on the floor—bald, bearded, and withered—was quite pale. The man who crouched beside him wore a surgeon's mask, an indistinct long-sleeve shirt, and black pants, and he held a knife. The camera zoomed in on the masked man who showed off each flat side of the knife, as well as its edge, as though hawking it for an infomercial. He showed his free hand to the camera, then pushed the tip of the knife into his index finger just far enough to draw a bead of blood.

The camera pulled back to capture the complete scene again. The masked man seized the pale man's arm by the wrist, held it up, and stuck the knife through the cold white flesh, then withdrew the blade.

No blood came from the pale man's wound. A viscous, yellowish fluid beaded up in the slit. The pale man did not flinch. Satisfied with his demonstration, the man in the mask exited the scene.

From the left of the screen entered a third man, bearded as well, but not bald like the man on the floor, nor as gray. He carried a long metal pipe, its weight evident in the way it resisted his grip in favor of gravity. It surprised her that this man was unmasked. Mitch and his organization must have had other means of ensuring the confidentiality of their "suppliers." Perhaps it was as simple as the implied threat he'd made earlier—likely made to anyone who would appear on camera—coupled with trusting that no one would believe them even if they were inclined to tell their story.

Her nausea grew as she thought of some wealthy stranger seeing her face on tape, pausing at a point of preference to study whatever emotion was most evident in her expression at that moment.

The man wielding the pipe knelt before the body and gingerly touched its forehead, almost as if checking for a fever. He bent over and kissed its cheek. When he rose, his eyes were shut tight. He took a deep breath, another, another, each inhalation coming quicker than the last as though building toward a crescendo. She could sense that he was keeping a scream chained inside his chest.

He raised the pipe and brought it down onto the pale man's head, throwing his body weight into the blow. Before this moment, the video had been silent, and she had unconsciously presumed no audio had been recorded. The ping of metal meeting skull made her shudder.

It is a strange and obscene thing to see a corpse beaten. She could not have guessed how unusual it would be until seeing it for herself. The body, of course, did not move as though enduring an assault, but rather as though the man who clubbed it was merely trying to awaken it from a stubborn sleep. The days-long dead do not react to anything done to them. They do not raise a hand to defend themselves or shrink from the next impending strike or yell or moan or otherwise indicate that they are suffering.

The man administering the beating made his own suffering known, however. His pained, pitiful whining began after the fourth strike. It was a primal pleading that predated language. The man seemed intent on not speaking, and she thought she understood this. She would not want her words captured on tape either. It would be enough to have your face exposed, your deeds and desperation documented for someone else's … pleasure? Curiosity? Whatever their motivation, there were people who would pay a fortune to possess this, and your words—your thoughts—were one thing you weren't obligated to give them during the process. But the man weakened. She could see that this was more difficult than he could have imagined. He broke.

"Goddammit, Billy, please!"

Another strike, now targeting the collar and upper chest.

"Billy, get up! You have to … damn it, please don't make me …" He turned to the camera, looked past it. "Why isn't it working? You said this would work. In the video you showed me, that girl came back almost right away."

Whoever he spoke to did not answer him. The man turned back to Billy, surveyed the damage already done—not visible on-screen due to the positioning of the camera—and retched. He gathered himself, raised the pipe again, and beat Billy across the chest. The crack of bone echoed. Billy did not get up as the man had implored. The man turned to the camera again.

"What am I doing wrong? Why isn't it working?"

Again, no audible answer.

"I can't keep doing this. There's not going to be anything left of him by the time I'm done. Just tell me what I'm doing wrong, please?"

The silence was suffocating, painful. The man dropped the pipe and turned to leave, then stopped himself. He screamed himself breathless, screamed with his entire body, screamed as if doing so would purge an illness from his cells. He picked the pipe up and turned to Billy again, delivering two more shots—the hardest yet—to Billy's skull, chips of bone flying with each hit.

As he raised his arm for another strike, Billy raised his arm to stop the attack. The same arm that the man in the surgical mask had cut earlier. Blood now streamed from the cut, but only for a second before it sealed itself. A warmer, healthier color overtook the paleness of Billy's skin. With one hand holding his attacker's wrist, Billy touched his face with his free hand and sat up. The damage done to his head had mostly disappeared already. The few cracks and craters that remained healed in seconds in full view of the camera.

The puzzled look on Billy's face was so profound it felt infectious, as though it could make you forget how to pronounce your own name if you looked at him for too long. He turned to the man who'd bludgeoned him back to life. The man whose love and want and will had unkilled him.

"Henry? What're you … Was I dreaming? I think I was just having the most awful—"

Henry hugged Billy as though he might vanish. His choking, ragged sobs turned the footage into something voyeuristic, more invasive than it had been just a moment before. As Billy, still bewildered, at last hugged Henry back, the video returned to static.

She stared at the screen for some time after, the men behind her in no hurry to turn off the set, take out the tape, or do anything else to disrupt her apparent trance.

The woman pictured herself in action, on the big screen of a buyer's private theater as they sat alone and watched her beat and rip and claw at the body of someone she loved until that body breathed again. In her mind's eye, she watched the watcher, the audience of one, who leaned forward in their seat and did not blink for a half minute or more, marveling at the woman on the screen who could commit such violence without a sound.

She turned to Mick and his colleagues. "What do we do next?"

The ghost town, much like the old campus, was not unknown or forgotten. It did not "hide in plain sight." It was simply neglected. Forty miles southwest of the city, not too long of a drive. The ghost town didn't have a notable history; it wasn't a place where industry had once thrived but then withered, or where some horrific calamity had killed erstwhile promise. It was alone in the middle of nowhere, one of hundreds of such places in Texas, which had a surplus of nowhere.

The meeting place was the two-story brick courthouse. Unused since the 1940s, it was not the ruin she expected it to be. The windows were caked in grime, but unbroken. Even under the moonlight she could see the bricks had been baked and bleached by a century of summers, but they weren't crumbling. None looked out of place. From what she could see as her car crept over the small hill leading into the ghost town, there was no damage to the courthouse's roof. The building, or at least the exterior, was surprisingly whole.

She parked behind the building. One of Mick's men greeted her, and she followed this man inside to a spacious, windowless room on the second floor. A former office, she guessed, now empty of everything save for Mick's men, their camera and microphone, and the mostly naked body of a familiar man lying on the floor. She had braced herself for the sight of this body and was pleased not to pause or gasp or otherwise outwardly react upon seeing it. Yes, she felt the insects flying and stinging her insides again, with greater urgency now than when she'd viewed the videotape days before, but that was the least of the reactions she could have expected. It boded well for her intention not to give the camera—the eventual viewer—any emotion when it came time for her to perform.

The man in the surgical mask—the same one she'd seen on the tape, or did Mick's men rotate in that role?—approached the body with his knife and authenticated the cadaver. That done, he stepped behind the camera, joining his colleagues.

Mick approached her before she entered the shot and held out a large rusty crowbar, hers to take. They had not discussed what weapon she would use, and, until this point, she'd started to worry that she had made a mistake in not furnishing her own. She could only guess their reasons for not telling her they would give her a weapon—much less *what* weapon they'd give her. Perhaps it was to further agitate her emotions. It wasn't enough that she would soon be trying to beat the soul back into the corpse of someone she loved and had lost so recently, but she'd be doing so with something crude and unwieldy.

She took the crowbar and gripped it tightly, the rust chafing her palms. The discomfort felt important, meaningful. If anything about this felt too easy, she was sure it would not work.

She approached the body, glanced at the director who stood behind the camera, and waited for his signal that she could begin. The director nodded, and she held the crowbar up above her head. She had avoided looking at the face of the man on the floor until that moment when she had to spot her target before the first swing. He did not look like he was sleeping, her loved one. He did not appear to "be at rest," despite the words appearing so often in the poem his mother had written and recited at his service. He looked like what he was: dead. Not a thing that you do, like rest or sleep, but a thing that you become. No longer human. No longer a son or brother or lover or anything that matters.

The crowbar seemed to gain weight as her legs and stomach and arms jellified. The burn and rush of grief rose from her chest, through her throat, into her cheeks and eyes.

Stop it. You will not give them this, she thought, and did not have to shut her eyes to picture the words in darkness or hold back tears.

The lights behind the camera blinded her to anything more than a couple of feet beyond them, making the room appear darker and larger than it was. She pictured herself on the screen of a home theater again, the buyer sitting in their seat with a glass of wine in hand, or holding a pen and pad, or nothing at all.

They think you're going to cry, or scream, or fall. You're not going to give them that. You're going to keep it all for yourself and for what you're here to do.

She swung, a clean, swooping golf swing that crashed the curved end of the crowbar into the corpse's temple. The crowbar bounced off the corpse's head, then off its shoulder, its skull undoubtedly fractured and its neck possibly broken, but there was no other movement. No reaction. It would take much more to bring him back. She had it all to give.

Their motel room awaited them back in the city. She had checked in earlier in the day, before driving to the ghost town. She'd needed to be sure the room and the location were as Mick had promised. The motel was small and quiet, one-story throughout. A place patronized by people with a vested interest in minding their own business.

Inside their room was their "payment package." A flat fee in the low six figures, which would amount to anywhere from 4 to 10 percent of the tape's sale price, depending on the bidding. More valuable, perhaps, was the paperwork that accompanied the money. New identities, complete with requisite documents. An obvious necessity for the formerly deceased, but also a welcome option for the one who reawakened them and wanted to join them in a new future, particularly if they were already a fugitive who needed to burn their past.

She'd sneaked a peek at her portion of the packet earlier and wondered how long it would take her to get used to her new name and learn not to respond to the old one.

Inside the car, her loved one shivered in the passenger seat. He had, at least, stopped repeatedly telling her "thank you" ten or so minutes ago.

"I can remember it," he said for the fourth time.

"Try not to think about it," she had responded the three previous times. This had only managed to calm him for a brief spell, so now she said, "What do you remember?"

"Being heavy, and being in the dark," he said.

"Heavy?"

"Too heavy to move. Not like I *couldn't* move—not like I'd lost the ability. Just didn't have the strength. Too heavy. That's how it felt."

She had no response to this, and the silence between them made her impatient with how long the drive was taking. She pressed the gas pedal a little harder. They were close enough now to the motel for her to feel as though they should have arrived already. The sooner they got to the motel, the sooner she could get to work on seizing the future, cease dwelling on things she wished had gone better, and on ugly but necessary acts.

The man in the passenger seat started to shiver and fidget again, as if all the sensations that came with living were an agitation to him, which she supposed they must be. She was surprised at how well she had accepted the reality of his revival. It was one thing to see it on tape, another to believe it was possible, and another still to experience it.

When his body had first lurched to life and begun healing, she'd been sure that Mick and his team had drugged her. It was beyond dreamlike. Dreams are far more disjointed. Seeing the body jump and its bones mend and its gashes close did not strike her as unreal, but hyperreal. Like she was undergoing a mental reawakening to coincide with witnessing a physical one. Everything in the world was more vivid and immediate than it had been moments before. The memories of everything she'd experienced prior to that moment instantly became a degree hazier and that much further removed from immediacy, to the point that later, in the car, she had to concentrate to fully remember why she'd gone through all this trouble and effort to bring this man back from the dead.

After reaching the motel and parking in front of their room, she came to the passenger side to help him out. His legs were sturdier now than when she'd had to guide him down the courthouse stairs and out to her car.

"They do not mean to be rude," Mick had said of his men, who had stood and watched without offering a hand. "They just do not feel comfortable coming into contact with those who have come back."

She had understood. They had no love for the bodies that were the central players in their films. If they *did* have love for them, they might not have needed people like her. The ritual was simple enough; they could have performed it themselves and saved an expense if not for the need of someone who loved the deceased urgently enough to bring them back.

She unlocked the motel door and allowed the man to enter first. He started to thank her once again, but froze when he saw the full-length mirror she had set up inside, facing the doorway. She stood behind him. Being a foot shorter than he was, she could not see his reflected eyes as he saw himself reading what she had written on the mirror with a black marker.

I KNOW
IT WAS
YOU

The room still smelled faintly of ink. She stepped inside and closed the door behind her. The sound of the door closing made the man flinch. He did not risk any abrupt movement. A thin, tattered lie was weaving itself together in his brain; she could just about see it coming together through the back of his head.

"Cassandra, wait—"

A pop of gunfire cut him off before he could finish. The bullet entered his back, passed through his heart, exited his sternum, and embedded itself in the mirror so fast it seemed to have occupied all these places simultaneously. He fell to the floor facedown. She stood above him, aimed carefully, and fired two more shots into the back of his head.

In recent fantasies she'd had of this moment, she'd pictured herself staring into his eyes so he could see how the love she felt for him had turned to poison because of his betrayal. So that he would know that it hurt her to do this, but she'd spent her energy back on the second floor of the courthouse, with the crowbar. She was too tired to turn him over so he could face her.

She lay on the bed. No one would come knocking at the door in response to the gunshots, at least not until after they had seen her leave. One of Mick's people would arrive then to handle the cleanup. She'd take off with her payment package soon. For now, she had earned a brief rest.

Beyond being glad it was all over, and feeling sore and worn from considerable exertion and lack of sleep, she felt an unexpected sense of accomplishment.

And of the many incredible, improbable things she had done to bring herself to this moment, she was most satisfied with having the discipline to not respond to her old name.

XII
יב
١٢
十二
12

THE DEATH/GRIP CHALLENGE

Originally published in *Strange Horizons* (May 18, 2020)

The award-winning talent assembled for *Death/Grip*, juxtaposed with the pitiful product, made an argument for it being the most disappointing horror film ever made. Many less competent films had preceded it, but *Death/Grip* didn't have the excuses of an inexperienced cast and crew, minimal budget, or rushed production. Watching it was like watching each member of an Olympic relay team trip and fall. It was sad, comical, farcical, and, by the end, seemingly conspiratorial.

Alicia wasn't surprised when it became her father's favorite movie.

"Have you seen the *Death/Grip* Challenge meme?" Benito Oliveira said.

"Yeah, it's pretty funny," she said.

"It's people pretending not to kill something with their off hand," he said, as though she hadn't responded.

"It's dumb," said Robert, Alicia's uncle. He was driving his niece to school, then taking his brother to a job interview at Robert's office.

"You've got no sense of humor," Benito said. "Alicia thinks it's funny, right, kiddo?"

"She's humoring you," Robert said. "I'm sure she also doesn't like being called 'kiddo' at her age."

"I can speak for myself," Alicia said.

Benito looked back at Alicia and winked at her. She smiled. Part of her hoped he wouldn't get the job, though he needed it. He had always been more boots and hard hats than suits and dress shoes. An eight-to-five tied to a desk and phone would be hard enough for him even without working for his brother. Living under Robert's roof *and* having to report to him might prove torturous.

Alicia took her phone out, searched for *Death/Grip* image macros, and found one of a man pretending to reach for a lone slice of pizza. He seized his left wrist with his right hand as if to restrain it. He bugged his eyes and drew his lips back in an exaggerated expression of horror. The text at the top of the image read "NO! I PROMISED MY WIFE THE LAST SLICE!" At the bottom was the most quoted line of the movie: "IT'S NOT ME, IT'S THE DEATH/GRIP!"

Alicia texted the image to her father. A few seconds later Benito laughed, a sputtering, breathy sound that made him sound like an old engine that ran on air.

"What're you laughing at?" Robert asked.

"You wouldn't like it," Benito said.

"Well, I hope you get all your laughs out now before the interview. Unless you're trying to tank it."

Benito reached over to put a reassuring stump on his brother's shoulder. Because there was no hand at the end of Benito's wrist, just a smooth nub. "Come on, Robert," Benito said, "don't you think I can *handle* it?"

Robert grunted and bit his lip to keep from saying anything. He hated any mention of his brother's long-lost, amputated hand. This just made Benito smile wider. He turned to wink at Alicia again. She was happy to see him happy. She tried to picture him maintaining that happiness while sitting two cubicles down from Robert for eight hours a day but instead saw the knot of his tie sloppy and loosened, his antiperspirant failing him as one customer after another rejected his sales pitch.

Then she imagined him sneaking a glimpse at the latest *Death/Grip* meme on his cell and stifling his laughter, and figured that would get him through each day. She shouldn't worry about him so much, though it was hard not to.

The author of the book that *Death/Grip* was based on wrote a blog post disowning the adaptation before its release. Many people online—even discounting the ever-present misogynist sect—deemed her an ingrate. Then rumors surfaced about how the film differed so much from the novel that it would only have character names and the basic concept in common. Then the first trailer showcased a less satirical and more somber tone than the novel. Finally, the film had its festival debut and early reviews characterized it as not merely bad, but gloriously so, on a level that only a failed message-horror film about a psychosomatic epidemic could reach.

Jokes at the film's expense didn't explode until the movie left theaters and came to streaming services. Its viewership soared, making it an even larger target. Soon, the *Death/Grip* Challenge meme was born.

Take a picture of yourself using your strong hand to keep your weak hand doing something evil. The more mundane the evil, the funnier the image. Add the appropriate text, and you were now part of the viral image macro sensation of the moment.

Alicia found a handful of the images amusing, usually those where people took a more creative approach to restraining their weak hand. Nimbly holding it underfoot or securing the thumb and forefinger with Chinese finger cuffs, for example. Most of the jokes were too obvious to be funny. The masturbation jokes grew stale within a day a two, as did most of the jokes about reaching for other indulgences—unhealthy foods, alcoholic drinks, and drug paraphernalia, mostly.

The more politically inclined took pictures of their rogue hand reaching for any book espousing an ideology they despised.

Despite typically being above such silliness, Alicia had to participate. Her friend Sam took a picture of Alicia in a store, reaching with her left hand for a DVD copy of *Death/Grip*. The top text stated, "NO! MY HAND THINKS PHYSICAL MEDIA IS STILL RELEVANT!"

At the bottom was the requisite quote: "IT'S NOT ME, IT'S THE DEATH/GRIP!"

She shared it and it briefly trended after *Death/Grip*'s lead actress reposted it, stating, "Okay, this one's not bad."

When she showed her dad how many likes and comments her post had received, he beamed like he was watching her walk the graduation stage two years early.

"You don't think it's a little strange?" Emily Oliveira said to her daughter over dinner. "He shares these images all day. It's a little much."

"He's just trying to stay sane at work," Alicia said. Benito had been offered the job at Robert's office immediately after his interview and started work the next day, a Wednesday. He posted two memes on the morning of his first day and three more in the afternoon. The next day he shared seven. Ten that Friday, more over the weekend, and even more when he was back to work on Monday. Yesterday, his fifth day on the job, he posted sixteen images and two videos during office hours, which Alicia figured had to be against policy. Was he trying to get fired?

Or was he just trying to keep his spirits up? Since he'd started working with Robert, he wasn't as upbeat in the car after school. He needed an outlet, and his missing hand was one of his favorite things to joke about. Something he *had* to joke about to keep from raging. *Death/Grip* and its associated challenge seemed uniquely suited to his circumstance and sense of humor.

His posts were getting grimmer because the challenge itself had taken a turn. People had graduated from restraining their rogue hand to pretending to punish it. Close-up images of damaged dummy hands—stabbed, burned, or broken—trended for a few days. Next came videos, the most popular being a man pretending to fry his hand on the stove. The video's creator insisted it was authentic, despite the hand looking like a ten-dollar Halloween decoration.

Still, it was all meant to be funny, so Alicia wasn't any more concerned about her father than she normally was.

"Wait, you're still following him on social?" Alicia said.

"Of course," Emily said. "We're still friends in real life, why not online?"

Alicia shook her head. "You should let him move on."

"It was *his* idea."

"Then you should both disconnect to let the other one move on."

Emily's brow furrowed and her head tilted as she prepared to go into a lecture, but she caught herself, took a breath, and relaxed. "You know, most kids in your position try to keep their parents together."

"It's way too late for that, isn't it?" Alicia said.

"Well ... yes, but that's not the point."

"If you weren't going to stay together because I *exist*, you aren't going to get back together because I say please."

Emily sighed and looked at her phone. Alicia pushed some food around her plate with her fork. After a brief silence, Emily gasped and nearly threw her phone across the counter.

"What is it?" Alicia said.

Emily gave Alicia her phone.

The video Benito had shared was titled "*Death/Grip* Challenge Gets Real for This Guy." In the thirty-second clip, a man knelt on top of his left hand, pinning it to the floor. The fingers twitched and stretched as though trying to free themselves. He held a hunting knife in his right hand. As he brought the knife down, the fingers tried to curl away from the blade.

The man sawed off his fingertips in two strokes. The blood and bits looked real enough, but Alicia was sure it was fake, as it came from the internet, which had an endless supply of false quotes, debunked claims, Photoshopped pictures, and faked videos. What bothered Alicia about the video was that her father had shared it. It wasn't silly or audacious enough for him to find it funny. Maybe the man in the video said something that made her dad laugh?

She turned up the volume on the phone as the video neared its end. The man raised his bleeding fingers to the camera and said, "Had to show it I was serious. Bet it won't go rogue on me again."

"Jesus, Dad, I hope you didn't think that was funny," Alicia said.

"Funny?" Emily said. "That's awful. See? I told you it was getting strange."

"You really want 'I told you so' points right now?"

"Could you talk to him about it when you see him, please? I would, but if I brought it up it would turn into an entirely different discussion."

"Sure," Alicia said. "I'll ask him about it tomorrow."

"And tell me what you find out. I just … I'd like to know."

"You're really worried about him."

"Just because you stop getting along with someone doesn't mean you stop caring about them," Emily said.

The video didn't last a day on the major social platforms—didn't last an hour on many of them—but in that time had already been viewed or heard of by enough people to become an inescapable story. Harold Pritchard of Portland, Oregon. Forty-nine years old, married, two daughters, owner of a small engine repair service. Nothing was known yet about what might have motivated an ostensibly ordinary, successful man to do what he'd done. That didn't stop the speculation. He had slapped his wife or one of his children. He'd groped his secretary. He was a hardcore fundamentalist punishing himself for onanism, because no matter how played out it was, the masturbation jokes would not die.

Alicia didn't care about Harold Pritchard. She cared about her father. She'd see him today after school. Until then, she'd have to wait and wonder. She didn't want to text him about the video, or even about how his day had gone. It was too easy to misinterpret a text. Even easier to ignore one.

At school, her classmates were back in on the *Death/Grip* Challenge, which had been on the doorstep of becoming last month's meme before Harold Pritchard's video. The question was not whether copycats would follow, but how far they would go.

"How long before someone really cuts their hand off?" Sam said. She sat with Alicia and Candice at the concrete benches in the courtyard during lunch.

"Another month, maybe," Candice said.

"Another month?" Sam said. "Hell no. End of the week. Probably some guy from Florida."

"It's *Wednesday*. You think somebody's going to go from zero to hand-off that quick?"

"Have you seen how crazy people are? Because people are capital-'cray' *crazy*. You never know what anybody's going to do, except that you always know that *some*body is going to do the *worst* sooner or later. With this, it's going to be sooner."

Candice shook her head. "I don't know. This guy just took his fingertips off. I could see somebody cutting some tendons or something, and then maybe working up to a pinky. Not their whole hand. Like if I lost my pinky tomorrow, that wouldn't be good, obvi, but after a while, I'd just be like, 'Oh well.' I'd miss it, but I wouldn't really *miss* it. But your whole hand? I feel like that would really suck."

"It really would," Alicia said flatly. Her friends looked at her, waited for her to say more. She knew they expected her to make a joke. She wasn't sensitive about her dad's hand. She shared his lightheartedness about it, but she wasn't feeling that today. She wasn't mad at her friends' jokes either; she was just worried about her dad.

Robert picked her up after school.

"Is Dad okay?" Alicia asked.

"He went straight to the guest room when we got home," Robert said. "Said he wasn't feeling well. I asked him if he wanted to come, and he said he didn't want to get you sick."

It reeked of a lie, but Alicia just said, "Oh." Less than a year ago, just before the divorce, Benito had picked her up one day as he always did, despite persistent sniffles and a dry cough. Alicia had called him Patient Zero and Typhoid Benny. He replied that he was suffering through the earliest stage of viral zombification and asked if she had it in her to put him down before he turned.

"Only if we make it as dramatic as possible," she had said.

Benito had smiled. "Well, tell your mother I love her very much."

"She knows."

"And tell your father he was one of the greats."

"Don't make me lie, damn you."

"Fine. Then promise me you'll tell your uncle he's an asshole."

"But … but I—"

"Promise!"

"But I already tell him every day!"

It hadn't been the first time they'd run that particular joke gauntlet when he'd been sick. Illness had never prevented him from sharing a laugh with her, much less sharing time. Either he was *very* sick, despite appearing healthy just yesterday, or something else was wrong.

Robert would not have lied about Benito being unwell, Alicia knew, but she wanted to blame him for her dad not being here. Hearing him refer to her dad's room as "the guest room" had annoyed her. At least Robert had stopped referring to it as "*my* guest room." A small change, but it was progress.

After a quiet car ride to Robert's house, Alicia went straight to Benito's room. She opened the door without knocking and found him in bed, atop the covers, phone in hand.

He turned to her. "Bobbito didn't tell you I'm sick, kiddo?"

"He did, but I wanted to see you. You don't look that sick. Do you need me to make you some soup or something?"

"I can make my own soup. Which, I guess, means you're right, I'm not really that sick after all."

"I didn't say you *weren't*, I said you didn't *look*—"

"I know what you said, and I know what you meant," Benito said. "Your dad's not quite as dumb as you think, kiddo."

"I've never thought that."

"First time for everything. Anyway, you didn't come in here to offer me soup, so what's on your mind? It's about what I posted last night, isn't it?"

Alicia sat beside him on the bed.

"What's going on with you?" she said. "I'm worried. Mom's worried too."

"I bet she is."

"Don't do that. She really is. Probably even Uncle Rob. Is it the job? If you don't want to work with him, you should tell him. I don't think anyone would blame you. You can always find another job."

He scoffed at the last part, though not with contempt, but as if he were swatting away an unearned compliment. "If I had known that sharing that video would be a big deal to you and your mom, I wouldn't have done it. Hell, it's not like it's the worst one I could have posted. You should see some of the others."

"Others?" Alicia said. "Where are you seeing other videos like that?"

"Dark web. I'm in deep."

"Dad."

"I joined a group for people like me. We watch them together."

"You mean other people missing a hand?" she said, speaking as frankly to him about it as he had always told her to. "Mom always thought you should join a support group. Mind if I tell her you're finally taking her advice?"

"She wouldn't approve of this group. We're probably a little more fringe than what she had in mind."

"Fringe like what? Militant?"

"Yeah. You ever heard of the Black Hand?" he said. "Well, we're the Lack Hand."

"Enough with the jokes. Especially when they're that bad."

"Okay. It's just a little private group for anyone missing a part of themselves. A foot, or an ear, or anything else. We're inclusive like that. And we all have our own stories about how we lost what we lost and why we have a right to feel bitter about it. The group was created by a psychotherapist who lost her right arm because of a drunk driver. She talks about how it's important for us to see every side of this. Some of us can laugh at it, some of us want to cry. Some feel mad enough to fight, or worse. The doc says it's important for us all to experience all of those emotions. She started sharing some of the self-harm videos with us a couple of days ago. She said it was good for us to get a jump on seeing them before they go viral. We can see them in our own supportive little space and get all our feelings out about it. I even get to talk about how mad it makes me sometimes. I've never been able to really talk about that with anyone. Not even your mom."

"You could talk to me," Alicia said.

"I'm not going to burden you with that, kiddo."

"I'm not really a kid anymore," Alicia said.

"I guess not. And maybe I wasn't all that sick today, but I sure didn't feel well. Still don't."

"Well, sitting alone in the dark won't help. Let's turn a light on. Maybe even get you into the living room, where there are some windows."

"Hey, we could watch that *Death/Grip* movie. I hear it's funny."

"Seriously?"

"Kidding. Let's see what's on Food Network. That never lets me down. Bobbito might even join us."

"We're sure we want that?"

"Be nice. He got me a job. I'm officially no longer a deadbeat."

"You never were," Alicia said.

Robert indeed joined them in the living room to watch television, and was even in a relatively good mood for a little while.

"I always wanted to take a cooking class," he said at the end of the second show they watched. "Ben, if I signed up for one, would you come with me?"

"Maybe," Benito said. "As long as they'll give us a little space to learn on our own. You know I like a hands-off approach."

Robert's face turned sour, and for once Alicia wished her father had shown a little restraint instead of needling her uncle.

"Don't you ever get tired of that?" Robert asked. "I know I do."

Benito held his stump toward his brother. "Hey, Bobbito. I'm giving you a thumbs-up, not a middle finger. Promise."

They continued watching television together for another hour, but hardly a word passed between them.

A yoga instructor from Charlotte posted a forty-second video in which she broke the fingers of her left hand one at a time.

In South Dakota, a construction worker with a nail gun put seven shots through his left hand.

A left-handed lawyer in San Francisco wrapped a string of firecrackers around his trembling right hand and lit the fuse.

None of these videos stayed long on the most popular sharing sites, but they were still easy to find.

Alicia had viewed these videos and dozens more. Seeing each person's bad hand convulse and cower almost convinced her that something more than mental illness or hysteria possessed these victims. It was as if the collective attention given to the film had pulled *Death/Grip*'s psychosomatic epidemic into the real world.

The alternative theory floating online was that Harold Pritchard's severed fingertips had been a blood sacrifice that brought the *Death/Grip* disease to life. Alicia made herself laugh this notion off each time it popped into her head, just as she made herself find and watch each of these videos as they appeared on LiveLeak or other shock sites. It was the only way she could keep tabs on what she knew her father was watching.

Benito hadn't responded to her text messages or calls for a week. She had asked her mother if she'd heard from him, and Emily had said, "I was going to ask you the same thing." The only information Alicia had on her father came from Robert, who picked her up from school on the appointed days, passing along that her father wasn't up for a visit.

"He still isn't feeling well?" she said.

"I think he's tired from adjusting to the job. It's an earlier wake-up than he's been used to. He doesn't look sick when I see him at the office."

"You don't see him at the house?"

"Not much. He stays in the room. I think he's just getting extra sleep."

Alicia didn't ask for more details. Robert sounded concerned, but not so much that he'd say more than, "Ben will be fine," if she pressed him.

She endured her father's silence until she was awakened after midnight by a phone call. When she saw her father's smiling face on the caller ID, she snapped out of her grogginess and answered.

"What's wrong?"

"Nothing's wrong," he said.

"You avoid me for a week and then you call me out of the blue this late? Bullshit there's nothing wrong."

"Hey, language."

"Don't 'hey' me. I've been out of my mind worried about you."

"I'm sorry. I didn't mean to upset you. I'll call back later—"

"Wait," she said, her heart pounding. "I'm sorry. Please don't hang up."

"I wasn't avoiding you," Benito said. "I've just been busier than usual."

"I get it. You're back to work."

"Yeah, there's that. And there's been other stuff."

"Like what?"

"The group I told you about," Benito said. "They're really helping me with some overdue therapy. I won't bore you with details. Plus I don't want you to hear your old man sounding weak."

"Don't worry about that. You can tell me anything."

"Your mother has a foot fetish."

"What? Oh, gross, Dad!"

"You said 'anything.'" He laughed, but it didn't sound natural. "Seriously, I'm sorry for not getting back to you before now. I don't have a good reason. And I don't have one for calling so late either. I just needed to let you know that your dad's okay. You shouldn't be worrying about me, kiddo."

"Of course I should. I'm always going to worry about you."

"Well, then I did a shit job of parenting. Kids aren't supposed to worry about their parents. It should be the other way around. So I'm sorry about that."

"Stop apologizing. I didn't mean—"

"Look, just tell me that you're not going to worry about me. Do me that little favor. Just have a little belief in your old man this once."

"I've always believed in you. I always will."

"All right then," he said, and she heard the smile in his voice. "That's all I needed to hear."

Alicia lay awake the rest of the night, wondering if her father was awake too, sacrificing sleep to watch more videos and chat with the people in his support group.

In the morning, she told her mother she didn't feel like going to school. Emily saw the fatigue under Alicia's eyes and said, "Are you coming down with something?"

"Just tired," Alicia said.

"Need me to stay home with you?"

"I'll be fine. I'm going to try to get some sleep. Just need to rest some."

Emily looked at her suspiciously, like she didn't trust whatever ailed her. "I'll take a long lunch to come check on you. If you need anything before that, you call me right away. I mean it."

"I'll be fine," Alicia said.

After her mother left, Alicia tried to get to sleep for close to an hour. It was almost a relief when her phone rang. She picked it up and saw her mother on the caller ID.

"Hello?"

"Hey ... hey, did I wake you?" Her mother sounded out of breath.

"No. I'm still trying to get to sleep."

"Oh. Okay. Okay. You should do that. I'm on the way home now and—"

"Already?"

"—I'll stop and get you something to help you sleep, all right?"

Alicia sat up in bed. "Mom, what's wrong?"

"Nothing, honey. I'll be home in a bit."

"You're lying. I can tell something's wrong. If something happened, you have to tell me." It occurred to her that it could only be one thing. "Is it Dad? Did he call you? Is he okay?"

"Just try to rest for now. I'll be home in a minute and we'll talk then."

Alicia's phone buzzed with a new notification. She looked at it hoping to see a text from her dad, an immediate sign that he was okay and that her mother was being cryptic over something less consequential. Instead, she saw a headline that read "First Fatality of *Death/Grip* Delusion?"

"Are you still there?" Emily said. "Alicia, what are you doing? Talk to me."

Alicia set her phone down. She didn't hang up to click on the link in the notification. Her mother would just keep calling back to interrupt her. Instead, she opened the drawer of her nightstand and took out her tablet.

The link brought her to a news site. A disclaimer at the top of the page warned: DISTURBING AND GRAPHIC CONTENT. In the center of the screen was a video thumbnail featuring her father's smiling face.

She tapped the play icon.

The warning at the top of the page repeated within the video, then her father appeared, facing the camera. She recognized the painting behind him from her uncle's dining room. She heard a stifled whimper coming from somewhere off-screen.

"Hello, everyone," Benito said. Dark circles hung under his eyes. His lips were chapped and his hair uncombed. "I'm Benito Oliveira, and I'm here to tell whoever needs to hear it that you've got it wrong. You see this?"

He showed his stump.

"I'd give a lot to get this back. Not an arm and a leg, obviously." He laughed as hard as he could, which amounted to a breathless cough. "But I'd give up a lot. And here you've got all these people destroying something that I had taken from me. For what? Because of a 'challenge' inspired by a stupid movie? No, it's something deeper. I think we're all starting to understand now. Something very real is happening to some of us. But for those of you who think it's a 'challenge' that you have to resist, that you need to maim yourselves to keep from doing something bad, you're wrong. You should just follow whatever this is. It's leading you to do something that will make you whole. In some cases, you know, in spirit, and in other cases literally. The good news is, it's not too late for any of us. I'll prove it in just a moment.

"But let's back up a second. I introduced myself. Let me introduce someone else."

Benito turned the camera to show Robert seated at the end of the table, bound to a chair by rope and duct tape. A long strip of the tape encircled his head to keep his mouth covered. Bruises marked his eyes and cheeks. A lazy stream of blood dribbled down his forehead.

"Dad, what did you do?" Alicia said.

Benito turned the camera back to himself. "That's my brother, Roberto. Mom called him Bobbito, but he wanted to be called Robert. And Robert is the kind of man who thinks he should always get what he wants. Even if it's a woman at a bar who's not interested. It doesn't matter that she's with some guys who've told him to back off. He doesn't care. He wants what he wants, and he'll fight for it. Even if he's so bad at fighting he'd lose to a one-handed man." Another dry laugh.

"But sometimes you pick a fight with somebody who's even more drunk and reckless than you, and they aren't interested in talking shit and fighting fair. They're willing to take it to another level. They got a big knife on 'em, and they've been waiting for a moment like this.

"Now, if you're Robert's brother, you know he's an asshole, but you don't think he deserves to get stabbed. So you step in, and in the course of things your hand gets so chopped up that the doctors can't save it, so they amputate. But at least you saved your brother, right? You did the right thing.

"And in all the years that pass you don't have any regrets. You just want one time to hear your brother say, 'I'm sorry.'"

The whimpering grew louder, became a plea, and Alicia knew that her uncle was trying to say the words that might have saved him a week ago.

"Or how about, 'Thank you,'" Benito said. "That would've been appropriate. Instead, the best you get is, 'I didn't mean for that to happen.' Like it was an accident, and I'm the jerk for holding a grudge. Because that's the kind of man Robert is. He never wanted to say thanks or apologize, so he didn't, and I made myself think that was okay and that I shouldn't hold a grudge. I never yelled about it. I never gave him the silent treatment. I never told him to let me get one clean punch to his stupid mouth. Hell, I even tried to make fun of it to convince him—and myself—that I wasn't angry. He wouldn't even get in on the jokes.

"Anyway, enough about that. You just needed to know why I'm going to do what I'm going to do. But here's how it relates to the 'challenge.' To *Death/Grip*."

Benito tilted the camera down to show an empty black leather glove on the table. With his right hand he opened the cuff of the glove, then slid his left wrist in just enough to be covered.

"Like I said, something real is happening to people. All these people hurting themselves feel it. They know. But they're misguided. They think it's a bad thing when it's really a blessing.

"For those of you wondering why I'm using the glove for this, my therapist suggested using a visualization aid. I've tried it without the glove, and it doesn't work as well. And I know that because of this a lot of you are going to say this is fake. I don't care. You don't have to believe it. I know one person who believes in me, and that's all I need."

Alicia trembled. *Don't put this on me. I didn't put my faith in you for you to do this with it.*

Benito reached with his right hand for something off-screen and brought back a chef's knife. He placed its handle in the palm of the glove and waited.

The glove's pinky twitched, then curled over the handle. The ring finger curled over the knife next, then the middle and forefinger in tandem. The thumb closed over them all to secure the grip.

Benito turned the camera to Robert, who screamed through the duct tape and fought with his restraints. Robert rocked in the chair until he knocked himself over, but Benito was upon him by then. Alicia was grateful that the table obscured the act, though it was impossible not to understand what was happening. Flecks of blood flew against the wall each time Benito brought his hand up. Alicia started counting the strikes because it seemed the only sane thing to do. She made it to sixteen before her father stopped, and he'd been over halfway through before she'd started counting.

Benito approached the camera and held out his gloved fist, still tight around the knife. With his right hand he pulled at the cuff of the glove to remove it. The glove lost hold of the knife and flopped to the table.

Benito stared at the place where his left hand had been. "That was *me*," he said. "*All* of me." Tears filled his eyes.

Alicia dipped her head and fought tears of her own. She wished she could disbelieve what she'd seen. But this was her father as he really was. The full version of himself that he didn't want to burden her with, not just the man who had made her laugh when he didn't make her worry. She had said he could tell her anything. This was *everything*.

Her thumb drifted over the video's replay icon, and she tapped the screen.

SAFETY IN NUMBERS

Originally published in *On the Premises* (April 2020, Issue 35)

I've been told that I'm one of those guys who never learns. I disagree with this, but it doesn't matter what I think right now. The man pointing a pistol at my face thinks that I'm the type who never learns. Right now, his opinion trumps mine.

"Can't be too mad at you," says Blake, the man with the gun. "If guys like you ever got a clue, I'd be out of work."

Blake's smile looks like a mouthful of broken porcelain. He's a stack of twigs held together by glue and strings, but that black magnum transforms him into a heavyweight. The three hoods standing between me and the door—Kinsey, Levy, and Wade—dissuade me from trying to run for it. Unless I want to try the window, that is, but my apartment is on the fourth floor. The impact with Gracie Street wouldn't be much fun and would only save Blake the trouble of flexing his trigger finger.

There's little for me to do right now except talk. Which is ironic, since talking in the interest of saving my ass is what put me in this predicament.

"Blake, listen, I don't know what you think you heard or saw, but I didn't say anything to anybody. I swear to God. I've never snitched in my life. I swear to *God. Please.*"

I see him grit those jagged teeth. His lips curl into a delighted sneer. I shut my eyes. I don't want to see this. Don't want to be here, sitting on the floor of my living room, my mind cycling through the slideshow summarizing my life. What the hell was I thinking, getting involved with guys like this? I do small grifts and courier gigs, light work for float money, not the heavy lifting that involves killers. My heart turns into a frozen fist. I wonder if the echo of the gunshot will stalk me into the afterlife, or if I'm sweating out the last seconds of the only existence anyone ever knows.

There's a sound, metal on metal. It's light, quick and impotent. It repeats twice before I recognize it. Once more and I place it. A *click*. I force my eyes open and see Blake staring at his gun like it insulted his mother.

He looks back at Wade and says, "Give me yours." Wade obliges. His gun's a gleaming work of silver that reflects light that isn't even present in the room. It's smooth and exotic, almost alien looking. This gun belongs in the Smithsonian, not in the palm of an angry gangster.

Even Blake seems seduced by the beauty of this pistol, staring at it like he isn't sure of its purpose. It looks too pristine to have ever been fired and he's not thrilled with popping its cherry on an insignificant snitch like me, but he gets over it and aims the gun at me. I stare down the barrel, unable to shut my eyes this time, and the nozzle is like a tunnel that I'll fall down forever. No light at the end of it, just blackness. Blake squeezes the trigger.

Then I hear that sound again. *Click*. A simple symphony of survival. I can't keep from grinning.

"Is this a joke?" Blake asks the gun. Then he looks at Wade and asks him, "This some kind of joke?"

I don't wait for Wade to answer. I jump to my feet and charge past Blake and his boys while they seem confused by my sudden luck. The front door is oh so close and I swear it takes a step toward me with every step I take toward it.

I hear Blake yell at his goons to grab me, but by then I'm already out of my apartment and dashing toward the stairwell at the end of the hallway. The footsteps behind me sound awkward and comical. Too rapid and furious to actually be gaining on me. Keystone Crooks stumbling over themselves. Meanwhile I'm moving on rails, gliding more than sprinting, my focus Ginsu sharp, and I know they can't catch me. I think of every chase scene I've ever seen in a movie and how I always thought I'd never let somebody catch me, because there's no way in hell they'd want to kill me as much as I want to live. Here I am now, proving myself right.

I make it to the stairwell and start bounding down the steps two at a time. I don't even look at my feet to see where they're landing. I don't have to. I feel like an athlete or a stuntman, a guy who's practiced this sort of thing every day of his adult life.

I don't hear Blake and his boys behind me anymore. I think they might have tried the elevator or the south-end stairs. Trying to head me off in the lobby. I wonder if I should take a detour, maybe get off at the second floor and try to get out through the hallway window. Do something unexpected.

No. If I just keep going like I am now it won't matter what they do because I'll be too far ahead of them. Once I'm outside I'll hop in a cab or board the first stopped bus I see. Or, if I have to, I'll keep running. I could run for days if it came to it. No need for rest or food or water. I'm not even winded. I can't even feel the metal handrail against my palm as I grab it to help myself turn on another landing. I'm going so fast that …

… that I should have been in the lobby by now. My apartment is on the fourth floor and I've cleared at least five flights. A part of me is saying, *Don't stop. Don't think about it. Keep running.* But another part of me can sense that something is off and is urging me to stop and figure it out.

My legs keep pumping, running on autopilot. I seize the handrail like it's the only thing keeping me from a free fall. My feet run out from under me. I go airborne for a second and then I drop. The back of my head hits first, then my lower back. I'm not a particularly clumsy person, but I've had my share of spills, and I have an idea of what the impact of concrete stairs on my head and back should feel like, and this isn't it. This feels like I landed on a mattress. It almost feels like I'm floating.

Get up. Get moving.

The urgency is flowing through me like electrified fire, and I know it's going to burst right out of me if I stay still much longer, but I force myself to pause for a moment so I can think. Something's not right. The lights are too close and too bright. I can see everything else around me with too much clarity. Every single crack in the wall, no matter how slim. Every wet stain on the floor, every speck of dust floating from the ceiling. I can see the damn antennae moving on the ants marching up the wall to my left.

But something's missing as well. For a moment I can't tell what it is, but then it occurs to me that those wet stains on the stairs aren't from water. This stairwell always smells faintly of urine. Living here as long as I have has desensitized me to the smell, but its absence is more noticeable now than its presence ever was.

My courage and confidence abandon me at once. I pick myself up and look back up the stairs. There is another reason why Blake and his boys aren't following me. A *real* reason that is dawning on me despite my earnest desire to deny it. This situation feels familiar. I've seen or read about something like this before. A story comes to mind, the name escaping me, something I saw in a TV show or a book, or maybe both. It was a story about a man with a noose around his neck falling off a bridge. He was being executed. Then a miracle happened, the rope broke, and he escaped. He ran from his executioners, ran for as long and as far as he had to, and he had almost made it home when suddenly he felt a crazy pain in his neck and everything went white … and it turned out he hadn't actually escaped after all.

I run back up the stairs. I don't feel so light anymore. I've got a thousand pounds of anxiety and apprehension piggybacking up the stairs with me. My knees and ankles throb with each step, my thighs and lungs are screaming that they can't take any more. It feels like I'm running upstream through a river with a grudge against me. I keep going.

I make it back to the fourth floor and into the hallway. The door to my apartment is closed. The silence in the hall is terrible. It's like I'm standing inside the ghost of a dead moment. Part of me would rather sit here and wait for whatever is going to happen to come to me instead of me going toward it. For better or worse, that part of me gets voted down, and I walk to the door.

The knob is stubbornly quiet as I turn it. The hinges too. The men inside are voiceless and motionless. The man sitting on the floor with his eyelids cramped shut and the agony of dread screwing up his normally handsome face is of particular interest to me.

"Holy hell," I say, but no one in the room hears me. I walk to the man on the floor who cowers before the man in front of him, the man with a black pistol. I get as close as I can to the man on the floor. My hands tremble as I reach for his face, too frightened to make contact. God. This is what I look like at the moment of my death? This is how I die?

Next, I turn to the man with the gun. Blake's expression beams with satisfaction. He's enjoying this far too much, probably doesn't look this happy when he's fucking. My stomach starts flipping and rolling and scoring tens in the floor routine from looking at him.

I feel redness glowing through my skin. Pure fury is a sensation I have never known before now. It blends with the terror stirring in my gut and makes for a nauseating cocktail. I look back and forth between my condemned self and Blake and I wonder, *Is this real? Or am I in hell?*

I look at the gun, and I think I can hear the bullet in the barrel. It hasn't quite picked up the speed to outrace sound yet as it moves down that tunnel toward my head. This moment is not perfectly still after all. Time is crawling forward, shoving the present into the past a microsecond at a time, and when this moment becomes history the other me that I'm staring at will have a fresh hole in his pretty face.

Except *I'm* the "other me," aren't I? The man on the floor is the real me, the real McCoy. What will happen to me when that bullet plunges into his head? What happens to a dream when the dreamer dies? I've got a hunch I won't like the answer, so I decide to do something about it.

It happens too fast for anyone else to react and that is what saves my life. As soon as I push Blake's arm to his left time moves at its regular speed again and the gun fires, missing the McCoy's face by an inch or two. Blake is still wearing that stupid crooked smile when I headbutt his mouth shut and snatch the gun from his hand. My forehead stings a bit from the blow, but I ignore it. Blake looks at me like I'm every nightmare he's ever known come to life. I've got his gun in my right hand, pressed to his cheek, and I hook my left arm under his chin.

His boys show off the reflexes of the comatose. I've backed into the corner with Blake as my hostage before they can make a move. Wade is the first to finally react. He opens his coat and goes for a boring black piece that's nothing like the gleaming dream pistol I had imagined him handing to Blake before.

I say, "Don't move!" He freezes. So do the other two. Blake has finally started struggling, clawing at my forearm trying to free himself.

In the opposite corner of the room, the McCoy is staring at me with wild eyes. I want to say something to ease his fear, but the truth is I'm almost as frightened as he is. I am a trespasser into reality. Everything looks too grimy and intense. I miss the sheen of the fantasy world that spawned me. I miss being immune to panic and not being able to smell everyone's sweat.

"I swear I'll kill him," I say. "If any one of you moves, I'll shoot him."

My strength surprises me. I've got this chokehold cinched like a boa constrictor. Blake's fighting more frantically now, his legs kicking, his fingernails digging into my forearm, but I'm holding all his muscle in my right hand, threatening to blow his brains out with it.

"Oh my God, what is this?" the McCoy says. "Who the hell are you? What's going on?"

I scream at him to shut up, and he cowers like a beaten dog. I turn my attention back to Blake's men. "Get rid of anything you're holding right now."

They're too dumbfounded to follow instructions. I know they hear my words, but they don't understand them. They're still struggling with how I even exist, so I'm speaking Greek as far as they're concerned. I point the gun at them, certain that this will resolve our failure to communicate. Everybody understands the universal sign language for *I'm seriously about to fucking shoot you.*

"All right," says Wade. "Look, you let him go, and we'll be on our way."

"Lose your guns, or I put one through his head." To emphasize that I mean business, I tighten my chokehold on Blake. A nice clean *crack* comes from his fragile, bird-boned neck. Blake emits this half-gurgling, half-groaning noise and suddenly he's dead weight.

Under my breath, I curse at Blake's inconvenient death, then drop his body and start firing. I shoot at Wade first because he's the closest. Unfortunately, the close range doesn't mean a hell of a lot for me, as I've never shot a gun in my life.

Still, out of five shots fired, two find a home in Wade's stomach and send him to the floor. Levy draws on me, and I'm praying for the McCoy to get off his ass and tackle somebody, or kick someone in the groin, or make some loud distracting noises. Do *something* to be useful. Instead, he starts for the door, which isn't the bravest thing he could do, but probably the smartest. Kinsey turns and grabs the McCoy by the collar and puts a gun in his face, leaving Levy free to blast me. And then the cavalry arrives.

Earlier, when I saved the McCoy, I said that it happened too fast for anyone else to react, but now that I'm on the other end of it I see that "fast" is an understatement. There's this blur of movement that seems to erase the moment and replace it with a new reality. There are two new men in the room who weren't here a fraction of an instant ago. Handsome guys, if I may say so.

One of the new arrivals grabs Kinsey and throws him through the living-room window. Kinsey's scream tells me that the fall to Gracie Street is every bit as unpleasant as I imagined it would be. The fourth "me" has tackled Levy to the floor and is trying to wrestle the gun away from him. Levy's a big man, and he manages to fight off my clone, punching him in the face with his free hand. Unfortunately for him, he's all out of teammates. I walk over, put Blake's gun to Levy's temple. Can't afford to miss. The shot cleans out his skull.

The gunfire has my head ringing like a bell tower, so it takes a while for me to hear Wade's grunting. I look at him. His hands make for lousy bandages. He's pressing against those holes in his stomach as hard as he can, but unless a couple of little Dutch boys show up to plug the leaks, the bleeding isn't going to stop. I remember reading somewhere about gutshots, how torturous they are, and damn if Wade doesn't look like he's in all kinds of pain. I point the gun at his head and fire. I may have recently become a killer, but I'm not a dick. No need to let the guy suffer.

It's just me, myself, the McCoy, and I left in the apartment. The McCoy is easy to single out. He's the sniveling mess crawling toward the door and looking at the rest of us like we're space invaders.

"Who the hell are you?" he says. "What the hell is going on?"

"Hey, relax," I tell him. "You're among friends, right?"

I smile at him and the other two, trying to dissipate the tension. One of the two new arrivals smiles back, but the other one, he's got a face of stone that Mount Rushmore would envy. I know what he's thinking. I'm thinking the same thing, and it's not *How did this happen?* It's *How does this work, all of us living in the same world together? How do we all get out of here?* It doesn't. And we don't.

I pop two rounds into the McCoy's knees. The clone who had been all smiles jumps back. "What the hell are you doing?" Smiley asks me.

Mr. Stone tells him, "Look around. Three bodies in the room, one in the street. And then there's the four of us. We can't all be here when the cops come, but one of us has to stay here to answer for it."

"But it was self-defense," Smiley says. "They were going to kill him. Us."

"Fine. *You* stick around to explain it."

The confusion on his face makes Smiley look younger than the rest of us, somehow. Like he's the kid brother who can't understand why the world just can't be fair all the time.

"What about the rest of us?" he says.

"Get out, go our separate ways," I say, "and make sure we never see each other again."

Smiley nods, but his eyes betray his uncertainty.

"Let's get going," Mr. Stone tells him. Smiley turns to walk out the door. That's when Mr. Stone puts the gun to the back of Smiley's head and fires. Smiley never sees it coming, so there's no chance of him summoning a clone to save himself. He drops dead to the floor. Mr. Stone kicks him over and fires six more shots into Smiley's face, leaving him unrecognizable. If we had time, he'd probably burn off Smiley's fingerprints, but this should be enough to leave the cops confused for a little while, or at least preoccupied.

He turns to me, and it's like looking into a cursed mirror. He's not just a clone, he's a version who went wrong. I figure he's mine—a copy of a copy—and Smiley belonged to the McCoy. I wonder if he's wondering whether he'd die if he shot me now, or if coming into the real world means he's no longer a dream dependent on the survival of the dreamer.

"You won't see me," he says.

"Likewise."

Mr. Stone runs out of the apartment, leaving me alone with the McCoy. I wait about thirty seconds, enough time for Mr. Stone to clear out. When I feel confident he's gone, I make my exit. I drop Blake's gun at the McCoy's feet on my way out.

Not so long ago, I was one of those guys who never learns. I've learned enough in the last five minutes to fill two brains. I've learned things I'd rather forget and other things that might save my ass yet again one of these days. For now, I know that I need to find someplace to stay for a while. I'll need to find a new identity, find some work, get some money in my pocket so I can get the hell away from the city and start over somewhere.

But before I get that fresh start, I know that I'll have to track down Mr. Stone and make sure I see him before he sees me.

MONSTER BITES

Originally aired on the *Nightlight* podcast (May 25, 2023, Episode 612)

The thing hunched on all fours in the grass was more shadow than substance, despite the moonlight. Elisa could not see which way it was facing but was sure it had eyes on her and Dandy. She didn't know whether to back away slowly, look for a large rock or stick to defend herself, or keep still and wait for the thing to lose interest. A dozen other thoughts passed through her mind. Among those, unexpectedly, was the fact that love had brought her to this moment.

Love led her to move in with Grace, outside the city limits, where every house had a septic tank and a couple of acres. Love made her a dog owner, too, the "stepparent" of Grace's dog, Dandy.

Elisa wasn't a dog person. She'd never owned a pet before moving into Grace's house, but the short-haired, brown border collie loved her and minded her better than she did Grace. Maybe because Elisa was less affectionate, never going in for a hug, refusing to speak to Dandy in silly voices, and giving out belly rubs like they were reserved for special occasions. That was Grace's theory, that Dandy worked harder for Elisa's attention because Elisa gave it sparingly. Elisa suspected it was because the little monster watched her make her food in the pressure cooker once a week, then package it and place it in the fridge. And because she was the one who walked Dandy along the snaking, mile-long trail near the house, instead of walking her a few laps around the park nearby, as Grace did. The little monster liked the park well enough, but she loved the trail. Grace had foot problems that gave her pain when she tried to tread that uneven ground. Elisa could handle it and until this moment had started to enjoy it. If she was going to live out here for love, she should try to love living here. Likewise, if she was going to be a dog owner, she might as well learn to be a good one, even though she found the dog more nuisance than companion.

Still, Dandy was a living thing—her sole responsibility with Grace out of town for the week—and even stubborn, smelly, and slobbery little monsters deserved to be treated well, didn't they?

Perhaps there were exceptions, like the thing in grass snarling at her and Dandy. "Easy, Monster," Elisa said to the dog, who usually responded to her saying "Monster" faster than she did to anyone else calling her Dandy. When she was being a little too much for Grace to handle, Elisa would say "Monster" in a forceful tone, and Dandy would settle down.

Then she would smile at Grace and say, "Ever going to learn to control your dog?"

"*Our* dog," Grace always said.

Elisa couldn't get Dandy to obey now, though. The dog stood stiff, hackles raised, a low growl coming from her. Dandy pulled as far as the harness and leash let her. Elisa started forward to move between her dog and the thing smothered in shadow, but when she moved, Dandy did so as well.

"Monster, get over here now," Elisa said, trying to sound less scared than she was, more assertive. Dandy still did not obey. The remaining quaver in Elisa's voice just made Dandy bark at the thing in the grass.

The shadow-thing moved, its shoulders straightening, its front taller than its haunches. It let out a throaty hiss for several seconds before the sound devolved into a clicking gurgle. Then, after a long breath, there was measured laughter, deep and mocking. The sound of a mouthless alien that thought human noises were risible. It made Elisa shudder and pull harder on Dandy's leash. To that point, she managed to delude herself into thinking the thing might only prove threatening if they made the wrong move or antagonized it. Its laughter told her that it took joy in scaring them. It gained something from her the longer she looked at it.

As if reading her thoughts, the thing said, "Close your eyes and see me better." Its voice was old, hoarse, and full of deranged glee. Worse, it possessed power. Elisa hadn't heard a voice with that much strength since she was a girl, when she was feverish, nauseous, and aching from an illness the doctors couldn't diagnose. An aunt she'd never seen before came to the hospital at her mom's beckoning when things worsened. The first thing she said to the crying Elisa was, "Quiet, child," and Elisa had obeyed as her pains instantly subsided. Her aunt's voice was that much stronger than her suffering. Later, after healing Elisa and taking some time to recover from the effort, her aunt—Margaret—explained to Elisa that she had been worse than sick.

"Medicine and science are wonderful," Margaret said, "but there are some things they aren't good for. Maybe one day that will change. For now, we still have to meet hexes with counters, threaten devils with banishment, or appease them or trick them."

Elisa visited her aunt whenever she could after that, but from then until the day Margaret died, Elisa could never get her to say exactly who or what had put her in the hospital. "Please don't ask about that ever again," Margaret finally said. "You're better off not knowing, and I don't like to think about all the things I had to do."

As she got older, Elisa heard bits of information that gave her a general idea of what happened to her. There'd been an ugly custody battle between her parents. Before she got sick, her paternal grandmother cornered Elisa's mother in the meat market one day and told her that if she really loved her daughter, she'd let the little girl go before something awful happened. Within days of Elisa getting better, her father and his mother went missing. They were never heard from again.

I don't like to think about all the things I had to do. Elisa was a teenager before she did the math that aligned her aunt's implied confession with her father and grandmother's disappearance, and trusted that Tía Margaret was right. She was better off not knowing everything.

She wished she knew a little more now. Some kind of spell to shield her and Dandy or buy them some time to escape. The shadow-thing spoke with the authority of a practitioner at least on par with Tía Margaret. As worrisome as the power of its voice was, the delirious delight in its tone was what made Elisa tremble.

"Close your eyes and see me better," it said again, and Elisa's eyelids got heavy. She started to fall asleep on her feet. As the darkness took her, she saw a weathered face shrouded by blackness. The face sported a toothy, tight-jawed smile, like it was holding a small, living thing inside its mouth, relishing the panic dancing on its tongue before it swallowed. Elisa thought it was a woman's face, though it could have been a man's. One thing she was sure of, this person was beyond old. Their complexion was gray, darker still around the eyes. Their face was more cracked than wrinkled. Thin strands of white hair clung to a mostly bald scalp like they wanted to fall away but were stuck there. The eyes were large, yellowed, and unblinking. She could see how many veins had popped in each eye as the face came closer.

Dandy barked twice, loud and sharp. This wasn't like when she went back and forth with another dog she saw at the park, or when she heard someone come through the front door. Elisa had never heard Dandy sound like this before but was thankful to hear it now. It brought her out of her daze just enough to see the shadow approaching. Its laughter filled the night.

"You're mine this time, girl. Who'll save you now? No one, no, no. I've got you this—"

The leash ripped free of Elisa's grip. The shadow's laughter turned into a surprised scream as Dandy leaped at it. Elisa was slow to react, still emerging from her stupor. She heard the dog cry out, then heard the creature Dandy was fighting do the same. That brought Elisa running toward the action. She shut her eyes and jumped shoulder-first at the taller figure in the grass, which became more solid and less of a shade at the moment of impact.

"Get away from us," Elisa screamed. She managed to pull Dandy from their attacker, then scooped the dog into her arms before running back the way they came in. Normally, Dandy resisted being picked up, but she didn't struggle now. That concerned Elisa, as did the wet spot she felt in the crook of her arm. For once, Elisa hoped the dog had just peed on her, but she knew that wasn't it. Dandy had yelped for a reason.

Behind her, not far enough for her liking, she heard the shadow person cry, "It bit me! Your disgusting rat bit me!"

Elisa did not look back to see how close her pursuer was. She heard them coming, though. Their steps pounded the earth with a rhythm that made her think they were back on all fours. She called for help and felt like she was screaming into a deep well. Her voice echoed and carried downward into nothingness. The neighbors couldn't hear her, she knew. She nonetheless screamed again, louder, and the well just got narrower and deeper. Was she imagining this, or was the person behind her somehow doing it? That living shadow. That witch.

"Don't use that word," her tía Margaret had told her when Elisa asked if she was a witch. "It's just as silly as saying werewolf or vampire. It's too limiting and too aggrandizing in the same breath. It describes something that none of us are. I am a practitioner and student in a field where there are no masters, and I accept that. Some of us learn to change shapes, some focus on spells, some try a little of everything, but none of that makes someone a witch, even though I've known too many who think of themselves that way. They think they're more than they are, that they can cheat death forever, when they can't even put off senility for more than a few decades. That's where the old stories of crones that know black magic came from, I think. I've seen what happens when minds in denial grow feeble with age. When they get weaker and the degradation accelerates. I don't usually think in terms of good and bad, because it all depends on who you're helping or hurting at the moment and their perspective. But those old ones who can't accept what's happening to them, and that nobody's immune to time—not even them—I swear they've never done good to anyone. They just get stuck in their denial, trying to relive old feuds, fight old battles, fix their history. Like they think they can trick time into believing they're as young as they used to be."

This all flashed through her mind in an instant, less a conscious thought than embedded knowledge. *You're mine this time, girl.* The one chasing her had said that a moment ago.

This time.

Who'll save you now?

God, that's what this was about? Elisa was some withered practitioner's old battle? History that their deluded mind was telling them to fix? How was she going to survive this? There was no one to save her now. Tía Margaret was long dead, and her closest protector was the poor, wounded dog. All she could do was run and hope.

She remembered pleading with her aunt to teach her something—anything—that would give her protection in case her dad and grandmother resurfaced and tried something again. "You don't have to worry about them," Tía Margaret assured her.

"Well, what about anyone else?"

"Are you planning to make enemies? Listen, the more you know, the more trouble you're liable to invite. And nothing I can teach you will protect you from everything, or even most things. All you need to know are the basics anyone needs to know. Try to be decent to people, be there for the ones who love you, and love the ones who are there for you. Sounds like a bad song, and I can't guarantee it will always help you, but I can't guarantee ninety-nine percent of anything else I could tell you either. And that last percent? It isn't worth the burden to know it. Trust me."

Now she was going to die. Elisa made it beyond the trail and into the street their house was on, but that didn't matter. She kept running because it was all she could do, but as she got close to home Elisa was still sure she would die. Getting into the house wouldn't save her or Dandy. She briefly considered running past the house because of this. She didn't want Grace to come home in a few days to find her and Dandy dead on the living-room floor.

She got to the house, went inside, and locked the door behind her. Even if there was no chance of surviving, she had to try. Dandy was shaking in her arms by then. For all Elisa knew, the little monster had been shivering in her grip the whole time, and she'd just been too scared to feel it. She set the dog down in the foyer and checked the damp spot on its hind leg in the dim moonlight showing through the front windows. The wound in Dandy's leg was a series of deep punctures and small gashes that formed a crescent. A bite mark? God, that shadow figure—a true monster—was more deranged than Elisa could have guessed.

She flipped a light switch to get a better look at Dandy's leg. The light immediately flickered out. She tried the switch again, then the hallway light near it, but the house remained dark. She rushed through the hall into the kitchen to try the light switch there but froze when she heard an angry, rising moan in the living room before her. The shadow person was there. Tall, thin, grayer than it was black, but still shrouded. Its face still hidden unless Elisa blinked. She did once, saw that awful, ancient face, and tried her best to keep her eyes open from then on.

"Your filthy rat bit me," the shadow said. "First, you escape me, then you have that thing bite me. I'm going to take my time with you. I was going to be merciful, but now …"

A feverish heat overcame Elisa from within. Sickness as thick and hot as boiling tar flooded her stomach. Pain sliced through her joints, and her knees buckled.

"Now I'm going to give you everything you missed the first time, and more. I'm going to give you everything I know, little girl. Before I'm done you'll—"

A rumbling growl made the shadow fall silent. The growl grew louder and made glasses and dishes near the sink crack. Elisa looked back toward the sound and saw a massive canine shape with distended limbs that bent more like a human's than a dog's. Dandy was far larger than she'd been a moment ago, and her huge, bared teeth were flatter, like a person's. When she stood on her hind legs and spread her arms to steady herself against the hallway walls, she looked stranger still. But it was Dandy, Elisa knew. She loved the little monster too much not to recognize her.

"What is that?" the shadow said, its voice unsteady. "That shouldn't be. What in the devil is it?"

Elisa managed to smile through her pain. "It's my dog that you bit, asshole."

Dandy emitted a hybrid barking, shouting noise that cracked the walls of the house and sheared a piece of the shadow's head away.

"Stop," the shadow cried, but it was talking to an angry beast that was just barely human enough to use the power that contaminated it. The bite did it. Like a vampire or werewolf bite, infecting someone else with accursed strengths and abilities. Except there were no vampires or werewolves, just practitioners, some of whom drove themselves so mad they might someday bite a dog. Elisa laughed when she realized this. It hurt to laugh, but not as much as it would have seconds ago, when the shadow wasn't on the defensive, and had all of its attention on her. They shouted, "Stop," again, and Dandy shout-barked in response, firing out some attack spell that made bones crack, and that Dandy didn't need to know the words for. All she needed to know was that the thing she was barking at was a threat to her and one of her favorite humans.

"Make it stop! Call it back," the shadow said to Elisa. She almost felt a grain of pity for them. They were so far past their prime, so powerless against anyone or anything capable of fighting back. "I'll leave, just call it back. I'll go away, please!"

Elisa was still laughing. She couldn't help herself. It was all she could do to keep herself sane. What she thought of before came to mind, how love had brought her here. Loving Grace, learning to love where she lived, even loving her damn dog. And what had Tía Margaret said about loving the people who were there for you, how that was a protection as effective as anything else she could teach her? That quote that belonged in a bad song? She laughed harder at that, which helped keep her mind from breaking at Dandy's thunderous shouts, the shadow's head-splitting screams.

It took Elisa several seconds to realize it when it was over. The foyer and hallway lights had come on. The house had gone silent aside from her petering laughter.

Quiet, child.

Was that just a memory, or her aunt speaking to her from the other side? It didn't matter. She followed the command and calmed herself, got to her feet, and walked to Dandy. The still-altered dog was bent over a very old man—Elisa saw that now—who was formerly wrapped in night but was now naked, broken, and still. Dandy lapped at a gaping wound in the dead man's neck.

"Monster," Elisa said.

Dandy turned, sat attentively, and gave Elisa a look that said, *I wasn't doing anything. I'm a good dog.*

Elisa smiled, started to crouch to get to Dandy's eye level out of habit, then realized she didn't need to. She coughed and cleared her throat to suppress another hysterical laughing fit. She looked around, surveyed the damage to the house, and shook her head at the body on the floor. What was she going to do about all of this? Where to even begin?

She held her hand out. "Thanks, Dandy. But you're going to have to change back. You know that, right?"

Elisa's not-so-little monster panted happily and licked her hand.

A STORY OVERHEARD IN A ROOM

Originally aired on *The NoSleep Podcast* (May 10, 2020, Season 14, Episode 13)

The numbers of the digital clock displayed 11:33. In five hours James would need to be at the airport to catch his flight home. He was tired, but he seemed to creep further from sleepiness each minute.

He shifted in bed, lying flatter on the mattress to take some pressure off his hip. The bed groaned as it did each time he moved. It was a stiff, quarrelsome thing, full of dips and mounds that collaborated to kill his efforts to get comfortable. Lying flat would soon prove to be hell on his back, and he'd have to shift again in ten minutes or so, and then again in another ten, and on like that through the night.

It was his fourth and final night of tossing and turning in this bed, but the first he'd spent wide awake in it. There was a time when he could have slept soundly on a concrete floor and been no worse for it in the morning. Now, though, the aches of a rough night's sleep followed him for days, if not weeks, and those accumulated pains prevented him from willing himself to sleep.

Other than the bed, there wasn't much in the motel room to complain about. It was small, its back wall taken up by floor-to-ceiling mirror panes, and it held the odor of cheap cleaning products. It was a vague smell, almost inoffensive, but noticeable enough to tickle the nostrils. James knew that it masked harsher odors. He remembered the smells of some of the other discount motels he had stayed in to cut costs during business trips and figured he should be grateful that this place was at least trying. Besides, he couldn't fault Roadside Suites—which advertised "Free Cable!" and "Renovated Restrooms!" on its marquee—for being exactly the kind of place he knew it would be.

The channel selection on the television was half as deep as what he had at home. He spent an hour with sitcoms that pulled a few smirks out of him but did nothing to cure his restlessness. Bored with the comedies, he searched for something else to watch. Channel surfing brought him to a British slasher film he'd never heard of. It had the dinginess of an untouched film from the seventies, back when movies looked like filtered dreams and were better for it, in his opinion.

The film was a reasonable diversion, though nowhere near the lullaby he needed. A small headache in the back of his head fed his insomnia and unsettled him more than anything on the television screen. He had a doctor's appointment waiting for him back home. He had already canceled an appointment earlier in the month and wanted to cancel again, but he'd promised his kids that he wouldn't put it off any longer. His son and daughter—recent college graduates who were sure they had the world figured out—insisted he see his physician about his headaches. James couldn't get them to understand that he could live more easily with the headaches than with any bad news his doctor might deliver.

The movie ended with a telegraphed final twist—the investigator's wife had been the killer all along—but did so with enough of a wink that James held no contempt toward it. When the second movie began—another British thriller that was part of an apparent marathon—he didn't change the channel.

The tone and the actual sound mix of the second film were quieter than that of the first. James had to turn the volume up to hear the dialogue for the relatively few scenes that contained dialogue. Chunks of the film passed with no words spoken. The lead character was an intrepid, naive man house-sitting a sprawling estate that couldn't have looked more haunted. The scarcity of plot and characters made it easier for James's divided and sleep-starved mind to follow what was presented. The first film had layered a fresh plot twist atop each body that the killer claimed, while this second film traveled a straight road with one exit. It kept his interest, but James found his attention wavering near the end, wanting something to happen. Then, in an unbroken thirty-second shot seen from the lead character's point of view, the house's resident specter painfully ripped itself from the massive portrait that had contained it while the hapless hero struggled even to gasp at what he witnessed, much less scream. James felt for a moment that he was there along with the man in the film. He held his breath unconsciously and backed himself up against the mirrored wall behind him.

The film faded to black. James smiled in appreciation of its climactic scare. It was now two thirty in the morning and his heartbeat was at a steady trot. Might as well stay up until he had to leave, he figured. Even if he could find a way to nod off now, he'd likely oversleep and miss his flight. Besides, he was interested in seeing what would come next.

The third movie opened on an exhausted, shoeless woman who limped her way through the stone streets of a town full of long shadows. The woman whimpered as she hustled along, but did not stop to pound at any door she passed, did not call out for help in the hopes that someone would at least come to their window. She went down an alley, then came to another that looked the same as the one she'd just left, only longer, then to another that was narrower. She heard something that sounded like scraping metal. She gasped, backed against a wall, and looked behind her, above her. If she saw anything, the camera did not reveal it, but something—the situation itself, it seemed—started her sobbing.

"Don't cry," an unseen child said. "It'll be okay."

James tensed. The child's voice had not come from the television. He turned and saw his reflection turning toward him in kind. The voice had come from behind him, from behind the wall. But it had been too clear and too close to come from *behind* the wall. It sounded more like it had bounced off the surface of the mirror.

He was just beginning to rationalize what he thought he'd heard—he was very tired, after all, and was up much later than he was used to—when the voice came again.

"You have to stop crying or he'll hear you," the child said. A soft-spoken boy, from the sound of it, though he spoke with an earnest composure that suggested he might be older. "You can still get out; you just have to be quiet."

On the television, the woman cried out again, louder this time, and James remembered that he'd turned up the volume for the previous movie.

"*Please* don't cry," the boy said. "He'll hear you. Listen to me, you have to look for a way out, and you have to keep quiet."

James slid to the edge of the bed, away from the wall. This had to be someone speaking to him from the next room. Someone's kid who'd heard the movie and was either playing a prank on James or was just profoundly confused and trying to be helpful. It had to be that, or something like it, even though it couldn't be that, because the voice was too clear to be coming from the other room. James had been in many thin-walled motels that couldn't keep the sounds of fighting, laughter, sex, or music from being heard next door, but never one with a wall so thin it let a child's whispers pass like smoke through a vent.

Behind James, the woman on the television screamed. Before him, the boy implored her to be silent. James stood and turned the television off. It was still possible that he was mistaken, and the voice was that of an unseen character from the film. It was possible that he had somehow imagined it being behind him. He watched the wall, waited.

"Hello?" the boy said. "Are you still there?"

James's stomach gurgled. He felt lightheaded. It occurred to him that this disembodied voice might have crawled out of the malady in his brain that was also responsible for his headaches.

"I hope you're okay," the boy said. "I hope you got away."

James walked to the small foyer and turned on the light switch, then reentered the room and looked around for signs of a microphone, signs that this was a dream, signs of anything that would give him the peace of knowing he wasn't losing his mind. Could this really be how insanity came to someone? So sudden and inspired?

He watched the spot in the mirrored wall where the voice had come from, just above the bed. He waited, almost daring it to return. He and his reflection stared at that same spot from opposing angles, eyes low like they were two men afraid or ashamed of making eye contact.

"Who are you?" the boy said at last, his words rushed, his tone stronger.

"Who are *you*?" James said, then shook his head. He wasn't ready to renounce the idea that he was speaking to a confused or mischievous kid who was in the next room. He needed to address this boy accordingly. "Where are your parents? Do they know you're up? Did they leave you alone in—"

"You're him, aren't you? You're *him*. Where is the lady that was crying? What did you do to her?"

"All right, kid—"

"Did you hurt her? What did you do?"

"—I'm calling the front desk. If your parents are there, you're going to be in a lot of trouble."

James stepped toward the phone that sat on the nightstand near the head of the bed. Near the mirrored wall.

"*What did you do to her?*" the boy said, and the mirror panes rattled as though he'd bellowed the words, though his voice was no louder than it had been before.

James froze. His mouth went dry. The mirror rattled again and he flinched.

It rattled once more, and a small crack appeared in the spot he'd been staring at. Surrounding the crack in the mirror was a small handprint that evaporated a second after it appeared.

"Where is she?" the boy said. "Did you hurt her?"

"I'm going to the front desk," James said as if he could fool himself into still believing he was speaking to some brat in the next room.

"No," the boy said.

James went to the door, reached for the door handle, and touched ice. He pulled back, looked at it to be sure—to remind himself—that it was an unremarkable motel door handle. He went for it again, pressed down. It held with a soft click, as though it were locked from the outside. He pressed down harder, pulled at the door to force it open.

"I won't let you hurt anyone else," the boy said. "This is the last time."

The temperature in the room dropped. James thought he felt something cold graze the back of his neck. He turned around and saw no one behind him. From the foyer, close to the door, his view of the damaged spot in the mirror was blocked by the corner of the wall. He could still hear the mirror being struck, though. He heard it rattle with each strike. He heard the small crack splinter and sprout limbs that sprouted offshoots of their own.

"I couldn't stop you then," the boy said. "But I can now."

"Okay, listen to me," James said. "You've got me confused with someone else, okay?"

"You won't hurt anyone else. No more for you. No more."

"Damn it, listen to me! That lady you heard was on the TV. She's not even real! I didn't hurt anybody. I've *never* hurt anyone."

"No more. *No more.*"

The lights in the room died. The crash and clatter of glass shattering filled the room. James turned back to the door, pounded on it, alternated trying to yank it open and force his shoulder through it. He felt pressure on the left side of his chest. He believed he was shouting for help, but he could not hear himself above the pulse pumping in his ears. The sentences that formed in his head made as much sense to him as possible under the circumstances, but he could not be sure they weren't spinning themselves into lunacy on the way out of his mouth.

Please hear me. Please help me. I am stuck in here with something that was stuck in the mirror. I am stuck in here, please get me out. I am stuck in here with something that thinks I've done something horrible. I am stuck in here with this thing that was stuck too but it's out now. Please help me. I am stuck here and it's out now. I am stuck here with it. I am stuck here. I am stuck here. I am stuck.

The door opened and James fell back onto the floor. The pressure in his chest became an enormous weight pinning him down as if his heart had become an anvil. He could only pull in short sips of breath. A hardening pain seized his lower jaw.

He recognized the two people who had forced the door open and barged in as the employees who worked the welcome desk. One of them, the woman, knelt over him. She talked quickly. James could not hear her any more than he could hear himself. He thought he read the words *heart attack* on her lips.

A strand of embarrassment needled its way through his panic. *Heart attack*. Of course. His exhausted, possibly tumorous brain—inspired by a string of late-night horror pictures—had conjured up its own work of scary fiction and subjected him to it. Frightened him into a hypertensive state and killed him with it. How foolish. How humiliating. If only he hadn't canceled that damn appointment ...

The woman looked at her coworker, shouted at him to get his attention. He stood behind her, his full attention stolen by something to his left. He was facing the wall. The mirrors.

The door slammed shut. As the woman jumped to her feet and the man facing the wall opened his mouth to scream, James felt an odd sense of relief as his life drifted away and he found himself surveying the scene in the room from outside his corpse.

At least it had been real. At least he hadn't died insane. Relieved at this he laughed, almost loud enough to drown out the boy's furious screaming.

A DEVIL WE USED TO KNOW

Originally published in *The Rack: Stories Inspired by Vintage Horror Paperbacks* (September 2024)

Enough seasons had passed for the seasons to no longer be what they once were. The world had changed since the thing had realized it must change its call, since it had last fed well. The cold no longer came when expected and departed sooner than it had when the thing was younger, healthier, and when it ate slowly to indulge in the distinct flavors of blood, marrow, and above all the essence that separated the humans from other animals. In those times, its preferred prey was still developing language and had no stories to pass down that warned of something in the woods. An animal that blended not only with the trees but the space between the trees. A predator whose call mimicked the laughter of children.

The trio of people the thing watched now were not children but may as well have been. Upon hearing the thing's new call, they tittered like babies. No, that was an insult. Children would have known better than to laugh at this new call.

The thing's stomach was too empty to groan, giving it rare cause to be grateful for hunger. The usual hollow noise of its starvation—

the sound of stone shifting deep within a cave—might have alerted the people creeping toward it that they were in danger. Made it easier for them to recognize the thing's eyes for what they were. Not part of the distant stars visible in the clearing, but darker lights that blinked just before you looked away, so fast you could convince yourself you hadn't seen them flicker. If people noticed that, they might sense the shape of the thing without having to see it. Shiver at the coldness of its breath, shudder at the idea of its army of teeth, all without being aware of what made them tremble, just knowing they needed to turn back.

The people fidgeted, spoke to one another in hushed voices, but did not come closer. Were they waiting for another call? Should it oblige their curiosity or remain patient? It could not afford to scare them away. Every second of delay was taxing, painful, but the agony of another famished season would be immeasurably worse.

It strained to remain hidden. Hiding demanded energy, as anything does, and malnourishment had exhausted the thing, as it would anything else. It had tried to sustain itself on everything from wounded birds to grubs. Larger animals could have been had, but by now were not even worth the idle effort of digestion. Spiders proved the closest thing to adequate. They at least had the wherewithal to set traps, employ deception. This made them cunning, clever, and cruel in ways that partly compensated for their diminutiveness. Still, anything that had no awareness of its soul—or even the concept of a soul—was insufficient. This included human corpses. Ideal sustenance came from living things that possessed sapience.

Not only had the world changed in the century since it last ate a proper meal but so had the people. It had recognized this later than it should have, adjusted its call after going hungry long enough to weaken. When had the sound of laughing children become a warning to them? *How*? Joyful innocence shouldn't indicate danger. It had worked for hundreds of years as the exact opposite. A mark of safety. What better beacon of security could there be than the happiness of the young? The thing could never have guessed this call would someday make people run. Even now, its memories of the humans freezing, then fleeing from the sound seemed impossible, a misremembrance, though the thing had seen this dozens of times before accepting it must try something new.

Laughter initially seemed an essential element to an ideal call. Why would someone run upon hearing that? No other creature heard one of their own so enthralled they had to make show of it and thought, "There is a threat present." But no other creature was human. The thing had taken human intelligence and emotion for granted. What made them a delicious and invigorating diet also made them less predictable, at least after centuries of easy feeding. Maybe it was the stories it overheard them telling one another, but the thing felt it was something deeper. A newly formed and better understanding of when something in the world was out of place.

It first observed this change in the darker humans, who eventually learned to avoid its call, but it hadn't concentrated on this because the lighter ones arrived soon after and ignored the warnings of the darker ones even when they appeared to ask for their guidance. That suited the thing well, allowed it to continue eating, maybe too hungrily. If it could change anything in its past sooner—other than its call—it would eat less. Resist gluttony and instead take even more time with the hot blood, the snapping bones, and the syrupy intelligence housed in each individual's skull.

The lighter-colored ones eventually gained the same understanding as the others of darker tones, some of whom were also foreign but nonetheless intrinsically informed of the lure of the monster's call. Likely they had a similar hunter they were warned of in their homelands. The lighter ones, too, must have had cousins to the thing in the places they were from, but had either lost knowledge of such predators or elected to think such things couldn't exist.

Now humans of every shade knew not to be drawn by the laughter of children. The laughter of men and women, in their prime or long past it, also drew no one. The thing remained in denial of this for too long. Laughter in the woods may be out of place, unexpected, but it was still an attractive sound, was it not? It believed for a time that its mimicry was too imperfect, that this was what chased the humans away. Not the idea of the sound itself, but the inaccuracy of the call. It worked diligently to make it as true as possible until the thing was sure the call was indistinguishable from that of an actual person's laughter. Still, they ran.

It adjusted, tried other calls, and discovered people were at least temporarily lured by a cry of pain. People would want to help the ones crying out. They would ask, "Are you okay? Where are you? Are you hurt?" The lack of a response beyond more crying made them wary. This, the creature understood. Their words meant something, and try as it might to form a proper reply, the only word it had mastered was, "Here." Effective enough to draw them in at first. When repeated, however, it sparked alarm. When said once, supplanted by more wailing, it likewise made the humans concerned.

"I'll come back with help," they typically said, or something similar. Then they ran before the thing could pounce.

Its imitations of screams did not work. Nor did its attempt to match the groaning of those exerting themselves on a trek in the woods. The thing even tried coughing. Had it the capacity for such a feeling, the thing would have felt embarrassment at how long it took for it to think of whispering.

No words were necessary for whispers. It was as if such sound was meant to not be understood, or to be mistaken for something else. A sound that people could tell themselves must be the wind rustling leaves, even when the wind was dead. A sound almost like the one the humans made when they hushed one another to listen more intently.

The thing pulled the sound from deep within its long winding throat now, with the four present humans remaining still and silent. It flittered its tongue to give the whisper the vibration of words. An approximation of language. Nothing as clear as its mastered "Here," and that was for the better. To them, it could be saying anything.

One of the men of the group came closer, separating himself from his friends. He had a large beard that seemed to pull his face down, draw his eyes into an ever-serious stare. When he blinked it looked purposeful, like he had never in his life let it be an automatic function.

"Trevor, come back here," one of the two women in the group said. She didn't sound like she meant it. Instead, she seemed to want him to make a discovery, venture into an encounter that would make for a wonderful story.

Humans and their stories.

The thing could smell the man named Trevor's curiosity. His boldness. His aspiration. Things that the soulless did not in the same way possess. No spider, clever as it may be, ever stepped toward an unidentifiable noise in the hopes that this would lead to a tale to tell. A legend its name would be attached to.

Trevor stepped into the clearing. The thing held its position. It had waited so long it thought this moment almost impossible. A deception of some kind. The human's thoughts were intoxicatingly sweet. The dormant, ever-present consciousness of the man's soul—so close—was ferociously luscious, almost as if it had teeth and hunger of its own and would eat the thing if not eaten first.

Now, the thing thought.

Trevor's friends would not try to save him, it knew. They had no weapons, no real grasp of the threat in their midst. They had come here behaving as though they were playing a game, akin to the imaginary children the thing pretended to be several human lifetimes ago.

Now now NOW.

The thing in the woods fell on the human named Trevor, its four jaws wide, its tentacular tongue uncoiling, its enormous, needle-lined stomach spasming in anticipation. Its satiation at long last soon to come.

The human Trevor vanished within its mouth, and with its dorsal eyes the thing saw his friends jump back, then go stiller than the trees surrounding them, then scream. Then run. Two of them first. The last, the girl who had spoken to Trevor earlier, called his name once, as though this could save him, then followed her friends as fast as she could.

Trevor struggled in the grip of curved, hooking teeth that he could not see, within darkness that seemed an outgrowth of the night sky. Fear, pain, and bewilderment made up the parts of his screams, and the thing wished it could disgorge him and eat him anew. Eat him a hundred times over to make up for lost, hungry years. Its teeth twisted and bored through skin, muscle, cartilage, and bone. It made hideous art of its meal, saving the brain for last so the human Trevor could distantly comprehend the reshaping of his body, grasp the absurdity of his transformation more than the pain of his thousand wounds, understand that his soul was so much more than his physical vessel ever could be, while simultaneously realizing that it, too, was now nothing more than food.

The thing ate too quickly, as all things would if starved long enough to catch sight of death. Even before it swallowed the last of Trevor's howling thoughts, it recognized this, but could not slow down, much less stop itself. It saved none of him for later. It licked its teeth clean, and as it now rested, as full as it had been in ages, it contemplated the idea of sadness over something lost. It was familiar with the concept through observation alone, having seen humans in times long gone return to the woods and cry not out of physical pain, but a different anguish. A longing for another person who had entered the forest and never returned. They would whisper names that the thing had felt in its stomach, in minds dissolving in acid.

It thought it felt something close to that now. As close as it could come to grieving. A great and hopeless desire to reverse time, relive something important and special. It could never have the human Trevor back. Never get another opportunity to take its time, pull him apart more methodically, as it would have in an earlier time. It could only ever remember him, what he provided in its desperation, and if it could have wept, it thought it might have done so this once, for this one human.

It was possible he would be its last meal. If the people were smarter, this would be the last warning they ever needed to avoid its habitat—even in packs—and to run away from any humanlike call coming from something unseen. But the thing felt more assured than it had in centuries that more would come. Something about humanity now—something it tasted in Trevor's thoughts—led the thing to believe that people wanted to be fooled. Wanted to disbelieve in creatures they could not see, fight, or even properly name, while also wanting to be proven wrong about their incredulity. They sought to flout any warnings, as well, and challenge their own mortality. These deep, defiant instincts had always been part of them, but never so prevailing. Something had changed in them. It made sense. Nothing stayed the same forever.

The seasons had changed, some shorter and weaker, some longer and harsher. The humans had changed multiple times, first growing more cautious, and now, perhaps, more reckless and curious, to a degree that made the thing salivate.

Because it, too, had changed. Better, it had adapted. A stone battered by wind and rain over time is altered, but true adaptation within a lifetime requires awareness. Intelligence.

The thing returned to its shelter and slept peacefully, without fear of waking up hungry. It was sure that it would not starve again for many seasons to come.

XII
יב
十二
12

NO HUNGRY GENERATIONS

Originally published in *Death in the Mouth: Original Horror by People of Color* (October 2022)

The bird looked like the last descendant of a prehistoric mishap. Fatter than a turkey and wild-eyed even after death, it had small feet and a golden beard on its chest that may as well have been a neon sign reading Shoot Here. Mother Nature must've been nursing a hangover when she made it and rushed the job, just wanting to get the day over with.

Mabel had never felt compassion for any animal the men of the family brought home after a hunt—circle of life and so on—but she felt a twinge of guilt looking at the plump carcass of this unfortunate thing. Hunting it would have been like playing dodgeball against a toddler.

She picked it up by its thick thighs. It was even heavier than it looked. Largest bird she'd ever cooked was a twenty-pounder. This one felt like it was north of thirty pounds. The neck was as fat as the end of a baseball bat, the body so round it was comical.

"Where in the world did you find this thing?" Mabel said.

"Woods, other side of the hill," her husband, Josey, said. "Don't think it's a turkey."

"I'm sure it's not. I can't say what it is."

"Us neither," he said, nodding to their sons, Brock and Bennet. "That's why we bagged it."

"*That's* why?" Mabel said. "How do we even know this thing's edible?"

Josey shrugged. "It's a bird. Big as it is, got to have some good meat on it." What he lacked in size, looks, and charisma, he made up in stoicism. If he ever somehow woke up in the middle of sky, found himself plummeting to the earth, he'd probably yawn, stretch, and spend his remaining moments thinking of how others had been worse off than him. To Mabel, there was something irresistible about how he neither worried nor impressed easily. Those moments when she raised a legitimate concern about one thing or another, and he just shrugged, as if to say, "It'll work out, and if it doesn't, we'll make the best of it," made her want to jump him on the spot.

She'd have him scratch that itch later. Right now, there was the question of what to do with this odd bird. Worst-case scenario, the thing would give off a scent during prep or cooking that would let her know it wasn't safe to eat. If she had to throw it out, it wouldn't hurt anything. They already had two good fifteen-pound turkeys cleaned and marinating—one to be roasted, one to be smoked—which was more than enough to feed the family and provide leftovers, especially with the ham she was also making. Josey, Brock, and Bennet had only gone out to see if they could find another bird because, what the hell, "more is more," and what was Thanksgiving for if not feasting? They were blessed with land that was generous, and it had taken generations for their family to come upon such stable fortune. In Mabel's view, turning down any gift the land provided made them ingrates.

"Need help with it?" Josey asked.

"Just the usual before cooking. Brock, go grab Gale. She told me she wants to see how y'all do it."

"I don't know, Mom," Brock said. "She says that, but she's really kinda squeamish."

"I'm aware," Mabel said, and Brock put up no further protest to his daughter witnessing the gutting and cleaning.

"I'll go get her," he said.

"Thank you," Mabel said. Then to all of them, "Go get washed up a little first. You all smell like you need three baths apiece."

Josey smirked as much as he ever did and kissed her on the cheek before excusing himself from the kitchen. Brock and Bennet followed. Mabel turned her attention back to the bird. Alone with it now, that unexpected guilt for what she was about to do returned. Shouldn't this thing be in the care and study of some scientist or wildlife expert? What if her men had plugged and bagged an endangered species? Now they were about to eat it. All but erase it from having ever been.

Taking a page from Josey's book, she shrugged it off, then waited for Gale to join her. The little girl was tougher than her daddy gave her credit for. That, or she was just trying to be tougher, which was good enough for Mabel. It reminded her of herself when she was that young.

The aroma was as appetizing as it was thick. Damn near oppressive, if such a word could be applied as a compliment. Hell, that didn't seem right at all, yet Mabel could think of no better description for the scent of the gilded non-turkey roasting in the oven. It was smoky-sweet, warm and tangy, and something else she had no word for, had never smelled before. It was meaty, but also light and flighty as the smell of pastries fresh out of the oven. One moment, it seemed to have hooks that dug in deep, then you'd sniff again and it would be gone, and you'd find yourself missing it so much, it ached. There had to be a word for this. Savory? She'd never quite known what people meant when they said something was savory.

Was this it? If so, she was upset at having missed out on this flavor all her life. If this bird tasted half as good as it smelled, this was going to be the best dinner she'd ever had.

"If one more person asks me when that bird's going to be ready, I'm gonna beat the lot of you unconscious," Mabel said after Bennet and his wife, Ellie, became the sixth and seventh members of the family to ask.

"Just as long as you wake us up when it's done," Josey said. That got a good laugh out of the household, although there was a hint of discomfort within the laughter, as if everyone was trying to convince themselves that the aroma wasn't getting to them. Mabel understood how they felt. She was in the kitchen with Gale and the girl's mother, Katie, putting the final touches on the rest of Thanksgiving dinner. Every minute or so she had to quell the urge to take the bird out of the oven, tear off a leg, and have at it. It felt like her stomach was a bottomless well and wanted no part of anything else they had prepared: five baked pies, two turkeys, a glazed ham, stuffing, collard greens, sweet potato casserole, mashed potatoes, roasted corn, cornbread.

When the food was ready, the family gathered around the two tables in the dining room. They had barely said a word to each other for the last fifteen minutes. During the blessing—which Josey rushed through so quickly that "in Jesus's name, amen" became "njeeznamen"—Mabel peeked at the beautiful bird at the center of the longer table. She saw that Brock, Katie, and both of Bennet's sons also had their eyes open and fixed on it. A predatory instinct switched on in her, and she wanted to leap across the table and pounce on the bird before the others got to it first. This quickly subsided, replaced by concern.

Get rid of it, she thought. *Throw it out, then throw away the trash can you threw it in. That thing is wrong*. The thought came and went like a lousy door-to-door salesman, full of initial bluster, then sheepish upon rejection. There was no way she was going to throw that bird out. Her family might tear her apart if she attempted it, which was further proof that she should get rid of the thing, but she couldn't see it that way at the moment. Beyond that, the anticipation of discovering a new, lovely flavor—feeling that dead muscle between her teeth, licking the juices from her lips—was almost unbearable. You could scrap waterboarding, electric shocks, and any other interrogation tactics. Just roast this bird, sit it in front of somebody, and tell them they don't get a bite until they tell you everything they know. You'd run out of ink and paper before they were half finished confessing.

Papa Clay, Josey's dad, handled the carving. He was pushing eighty and suffering from a life of landscaping labor, booze-fueled partying, and, much more recently, rheumatoid arthritis. His hands shook when he took the electric carver to the bird. It took everything in Mabel not to yell at her father-in-law to hurry the hell up or pass the carver to his son.

Any other year, she and Josey made sure Papa Clay was served first, then they helped their sons and daughters-in-law make plates for the children. Now, though, when Papa Clay was done, Mabel speared a piece of breast meat with her fork and took a bite before it made it to her plate. Josey didn't bother with a fork, grabbing a handful of breast meat instead. Apparently, seeing where this was going and realizing she might be left with scraps if she waited for the adults or her older cousins to feed her, little Gale jumped up on the table and scrambled to get at the bird. By then, everyone was digging in, all with their hands, which was a blessing, because if any of them had taken Mabel's lead and used a fork, someone would have gotten stabbed.

What prevented them from truly fighting each other was that it would take away from precious eating time. They were content to shove, grunt, throw an elbow here or a kick under the table there, until they could stuff their mouths and be overcome by the taste for a moment, eyes rolling back, obscene sounds of delight coming from them. Then they would swallow and be consumed again by the thought of eating more.

Part of Mabel, well past being appalled at their primitive, unmannerly behavior, was frightened by what was happening. But that small piece of her normal self was like a single, quiet cry for help amid a crowd roaring with laughter. The intensity of the bird's flavor occupied every sense she had. It made her skin tingle; it made her hear cool whispers that tickled her inner ear. She saw everyone and everything around her shining like they were made of sunlight, and each time she swallowed a bite and all those feelings went away, it made her want to cry, until she set her sights on the next bite.

The family reduced the carcass to bones in just under ten minutes. Mabel felt exhausted and overstuffed, and a little regretful that they hadn't saved any for later. Then, like the others, she fell asleep in her chair as though drugged, leaving the remaining food untouched.

"Gramma, I don't feel good."

It was Gale, nudging Mabel's shoulder to wake her up. Mabel had heard the girl's voice in a dream she was having, in which she saw a gaunt, sallow face that barely resembled her granddaughter accompanying the voice. When she woke up and saw the girl was still her rosy-cheeked self—a little sad-eyed, but nothing worse—a wave of relief hit her hard enough to restore her mind. She pushed her chair away from the table and surveyed the room. Daylight still beamed through the windows. She hadn't checked the exact time before dozing off but knew they set the table a little before two that afternoon. She looked at her watch, saw that the date hadn't changed and that it was almost three o'clock. At least she hadn't been out for too long. Around the table, everyone else was either dead asleep or groggily waking up.

"I don't feel good," Gale said again.

A gripping pain tightened Mabel's stomach. It wasn't unfamiliar. Once upon a time, when she was much younger, she'd known what it was like to go a day or two without eating. She would never forget the hollow pain of going hungry. But that didn't make sense, given how she had just gorged herself.

"I don't feel so good either," she said to Gale. "Probably none of us will. We all ate too much."

Gale shook her head. "It's not that. When I woke up, I was hungry. I was so hungry it was like ... it was like when I got in the ivy and couldn't stop scratching. Remember? It was like that, but with being hungry. I felt it all over. I had to eat something. I wanted more of that bird we made, but there's none left. So I ate some turkey instead, and it tasted so rotten I wanted to spit it out, but I had to eat something. But now I feel sick. It's getting worse and worse, Gramma. I think I might need to ..."

The child choked down a burp that Mabel knew was a precursor to her throwing up. She stood up, took Gale by the hand, and rushed her down the hall to the nearest bathroom. She held Gale's hair back while she purged. Long retches racked the girl, curved her back and made her sob in pain when she could catch her breath between heaves.

We made a mistake, Mabel thought. *I knew I should have thrown that thing out. I knew it.*

The sound of someone else in the house getting sick reinforced this belief. Then she heard two others retching.

Mabel called out to the household, "Y'all, don't eat anything else! Something's wrong with the food!"

That wasn't the real truth, she knew. Nothing was wrong with any of the other food. Gale had said the turkey tasted rotten, but that couldn't have been true. No truer than the stabbing, brutal hunger Mabel was fighting against now. It tried to pull her from her granddaughter, draw her back to the dining room to eat the first thing she saw. Ham, pie, greens, anything. But even thinking of what those things smelled like, seeing them in her mind, made her gag. It was like she saw them with flies or worms crawling out of them. Smelled them after they'd been outdoors for weeks. Still, she had to try to eat something soon. She was so hungry, she was getting a headache.

Someone knocked on the bathroom door as Gale spit up the last of what was in her stomach. "Who's there?" Mabel said.

The door opened and Josey walked in. The only thing that could have made Mabel forget about eating, even for a moment, was the look on his face. She recalled the time Josey helped a woman who went into labor at the state fair deliver her baby before paramedics arrived. The whole time, he had looked like he was talking to a neighbor about the weather. The same went for the time Josey told a knife-wielding man at a bar that he either needed to come on with it—get to fighting—or go home and get a head start on sleeping off his hangover. She had thought Josey was incapable of getting scared. As it turned out, he was saving all of his fear for a moment like this, when he needed to say more with his wide eyes, parted lips, and heavy breaths than he could with a ten-minute speech.

"We're in trouble, Mabes," he said. "Something ain't right."

"I'm aware," Mabel said. When Gale whimpered, Mabel put her arms around the girl and brought her close but resisted the urge to say things were going to be okay. She couldn't see how lying to the girl would do any good.

It didn't take long for the family to sample the remaining food and discover it all tasted contaminated or spoiled, to put it mildly, and that swallowing any of it made you ill. Bennet, Ellie, and their two sons remained in denial long enough to make themselves sick thrice. Everybody else took their first and only experience as all the evidence they needed.

"What's happening to us, Mom?" Bennet asked. "I feel like I haven't eaten in a week. I'm exhausted, I'm hurting. I don't understand what's going on. You think maybe that bird gave us some kind of food poisoning?"

"Could be," Mabel said, though she didn't believe this, and saw on their faces that no one else did either. Food poisoning. If only they were so fortunate. They could go to a hospital for that. The bird had done something else to them, and none of them could pretend otherwise. She sighed. "I really don't think that's it, though. I wish it were that simple."

"What are we gonna do?" Brock said.

"Y'all said you found that bird where, again?" Mabel asked. "Other side of the hill?"

"In the woods out there," Josey said. "Where we should've left it."

"Too late for that," Mabel said. "If there was one of them there, there has to be more. And we all need to eat something soon."

"I'm not sure that's the best idea."

"I don't have a better one, Josey. Do you?"

He shook his head, and if his headache was as bad as hers, she thought that must have been blindingly painful. But he didn't show it.

"You're right," he said. "Boys, get your rifles. Let's go."

"Let's all go," Mabel said. "We need as many eyes looking out for it as we can get."

Brock said, "That ain't the best thing to do when you're hunting, Mom."

"No, she's right," Josey said. "We don't have to worry about scaring it off. That thing didn't even turn its head when it heard us, remember? It stood there and waited like it wanted us to get it."

You should have told me that, Mabel thought. *I would've trusted my gut and gotten rid of it if I had known that*. But she couldn't know if that was true, and blaming her men for doing what she was normally happy to see them do wasn't a productive course to take. "You heard your father. We're all going. Come on, we're all in this together."

A few minutes later, as they shuffled out of the house like malnourished prisoners on a forced march, Mabel gave the beautiful house she and Josey had built a long look. She hated to leave it in such poor shape, with some of them having gotten sick on the dining-room floor, others in the kitchen. What would other people think when they saw how her family had left the house? Lord, why was she thinking of it that way, like it was going to sit there unoccupied until some friends stopped by to check on them and were stopped dead at the door by the smell? Why was she thinking of it like they weren't going to come back tonight, or at all?

The hunger had teeth. It ate her alive as she walked. Enduring it, and being in the woods where her men found the bird, gave Mabel excruciating clarity about what had happened to her family. The suffering was like a darkly religious experience. Enlightening in a hideous way. She thought she understood now why sacrifices were once common, why some even volunteered for it. Why some zealots practiced self-flagellation or wore hair shirts. Pain had revelatory potential. It wasn't worth it. Mabel would rather remain ignorant. Moreover, she'd rather her sons and her grandchildren didn't have to go through this.

They hardly spoke as they walked, save for the rare occasion when they mistakenly thought they saw a large bird with a bright beard behind a tree or in the brush. Their collective silence told Mabel more than she wanted to hear. It told her they were all stuck in their thoughts, probably thinking similar things. Like how they were all just made of meat and blood encased in skin. Ingredients. That's all any living thing was. An eater made of parts meant to be eaten. Destined someday to be soil for plants, or nutrients for bugs, or fuel for a fire if you elected cremation. Before your time came, though, if you went long enough without eating, your own body would turn you into food, eating whatever it could spare, for as long as it could.

These were simple truths. Common knowledge, even, except most people never thought about it. Mabel couldn't get it out of her mind, along with a few other things. Like how nature—or whatever held seniority above it—might try to curb humankind once it got too voracious. How long would it let people devour more than their share? Let them believe that they were so much more than mere flesh? Why not use their appetite against them? Few among them would resist eating something so delicious it not only made everything else taste rancid, it made your body awaken to the truth of its decay, the truth that it was fated to be a meal far less memorable. Even if they knew ahead of time what would happen, they'd still take a bite.

Mabel imagined Mother Nature grinning at her plot, thinking, *Since you all can't help yourselves, here you go, help yourselves.*

The echoing clap of a rifle shot brought Mabel out of her thoughts. She turned back to see Josey pointing his gun at Papa Clay. The older man was dead on the ground, a bloody hole in his chest. Josey's shoulders slumped. He sniffled once before straightening up and turning around.

"He asked me to," Josey said.

Mabel narrowed her eyes like she couldn't make out what she saw, then something told her to look around, pay attention to her surroundings. For the first time, she noticed that dusk had settled in. When had they left the house? No later than four o'clock. They had been walking in the woods for a couple of hours. For an arthritic old man whose body told him he was starving, it might as well have been a couple of days. His pain was more than he could bear. That, or seeing three generations of his family as they were—food in waiting—was too much for him. Mabel had no doubt Josey told the truth. Papa Clay asked to be killed, even if no one else heard him say the words.

The children whined at the sight, too weak to muster a proper cry. Mabel saw Brock and Katie sharing a glance and nodding at each other. Brock winced from the movement.

"Momma," Katie said, pushing Gale toward Mabel, "would you take her, please? Brock and I … um …"

She turned to Brock, who said, "I think we've got to split up if we're going to find this thing. We got to find it fast before any more of us … Well, we have to cover more ground. But it's getting too dark, and I don't want to accidentally shoot Gale out here. She'll be … she'll be safer with you."

Tears filled Mabel's eyes. "That's not a good idea. We should stick together."

"Mom, it's okay," Brock said. "I know you'll take care of her."

"Listen to me, boy. I'm your mother. Tell him, Josey. We have to stay together."

Josey was barely present, though. He was still looking at his father and didn't react when Mabel called on him.

"Keep looking, Mom," Brock said, "and if you find that thing before we do, please take care of Gale first, okay?"

Then he turned with Katie to make their own path, away from the group. Mabel moved toward them, intending to run after them, but she was in no shape for that, and when Gale grabbed her wrist, she stopped.

A few minutes later, after the group returned to walking and searching, a gunshot sounded off in the distance. Mabel let herself hope for a moment that Brock had found the bird and killed it. She started to say they should turn back to find them. Then the second shot rang out. She knew it wouldn't take two shots to bring the bird down, and that the odds that Brock and Katie had found two of those things were infinitely slimmer than the likelihood that they'd found their own way out of this misery.

Bennet, Elaine, and their boys stopped to rest around midnight.

"Go on ahead, we'll catch up," Bennet said.

More than she wanted to tell them to keep on, that they had walked too long to give up now, Mabel wanted to lie down with them. She couldn't do that, however, any more than she could make them keep going. She had to look after Gale. So she gave Bennet, Elaine, and her grandsons each a kiss, then let them go without a fuss. Let them have their peace instead of dying with the knowledge that they were breaking her heart. They probably knew that, anyway.

Mabel knew she wouldn't hear shots after she left them. They would let death come to them on its own, in its own time, and it would not take long.

Josey trailed her and Gale as they walked toward the moon like it was there to guide them. Mabel made herself think Josey was protecting them from any threat that could creep up behind them. As if it wouldn't be a mercy for a cougar or coyote to accelerate inevitability, free them from their final illusions of survival. Maybe Josey lagged because he was thinking the same thing, that ending things soon and swiftly, as he had with his father, would be the last and best thing he could do for his remaining family. He was back there unsure of who he should shoot first, torn up by the decision. He would lose his nerve if she looked back at him, so Mabel kept her eyes forward, kept Gale moving with her, kept praying for Josey to have strength, for his aim to be true. She did not pray for salvation. Not until she saw the soft, golden light seeping through the branches ahead.

Her heart almost stopped, and she willed herself not to faint. She begged God to let this be real, please don't let it be a mirage. *Please, Lord.*

The trees made a hushing sound as a breeze passed, carrying with it a scent that made Mabel's mouth water. It smelled fresh like fruit, but more succulent. Warm as well. Her stomach growled and she held it like she believed it would open a mouth of its own if she didn't put her hand over it.

"Gramma … Gramma, I smell food," Gale said, panting with excitement.

"Me too," Mabel said, beginning to wonder if this was a trap. What else could it be? They were just food themselves, after all.

Nothing more. What was more likely—that they had lucked upon something as irresistible as that one-of-a-kind bird, or that they were being baited by a clever, unknown predator? Didn't their hunter know, though, that deception wasn't necessary? Their prey was ready to fall down, too famished and weak to fight or flee. This trick was pointless, and crueler than killing.

"Josey, do you see this too? And do you smell that? It's like … I can't tell what it is, but we've got to try to get to it, don't we? Josey?"

She knew before she turned around that he wouldn't be there. How long ago had he left them? Why hadn't he at least given her a chance to say goodbye? She knew the answer to that last question. She would have wanted to stay with him. Then she would have come to her senses, remembered that she owed it to Gale to keep going, but they would have lost some time, and who knew how much more time they had? Every second might be valuable, and she'd have spent minutes trying to talk Josey out of giving up, then talking herself out of staying with him, then finally telling him to hold her seat at the table wherever he ended up. Those minutes might have cost them this moment, this chance.

"Thank you, Josey," Mabel said.

Gale pulled Mabel's arm to get her moving again. "Gramma, come on. We're close. We can eat and take some back to Momma and Pop and everyone else."

"Yes, we can," Mabel said, getting more lightheaded with each step toward the light. She could hardly lift her free arm to move the thin lower branches of trees that brushed and scratched her face. Barely had the strength to duck beneath the ones she couldn't push away. It was all she could do to keep from dropping to her knees, knowing Gale would try to drag her the rest of the way.

When they broke into a clearing, they slid down a brief slope that brought them before a sprawling tree with a shimmering, bright yellow bark that almost looked metallic. Its unnatural shine stung Mabel's eyes, and the aroma emanating from it was so tantalizing she thought its source must be evil. Nothing good could come of something so tempting.

As her eyes adjusted, she saw things that whittled at her sanity. The tree's size spoke to its age. It had to be ancient to have grown so wide, to have structural roots larger than the trunks of every other tree nearby. But it couldn't have been here all this time. They'd have seen this glow before. They should have seen it earlier tonight. It was as if it had hidden itself until it wanted to be seen. What had brought it to life now, at this time of year? The answer was in the question. It was the time of year. What the family did every fourth Thursday in November, that's what brought it to life. It was the day they were least apt to question any bounty granted to them, no matter how unusual. They would count it as a blessing and be thankful for their giving land.

Large, bulbous protrusions grew from some of the roots. Oval-shaped and speckled, they did not look like they were made of what the rest of the tree was made of. When one shuddered and cracked, Mabel understood what they were. Eggs. She didn't need to see one of them open up to know an ugly bird, identical to the one they had eaten, would emerge. The realization should have made her sick, but it just made her salivate more. If only she had the tools on hand to clean and gut one of those birds, the energy to build a fire. She'd break the rest of the shell open with her hands to get to what was inside, have it roasting over a flame in no time.

"Gramma, help. I can't reach." For a moment, she couldn't tell where Gale's voice came from, and the last reserves she had were spent on panic. She circled the tree and found the girl on the other side, trying to climb one of the lower branches to get to hanging clusters that looked like fist-sized, blue strawberries. Mabel looked up and saw a variety of oversized fruits, all in strange or vivid colors. Silvery grapes, apples with mirrored, ruby skin. The tree trembled, seemingly of its own accord, and sent down a wave of enticing fragrances.

"Gramma, please," Gale said.

"I'm coming," Mabel said, but as she stepped toward her granddaughter to give her a boost, a root caught her foot, and she collapsed against the tree.

Not now, she thought, as she felt her consciousness start to fade. *Not this close. Let me just help her. After that, take me away. But let me help her, for heaven's sake, I'm begging you.* She wasn't praying to God, but to the tree, and knew immediately that it heard her.

She didn't feel the piercing at first, then felt every place that a root was jabbing through her all at once. A tingling sensation spread through her, followed by a softening of her bones and slippage of her skin. It was agony, but nothing she couldn't tolerate for the rest of her life, given how short that would be. She refused to scream. If her courage broke, Gale's would too.

"It's okay," she said as Gale stared at her. Mabel wondered if she'd only mouthed the words. She couldn't hear anything anymore. Her senses faded by the second as the tree fed from her, which was good. It lessened the pain. She thought the tree did this deliberately. Whatever its agenda, it didn't want her to suffer. Just to be sustenance.

For Gale, it wanted something else. It wanted to nourish and adopt her. Bring her up for some other purpose. Maybe to lure others here to be made food for the woods and its inhabitants. Maybe to help the tree keep others away. Mabel only understood that the tree wanted to keep Gale alive. She could not tell if part of her consciousness—her protectiveness—was infecting the tree while it devoured her, or if it had planned this for Gale all along. Her head said it was the latter, but her heart said the former, and she made the choice to believe that. She deserved that minor relief before dying, didn't she?

She raised her hand to touch Gale's face—let her know she would be fine on her own—but shuddered at her own reflection when she saw a large, jewellike apple sprouting from her palm.

Gale hesitated only a moment before ripping the apple from Mabel's hand and biting it like it was the neck of an animal she meant to kill. Its juice was a lighter shade of red, and it spilled down Gale's chin. The little girl shut her eyes in bliss before taking another bite, then sat down and held the apple close like it was a favorite doll and she was pretending it was her child.

If Mabel could have smiled, she would have, but she was more soil than human now, and her consciousness joined her body and crumbled into the earth.

XII
יב
12

THE GENIE AND THE INQUISITOR

Originally published in *Fantasy Scroll Magazine*
(February 2016, Issue 10)

Gray smoke billowed from the broken glass ornament, and from the smoke emerged a face. The chin appeared first—a sharpened cone with a beard pointed like pencil lead—then the grin, wide and bright, two parallel rows of pristine teeth. The eyes blinked, then opened, circles of clear water with tight blue orbs for pupils. The genie pitched its head back and laughed, a raucous sound, like boulders racing down a cliff.

"Come!" it said, its voice rumbling and welcoming. "Surely you know what I am. There have been stories of my kind as long as there have been stories! Surely you must know, or must I tell you?"

The man shook his head. He was short and plain. He spoke with a meek but clear tone and the hasty cadence of an uncertain salesman. "No need to explain. I know what you are."

"Well then, come! Wish! Surely you've dreamed of this moment. Do not be overwhelmed, and do not doubt this is real. Come, make your first wish!"

"Why the rush? Are you in a hurry?"

The genie chortled. “Are you not? Your dreams await you, dear man. Come!”

“Yes, yes, ‘come make my first wish.’ I only get the three, don’t I? Isn’t that the rule?”

“It is.”

“So why the rush? Wouldn’t it be wise for me to take a moment? Be sure of what I want to wish for?”

Another avalanche of laughter. “Trust me, dear man. I’ve met many of your kind. You’re all interesting in your own way, and yet you all have an unbelievable talent for outsmarting yourselves. The wish you should speak is whatever has lived in your heart the longest. Whatever you’ve envisioned wishing for in this very moment, which I know you’ve dreamed of, as all of your kind has. Happiness is not born of the mind but of the heart! What you *think* you’ll want, you’ll come to regret. What you’ve *yearned* for is what you’ll cherish.”

The man shook his head, removed his glasses, and rubbed his eyes. “You really are all the same,” he said.

The genie narrowed its eyes. “What was that?”

The man put his glasses back on and stepped forward. “You want my wish, here it is. I wish for you to answer any question I ask you with absolute, unambiguous honesty.”

A brush of wind seemed to pass through the smoke, scattering the djinn’s face into a scowl.

“I’m not sure I understand. You wish for me to … ?”

“I won’t repeat myself,” the man said. “You heard me. You’re suspicious too. It’s an odd wish. But it is what I want. I won’t reconsider or rephrase. Now grant what I’ve wished for as you are meant to do.”

His last words held no true sway, but as a reminder to the djinn of its role, they were effective as a command. The genie composed itself and nodded. “Granted,” it said. Then it forced a broad smile, one worthy of a devil that had come upon a trove of unclaimed souls. “So what questions do you have for me, little man?”

"If I were to be careless in how I phrased my next wish, would you use that as an opportunity to turn my wish against me?"

"What precisely do you mean by turning your—?"

"You know *precisely* what I mean."

The genie remained silent, though its wraithlike face appeared to harden around one eye. Small gray pustules budded where its once-smoky countenance had solidified.

"You're going to make me elaborate," the man said. "Fine. If I were to ask for a sum of money but didn't specify how the money should come to me, would you take the liberty to provide the money in a way that you know will bring me harm? Let's say, give me the money due to an accident. I do have insurance that covers me for death and dismemberment. I didn't specify that I'd have to live to enjoy my money. Or that I'd have to remain physically intact. Or perhaps the money would come to me by illegal means for which I'd soon be convicted. Rich men can still go to prison once in a while, where their money's no good to them. But that wouldn't be your concern. You'd have held up your end, right? At least technically."

The pustules under the genie's left eye had clustered and grown so thick that they forced the eye shut.

"Those possibilities are all dependent on your definition of careless," the genie said.

The man sighed. "You're dodging the question."

"No, I'm telling you the truth. That is what you asked for." The malformations sprouting in the genie's face began to fade and the genie could not mask its relief.

"No," the man said, "I asked for honesty, not truth. The truth is merely factual, and facts can be used to deliberately deceive. Honesty is truth that is free of deceit. I wished for you to be *honest*. You're violating that wish."

A convulsive snarl curled half the genie's mouth. It fought to remain silent, to remain as it wanted to appear, but the infected pustules re-formed on its face, migrating and ballooning into larger deformities. The pain was soon apparent, but the genie continued to fight to defy its calling, deny a granted wish, until one of its eyes snapped open like a snake's mouth and revealed rows of bent needle-thin teeth. The genie emitted a short scream that could have sheared iron. The man plugged his ears, winced. Then he laughed.

"Outsmart ourselves," the man said. "That's what you think? Well, who's being outsmarted now?"

"I am," the genie roared before realizing the question had been rhetorical. But providing an honest answer released it from the torture of violating its purpose. Too much damage had been done for it to reassume its previously adopted form, however. It now stood naked before the man, a bipedal mass of huge gray worms melting into and devouring one another, consuming and expelling themselves. "What do you want?" the genie asked.

"I want my initial question answered," said the man.

"Yes," the djinn rasped in a hundred voices, more a spasm than a response. "*Yes*. I'll take any wish you speak, any dream you desire, and turn it into a nightmare. Do you know what I am? Do you know the wrath you have provoked, little man?"

"Not any wish," the man said. "But we'll come back to that. For now, I have more questions. Why would you want to turn a man's dream into a nightmare? What could you possibly gain from doing that?"

"Watching your kind suffer is its own gain," the djinn said, and tried to laugh but succumbed to a fit of retching instead. The throng of worms fell to the floor, growing arms to brace itself, its thin legs folding under the weight of its hopeless defiance. "It is … a delight … to watch you suffer—"

"Please stop. Save yourself the misery. You're well past the point of impressing or intimidating me. For heaven's sake, look at you. Look at what you were when you first showed up and look at what you are now. What you truly are. If I wasn't so disgusted, I'd be embarrassed for you. Do yourself a favor and just answer honestly."

The djinn tried to stand and failed. A large, misshapen head sprouted from the top of its torso and flopped to the floor, the neck a wilted, wet stem. A shiftless blue eye surfaced on the side of its head, blinking slowly as if drugged.

"Answer the question," the man said.

"I do it because ... *because.* We do it *because* ... Stop this ... please."

The man smiled. "'Because.' That is your answer, isn't it? You don't really know why you do it. Twist people's wants and hopes. There's no point to it. It's just what you do. Just 'because.' I keep waiting for one of you to give a more satisfying answer. But at this point, I'm thinking you're all the same."

"One of us?" the genie said, its back and chest heaving, its arms trying to push its body upright. "One of us? How many? Who are you?"

The genie's eye burned into a shade of red the color of pain. "How many of us have you done this to? Who are you? How have you done this?"

"I'm not finished," the man said. "Next question: What is the one thing you fear most?"

The genie shrieked and shriveled, its limbs recoiling into its body. "Please! Please stop this! I'll grant you any wish, and I'll leave it a dream. I promise, no nightmares, no corruption, only what you ask for as you want it. I swear. *Please!*"

The man stood over the djinn's head, stooped to look into its eye. He knew he needn't ask again or coax the genie to answer. Its agony would compel it to do so.

"Alone ... forever," the genie said. "What I fear most ... I cannot die ... none of my kind can die. Ever. We exist ... across ... worlds. Can never die ... and are always found. Always. But to be lost forever. Alone forever ... that is ..."

"It's okay," the man said, going down to one knee and lightly patting the genie's head. "You don't have to say any more. You've been very honest. And that answer is one I actually haven't heard before. So thank you for that. Now I'd like to make my next wish. My last, in fact. There won't be a third. But before that, there is just one more question I need answered. And remember, truth without deceit.

"Now, how exactly should I phrase my next wish to ensure that your worst fear comes true?"

Too weak to scream, the genie wept and simpered and tried to slither away from the man. But the resistance did not last very long. There were, after all, rules to obey. And there was a final question to be answered.

A week later, after a pleasant dinner with friends, the man returned home and treated himself to a glass of wine. One glass soon became four, which soon became an empty bottle, and looking into the empty bottle made him think of the first djinn he'd encountered. The one who'd given him a hard lesson in the danger of carelessly worded wishes. The one he was still acquainted with.

While the bottle reminded him of that first djinn and all that he'd lost and learned with that first wish, it was the wine that inspired him to wonder if they really were "all the same." Likely so, but perhaps not. Exceptions could exist, after all.

With this in mind, he went upstairs to the second floor of his home and unlocked the hall closet. Something on the floor—something shapeless and as thin as a day's layer of dust—shivered to life and slunk away into the corner.

"Sorry, I know it's a bit late," said the man, leaning on the doorjamb, "but I was thinking I'd like to meet some more of your kind. I'd like to see if they're any friendlier. Or see if they're like you and all the rest I've met. Come on, you're not really going to make me ask, are you? Okay, fine. Just remember: honesty.

"Now, where can I find another one of you?"

EVERY TIME YOU LOOK AWAY

Lincoln had long tried to imagine something comparable to the dread of seeing a ghost, something he could use to describe the feeling to those who would never understand.

"Imagine falling over the side of a cliff, the exact moment when you realize you're *over* the side, and gravity isn't giving you back. Nothing is there to catch you, there's nothing for you to grab onto. There's got to be an instant where you realize, 'This is it.' That's close to what it's like."

What would he say now to the people he'd given that little speech to before? "Try to imagine something worse than what was already worse than knowing you're going to fall to your death."

What could he compare this to? Nothing but itself, if he was to truly be accurate. The feeling was not a singular thing, but a mosaic of tangible, awful sensations. Lightheadedness that made every second of consciousness a miracle. A pain in his chest like his heart had grown too dense and was collapsing, threatening to bring the rest of his body with it, crush it all down to a pinpoint. A tempest in his stomach sitting atop a strange void in his loins. All held aloft by legs he could not be sure still existed, even if he could bring himself to look at them, rub his hands over them, verify that they were there.

More entrenched and severe than any of these was the thought that brought his hopelessness to heights far beyond the reach of oxygen.

I shouldn't have come here.

The walls to his left and right had changed. The wall behind him had changed as well, but his peripheral vision gave him immediate confirmation of the changes to the walls on either side of him. The painting to his left was no longer a tall portrait, but a wide landscape. Yellow wallpaper plastered the formerly stone wall on the opposite side, which hadn't been stone two looks ago, much less yellow. It had originally been white. Then it had been black. Faux brick before becoming wood.

I shouldn't have come here.

Yet here he was, in a hotel room reputed to be haunted by people who only shared their experiences in chapbooks, or in old obscure articles from defunct niche magazines, or in person, in private. Never on the more easily researchable areas of the web, or even in the more hidden, far corners of it. That increased the risk that your experience could catch the wrong attention, spread, go viral. Invite ridicule and—worse—interest from the insincere or ignorant who claimed they wanted to know more about spirits and the supernatural. Time wasters who only wanted more views or listeners for their shows, and didn't care about properly investigating phenomena or even documenting and cataloging experiences.

The management and owners of the hotel—current and original—also had no apparent knowledge of the room's true nature. There was no record of them trying to exploit the room's history to attract ghost hunters, nor evidence of them trying to keep the room unoccupied. If they read or heard any stories about the room, they must not have believed them. And if they hadn't experienced anything themselves, they had no reason to believe. To *know*.

Lincoln was not a believer, he was a witness. You didn't call someone who'd seen a murder a believer in killing. Lincoln had seen his first ghost when he was fourteen. The second, while pursuing validation of that first experience, when he was thirty. As horrible as those experiences had been—the first in particular, with his great-grandmother staring at him despite having her back to him—he was nonetheless compelled to continue chasing spirits. Feel as certain as he could, for as long as he could, that his mind hadn't fractured in the moment.

Oddly, all that he could liken this illogical distrust of his experiences to was a description he'd heard of what it was like to surf. An enthusiast he'd met in Minnesota had told him about it. A transplant from San Diego so committed to surfing that he braved the freezing waters of the Great Lakes after winter storms.

"Every time I come out of a wave, I feel like, 'Did that really happen?' Then I have to go after another one to prove it was real, and it never stops," the man had said. Lincoln thought that approximated his ghost obsession, except he wasn't pursuing a thrill. He understood what he was chasing less than he understood that he couldn't stop looking for it.

Here, in room 414, he'd found something far beyond what he knew existed. Ghosts were terrifying, but not truly uncanny once you accepted them as reality. Souls carried on. What we think of as life is a phase. Death is a transition. There were ancient religious texts and personal testimonies from the earliest written records that supported this. But nothing Lincoln was aware of spoke to what was taking place in the room.

He forced himself to look at the wall to his left. Better that than to look down, or look up, and he could only face forward, unblinking, for so long.

The Renaissance-reminiscent painting of a Victorian nobleman that had been there when he'd last looked was gone. There was instead a huge painting of the cosmos, something created by street artists who used buckets and aerosol cans in front of a small group of onlookers. Lincoln could smell the spray paint as if it hadn't yet dried.

The wall that had been behind him, which had been blank particleboard the last time he'd looked, now had twin doors built into it. An escape, perhaps? How had he come into the room? He'd turned around enough—and the room had altered more than enough—for him to have forgotten. Those who had been here before had said the room might do strange things if one stayed too long. None of them specified what those strange things were. Had they left before it came to this? They must have.

I shouldn't have come here.

This was true, but what should have dominated his thoughts, he knew, was *I shouldn't have stayed this long.* Making the mistake of coming here was just that: a mistake. He could blame it on the vagueness of the warnings. Staying here for thirty days despite the menace dripping into him each night, accumulating in a manner that was both insidious enough to deny but too evident to ignore, was a decision. Something he deliberated every night, every morning, every other hour since he'd checked in. Stay until he was sure of what was happening or leave before it was too late.

He did an about-face. The yellowed wallpaper was gone, replaced by a huge sheet of tin that held his almost featureless reflection. He wished it was fully featureless.

It was strange to panic over something as mundane as a hairstyle, but his heart went from an imploding clinch to a short-stepped sprint. He'd taken to shaving his head years ago, at the first signs of a retreating hairline. The reflection in the metal had the kind of natural, slightly uneven afro he had long admired in anyone he saw who had one. Focusing on and studying his features for longer, he suspected his shoulders looked wider, his arms a little longer, and his hands a little heavier than they ought to, and overall he looked too thin. These bodily discrepancies, however, could be chalked up to an imperfect reflective surface. The hair, however, was too broad, wild, and present to be explained away. It was there. Part of him that should not be.

In the corner of his eye, to his right, he now saw a mirrored wall. His jaw was so tight he thought his teeth would break. This couldn't be a coincidence. The room wanted him to see more than the changes it was going through.

It wanted him to see himself.

It sensed that he was avoiding looking down at his legs, resisting even a quick glance at his hands.

It wants me to see myself. What he looked like after he looked away, then looked again.

Lincoln grunted, spat. A tear filled his eye, and he blinked it out, down across his cheek. It didn't get past his beard. He didn't have a beard. But he still felt a spot of dampness absorbed into the coarse, scratchy hairs on his face.

Deep breaths did little to ease his anxiety. His heart pumped like it was a valve working to empty the flooding in his chest.

Lincoln turned right, looked at the mirror, faced what he dreaded, as he'd been driven to do since he was fourteen, but what he saw—lighter skin; straightened, long hair; freckles and other features he didn't possess—startled him into shutting his eyes.

That was a mistake. Damn it, now he had looked away from everything. Nothing would be as it was when he opened his eyes. None of the walls, nor the floor and ceiling. And as for himself . . .

He felt smooth, almost glass-like. A colorless, untouched surface, waiting to be filled in by the next glance, then altered by another glance, and then another.

He kept his eyes shut, moved forward, felt around. Maybe reality would reset as long as he wasn't looking, conjuring impossible changes just by witnessing what the room wanted him to see. Or was it that the room invited him to create these changes? Was the room doing all of this itself, or using him to do it? It didn't matter. Something to ponder much later, days later, after he got out.

His palms found a wall and he felt for a door first to his right, then to his left. His fingertips grazed a door hinge, and he pulled his hand back like he'd touched an animal's fang, then reached for where the doorknob should be. He found it, but it would not turn. Not as though it were locked, but as though it were a show handle, never meant to turn. He pulled hard, his adrenaline driving him to believe he could rip the door from the wall if needed, but it did not budge.

"Help me! Can anyone hear me? Help!"

He hammered at the door with a fist, and it moved forward, creaking open.

Hotel room doors don't open into the hallway. This was true, a thought he couldn't argue with, except to say that this room was far beyond ordinary. It was possible that the room was tricking him in some way. Inviting him to step through into a different, deeper hell. But Lincoln feared having the doorway disappear if he opened his eyes more than he feared walking into a trap. He was already stuck in a trap, how much worse could it be, whatever was beyond the door? He knew how much better it could be.

Lincoln walked forward, arms still outstretched. When he touched another wall, he took a few quick breaths, then opened his eyes. Without needing to look left or right to confirm it, he could tell he was in the hotel's hallway. The room was behind him. He was out. All he had to do was not turn around. Even if he did, it couldn't hurt him if he wasn't inside, could it? He wasn't going to risk being wrong about that. He looked right and saw a softly lit Exit sign hanging from the ceiling. Another sign below it and to the left read Stairs.

As he walked, he thought he saw something shimmering on his left wrist. A watch? Gold? He never wore a watch, much less one that would shine in the light. His pulse quickened and he lifted his head slightly to avoid seeing any other part of himself. This made taking the stairs a little tricky, but that was preferable to looking down, and taking the elevator wasn't an option. Elevator cars often had mirrored walls. He couldn't remember if this hotel's elevators had them or not. Had he been stuck in the ever-changing room 414 long enough to forget that detail?

He took the stairs with more impatience than care. Three flights down, at the ground floor, he came to the end of another hallway. To his right was the side exit into the streets of downtown. To his left, a walk to the hotel lobby.

The lobby likely had at least one mirror. Perhaps multiple. That seemed standard decoration in a hotel lobby, at least when Lincoln pictured one in his mind. Several mirrors and various other metal-plated, reflective ornamentations.

Lincoln exited the hotel and sucked in city air polluted with trash and traffic fumes that nonetheless felt clean in his lungs. It was air from outside the hotel. It tasted like clear water to him.

He looked at the sky and absorbed the sunlight as he stepped toward the sidewalk. For a second, the noise of cars and pedestrians passing was beautiful to him. For a second. Then someone yelled, "What the hell?" and he knew they were speaking of him.

It was not intuition. He knew because he physically felt it. In his left hand and his right, and not in the same way. One formed a fist against his will, and the other was missing a finger. The pinky? The ring? He didn't want to look down to confirm at first. It dawned on him an instant later that it didn't matter.

Others were looking. Then looking away before looking again.

His feet were different sizes, and he had different footwear. A sneaker on his left foot. A sandal on the right. Then one was barefoot. Then one was booted.

The apparel changes were noticeable, but not as alarming as the anatomical changes. The molding of his flesh, far deeper than his skin. If a person saw him as heftier one moment and thinner the next, his organs and bones had to shift to those changing perceptions. This applied to growth and reduction by any measure, and in any direction. Two inches wider. Four inches taller. Then smaller, and smaller still, before sprouting back up and out.

The room had infected him. The room whose features changed every time he looked away and then looked again. That was part of him now, and now he was outside, where seconds ago his freedom had felt good enough to make filthy air refreshing. That was before the many strangers passing him by did what people do. Look at someone and then, if you think you might recognize them, or if something about them catches your eye, or even just out of habit, do a double take. And every time, with each look, something about Lincoln changed.

He heard the screams coming from those who must have glimpsed his features twisting and churning, but the sound warped and echoed in ears that shifted on the side of his head, grew and shrunk, sometimes disappeared altogether.

He tried to return a scream of his own, but his mouth shut and opened and split the difference against his will, morphed by the many people who each saw him their own way, then saw him another way when they looked again. Trying to speak through this only made him bite through his tongue a dozen times or more within a few seconds.

All that remained unchanged within him was his mind. His skull reshaped, and the size of his brain adjusted with it, but his mind held, and the speed of thought allowed him to feel everything happening to him. It was too swift to be painful; his body changed too rapidly for its pain receptors to keep up with the perceived damage, but in a different, more substantial way, it was worse than anything he'd felt before.

What could he compare it to? He would sell his soul to trade this feeling for the dread of falling to your death, or even that of seeing a ghost.

If only he could find an apt description for his agony, and the physical means to communicate it, maybe he could convince everyone to look away long enough for him to leave and go someplace where he could never be seen again.

WHEN YOU PUT IT THAT WAY

They rarely made each other laugh, but they made others laugh, which was good for their marriage, wasn't it? The kind of thing that could get you through the in-laws ruining yet another Thanksgiving, or your daughter crashing the car through the garage door, or the neighbors' nerdy kid ensnaring you in the issue he has with the school bully.

Where the hell were that kid's parents, anyway? One of those questions that came and went as the laughter brightened his mood. If other people could find humor in his situation, no matter how frustrating or absurd, why couldn't he?

His family even had a little in-joke for when one of them summarized the events of the day. Jeremy said it most often, but Jenna, his wife, and their daughter, Kylie, sometimes got in on the act. Usually, though, one of the two most important ladies in his life would be itemizing the day's damage after he had just tried to put things in perspective and offer the upside that life could always be worse. That's when he would make one last attempt to lighten things up.

Just moments ago, Jenna, close to tears, had said, "Really? How much worse can it get than our daughter getting suspended from school? She got caught cheating, attacked the boy who reported her, then *slapped me* when I confronted her, Jerry! This is serious. I need you to be on my side for once. Kylie's starting down a bad path. I'm worried about her."

He took a deep breath, gathered a thoughtful, passionate response in his head. No, not a response, a *pledge*. A dedication to his wife, and to his daughter as well. This was no joke. He was going to do better this time. He wasn't going to let Jenna take the weight of the responsible disciplinarian. And he wasn't going to let Kylie down, either, by failing to be the serious, concerned father she deserved and needed right now. He wasn't going to do that …

But the space in his mind was made of too much silence, which occupied too much time. Mere seconds, but more time than he could stand, especially when he added those seconds to how long it would take for him to bare his heart to his wife. How long he would go without hearing laughter. Surely it wouldn't take as long as other moments when he'd been sincere with her, like when he said his vows during their wedding, or when he proposed and said exactly why he wanted to spend his life with her, or when Kylie was born and he must have been overcome by joy and awe that left him speechless.

Strangely, he couldn't remember those moments. The laughter of others, however, was a floating, disembodied happiness so loud it seemed impossible that he wasn't performing before a rapturous crowd. He remembered that laughter, or, more so, could not forget it, as it accompanied every aspect of his life. The laughter of the unseen audience was essential to him. It was oxygen. He felt himself fading in the absence of it, so he said what he knew would bring it back.

"Well, when you put it that way."

Jenna stiffened and her eye twitched. "What?"

He almost didn't hear her over the jovial response from the people who were always watching and listening from behind a wall he couldn't even see.

He smiled. She'd heard it how many times? A hundred? At least. She'd always greeted their in-joke with a smirk and headshake, an eye roll at worst. Not this time. Her eyes burned with fire as invisible yet present as the voices that laughed at their ups, downs, quips, trips, and falls.

"Well," Jerry said, "I was going to try to say that things with Kylie could be worse. Then you mentioned her suspension, and her slapping you, and … when you put it *that* way."

With hindsight that would only survive another minute before dying with him, he would acknowledge that he'd picked a poor time to say this, considering she was preparing dinner and holding a large chef's knife. After she darted the blade through his cheek, he wondered how often she'd wanted to do this before, prevented only by not having a weapon in hand.

He read shock in her face at what she'd done, but also a release and relief. Even exhilaration. A bit like she was falling but was tied to a bungee cord. In fact, her expression wasn't dissimilar to that of the neighbor's kid that time he coaxed Jerry into joining him on that slingshot ride at the fair. The invisible audience hadn't just laughed then but cheered as Jerry conquered his fear of heights.

Now they gasped. Then chuckled.

Jenna withdrew the knife and Jerry saw droplets of his blood jump onto her shirt.

"'When I put it that way?'" she said. "How about when I put it *this* way!"

She slammed the knife down through his trapezius muscle. He felt the blade scrape his collarbone and heard the crowd laugh at her spin on their old joke. Or maybe they were laughing at his pain. That wasn't unusual. They'd laughed before when he'd stubbed his toe, hit his head under the sink, took a tennis ball to the groin. This was different, though. Surely they could tell the difference. Maybe they just didn't want to. Maybe they were like him and couldn't stand the effort it took to differentiate between a moment that called for empathy and one that called for levity.

"What if I put it *this* way, Jerry," Jenna said, plucking the knife free to plunge it into his chest this time.

"How about *this way*," she said, stabbing him in the stomach.

The laughter became explosive. Jerry pictured the entertained crowd shutting their eyes tight, crinkling their faces, and holding their stomachs not unlike how he held his, but entirely unlike why.

THE REF

Laz Marron returned to the table with the rye whiskey Brian had ordered, as well as the question he'd wanted to ask all evening. "You think it's better to die drunk or sober?"

"Shit, what are you asking me that for?" Brian said, taking his drink and knocking half of it back before setting down the glass. "We're having a good night. Jesus, who wants to think about that? Why would you ask that?"

"I got a reason. You can probably guess."

"Come on, Laz."

"Just answer. And don't say, 'It doesn't matter, neither is any good,' or anything like that."

"But neither is any damn good," Brian said, laughing loud enough to draw attention had they not been the only two people in the bar, minutes ahead of closing time. "People dying whichever way probably wish it was the other way, or no way. Fine, I'll say sober. But honestly, it's like you're asking if I'd rather eat a bug or a rat. Yeah, it's easier to choke down the bug, but who took steak off the menu?"

Laz's polite smile turned into a short-lived scowl when Brian immediately finished the rest of his whiskey. It was like he'd seen someone else spit in his friend's drink but hadn't had time to warn him. How Brian could inhale liquor that smelled like burnt medicine was a marvel. Brian wiped his lips and gray beard, though Laz was sure he hadn't wasted a drop. As the man he first met forty years ago at the Leyandas Boxing Gym moved on to his pint of amber lager, Laz nipped at his own drink carefully, like there might be crushed glass in it.

"About that reason," Brian said, "do I need to be worried about you?"

"Maybe," Laz said. "Probably." He sighed, smacked his lips, glanced at the disinterested bartender as though he might be eavesdropping. With a lowered voice, he continued. "You might get a little upset with me about this. You might even want to hit me. But I hired a guy recently. A hit man. Well, actually I hired a guy to find—"

"Wait, what? You paid somebody to—"

"Listen, I paid this guy to find somebody for me who could kill people for hire. I paid a lot, everything I had saved up, because I wanted somebody really good. You know, you read these stories and it's always funny to me when somebody pays like two or three grand for a hit man and their plan goes to shit and they get caught. Of course the plan fell through, you went cheap on something that should cost a fortune. Two, three grand? That's what, half the down payment on a small car these days? Hell, that's a little depressing to think about."

"Hey, stay on topic," Brian said. "What the shit, Laz? Who the hell would you want to get ... Whoa, something to do with Harper? Somebody else giving you shit about that?"

"Pretty much, yeah."

"Jesus, some people. The man's own mother and children can forgive you, and that isn't good enough. Let me guess, whoever it is, they're not even a relative. Or if they are, probably a third cousin or his nephew's nephew or some shit."

"Or just me."

"Yeah, or just … *what*?"

Laz nodded, squinted past a pain in his eyes that almost felt like fatigue, and was related to it.

"What do you mean 'you'?" Brian said.

"I mean me. I hired a guy to kill me. I can't do it myself, and I wanted it done. I *needed* it done."

"Jesus Christ, Laz, what the shit? Are you serious? This is one fucked-up joke if you're joking."

"I'm serious."

Brian rubbed his beard again, leaned back in his chair, stretched, looked ready to get up and pace the hard floor of the bar from the bathrooms to the front door. He was always expressive, demonstrative, but when he'd been drinking he almost ventured into performance.

He pointed his finger like he was trying to throw it off his hand. "You weren't lying when you said I'd want to hit you. I want to jump across this table right now. What were you thinking?"

"That I was tired," Laz said.

"Oh, that's it? Tired? After all this time, *now* you're *that* tired?"

"I've been that tired for all this time. Tired and pissed off. Every time I look in the mirror, I want to drag the other guy out and beat him to death. If you didn't know that, then we aren't the friends I thought we were."

"That's a fucked-up thing to say. That's a hell of a thing for you to say to me."

In the ensuing silence, Laz could hear the clinking of glassware as the bartender started cleaning up early, knowing no one else was coming in. His only two customers—two irregulars—had braved icy roads and a cutting windchill to be there.

The night Harper died hadn't been quite this cold, quite this harsh, but close enough for Laz to feel it was fitting. What was it people said? History doesn't always repeat, but sometimes it rhymes. Something like that. In this case, the rhyme was imperfect at minimum.

Similar to Brian, Laz had been too stiff and slow to have any success as a boxer, even as an amateur. That was okay. You could still involve yourself in your passion and even make a solid living working within it despite never quite living your dream. He'd made it as a ref, after all. A good one, for years, before the Harper fight.

Building relationships in the fight game meant being two or three degrees removed—at most—from lifelong criminals. Laz didn't know if that also applied to other fields, though he imagined being a producer in the music industry, or a big enough businessman on Wall Street, meant the same applied. But he could only say for sure that it was true for the world of boxing. Knowing somebody who knew somebody who would kill someone for five or six figures was one of the grim perks of spending three decades as a referee, working some pretty big fights, and even a handful of title fights.

He had little memorabilia and fewer memories from those events. Anytime he thought of being in the ring, he could only think of that night in Chicago. Punch after punch landing on Scotty "All Heart" Harper's chin. His temple. The bridge of his nose. Goddamn, why didn't he fall sooner? Why did his body hold up until a few seconds after the bell at the end of the twelfth? Why had he been too tough to drop, but not tough enough to survive?

Stupid questions. Pointless. There was only one real question that mattered. One question that reporters and spectators and even some other fighters had asked the next day, as soon as news broke that Harper had died in his hospital bed.

Why didn't the ref stop the fight?

Others shared in the scorn and blame. Harper's cornermen, the ringside doctor, and the fight's promoter among them. But Laz was closer to the action than them. Close enough to effectively be part of it. It was part of his job to see when a fighter was out on his feet, a zombie boxing on autopilot while his brain was collecting more damage than it could recover from.

Why didn't I stop the fight?

He refused to rewatch footage from the bout, and at times he struggled to distinguish his memories of it from his nightmares. Harper's eyes rolling back, his neck snapping from each punch. Laz coming close to stepping in and calling the fight, then watching Harper return a shot or two, looking like he had the slimmest chance of mounting a comeback. He'd chosen to let the fighter called "All Heart" live up to his nickname. Except that credited Laz with making a conscience, defensible decision, and he had no real memory of thinking that clearly—or thinking at all—when he looked back on what happened.

"You can't still be killing yourself over that," Brian said. "Shit, you just *literally* tried to kill yourself over it." He looked over one shoulder, then the other.

Before Brian could say it, Laz addressed his concern. "The guy's not still out there. He's not going to show up here and shoot me, then take care of witnesses or anything."

Laz saw his friend's tension deflate, then he added, "He already came to see me."

"What? Holy shit." Brian leaned forward. "What happened? You … did you kill him?"

Laz shook his head. "God no. If I spent *that* much on a guy *I* could kill, I'd be out there tonight trying to find the bastard who conned me. No. I spent about a week getting drunk after I got word that the man agreed to the job. I thought different from you: I thought it was better to die drunk. But my nerves were up, so I could never really get there before I got nauseous and threw up, no matter how much I tried. It didn't help that I kept feeling like there was somebody hovering over me. Whoever was sitting at the stool next to me at a bar, whoever was next to me at a urinal, the guy behind me in line at the deli, they all had me bracing myself. Like, 'This is it. They're the one. They're gonna give me what I paid for.'

"But I also kind of knew it wasn't going to be someone I noticed. I spent a hundred thousand dollars on this. Emptied my savings.

Whoever was worth that wasn't dumb enough to shoot me in the men's room at a full bar. And I had this weird feeling the whole week that someone was following me, but they were hiding perfectly. It was like I grew an extra shadow smart enough to hide in my first shadow."

Brian shivered and Laz smirked, wet his lips again, then set his drink down. "Yeah. Turns out this guy was that good. Worth the money. Hell, I think I must have gotten a discount. He really had been following me all week, and maybe I had noticed him and unconsciously convinced myself I hadn't, because I didn't want to know it was coming. That was half the point of paying someone else to do it, besides not having it in me to do it myself. Anyway, a couple nights ago, I come home and my living-room light's on even though I never leave it on, barely even bother turning it on when I'm there. It's hot as hell inside, for some reason, and there's somebody sitting on the couch."

"The guy?" Brian said.

Laz nodded. "My first thought was, 'This can't be him.' I'm expecting somebody so white he's invisible. White, medium height, medium build. Hair that's sort of between blond and brown. A guy who doesn't stand out. This guy, though. Long black hair. Almost this kind of sunburnt skin. Not like he's brown, not like me, but like maybe one of those white guys who's gone past getting too much sun. Almost like those bodybuilders who bronze themselves up for a competition, except more natural looking, but stranger looking too? I don't know. The point I'm trying to make is if you saw him you'd notice him, you'd be able to ID him in a heartbeat, so I imagine he has to be extra good at what he does to still be out here doing it without getting caught. He's got this solid, hard jaw, like—"

"You hit him?"

"No, but I could've bruised my knuckles just looking at him. Let me finish. I'm saying this was a hard-looking dude. Bad-man energy coming off him. He's filled out, he looks tall even when he's sitting down, and he's got the coldest eyes you've ever seen. I mean look, we've seen a lot of tough-looking guys, and some of them lived up to appearances, and some would have been better off taking ballet. Trust me when I say this guy looked more like a killer than anyone we've ever seen.

"I froze up when he looked at me, and even though I didn't want to see it coming, a part of me thought it would be better this way. I'd get a quick prayer out. Really confirm that I'm good with this. I was about to say that prayer in my head when the guy pointed to my couch and told me to sit down. I felt like I had to do it, so I did."

"And then what?"

"He talked me out of it."

Laz let this last comment linger, watched Brian take it in and twirl it around in his head for a few seconds. Lacking words for a moment, Brian took another drink, let the lager water his tongue so he could grow something to say.

"This feels like a bad question, but did you at least get your money back?" Brian said. "Because if not, if you need some help, you know I've got you."

"He paid me back," Laz said. "Well, in his words, he hired me for a 'future favor.' When he told me he wasn't going to do the job and was giving me the money back, I told him I didn't want it, I wanted what I paid for. That's when he told me he'd been watching me for a week, and that he didn't kill guys like me. It would be bad for his rep and business, he said."

That wasn't all the man had said. Far from it. But Laz didn't want to share that with Brian. He wondered if he'd shared too much already, and if something deep within him had intended to. Share enough to warn Brian off, make him call it a night already, get home while he could.

"Bad for his rep?" Brian said. "Like he's got an honor system? He doesn't kill women or kids or, what, guys who think they deserve it when they don't?"

"Something like that," Laz said.

You're not the only one I've met like you, the man had told him. *I met a bus driver in Arkansas who thought she should die over an accident that killed two kids, even though the other driver was the one asleep at the wheel. I had a nurse hire me because she gave the wrong medicine to a pregnant girl who's still in a coma, but from my investigation, the machines and computers at the hospital were at least half at fault. I don't kill people like that. There are people far more deserving. I'm sure you know someone.*

"So, what kind of favor do you owe him?" Brian said.

"Something soon. He made it seem like he'd done this before. Like he'd bought a 'future favor' off a lot of people. I got the impression he wasn't just a killer. There's more to him."

"Shit, a *lot* more from the sound of it. Well, hell, here's to him." Brian raised his pint glass and Laz raised his tumbler. They clinked glasses and Brian added, "And here's to you being here. Damn it, Laz, don't ever do something like that again. Jesus, man. I can't even … Just call me when you get to feeling like that. I'll make the time. We can get out, have a night like this. Take your mind off everything. We're having a good night, aren't we?"

"It's been a good night," Laz said. "But I can't just drink it all away every day. I'm not built like that. I'm not like you."

"Bullshit. You're stronger than me."

"Yeah? You ever come close to killing yourself over what you did?"

Brian took a deep breath, a deeper drink from the pint, finishing it. Then he got up, went to the bar, and came back with a short glass of whiskey. He took care of half the whiskey before he finally answered Laz. "No. Can't say I have."

"Didn't think so. Like I said, I'm not like you."

"It's different. Nobody knows about my shit. Yours, anybody in the world can read about it, or watch the video. You've had these hack reporters and internet trolls blaming you for Harper all this time. Maybe if I'd had to deal with that, I would've had a mind to check out too. I guess I'm lucky that way."

"Yeah, but yours was more … you were more involved," Laz said. He saw Brian's eyes dip like they were searching for a place to hide. "Shit, Brian, we don't have to talk about this if you don't want to. I'm sorry."

"It's all right. Don't apologize. If it helps you *not* feel like you should kill yourself, we can talk about it all day."

"Okay. Thank you." Laz stilled himself, got ready to take a step over a ledge, fall all the way into the decision he had to make. His stomach was close to cramping. He clenched his fists for a second. This feeling was a perversion of what he'd felt before every bout, dating back to when had the big red gloves on, and up through the times he wore a sky-blue shirt and bowtie instead. This wasn't the exhilaration of possibility, though. It was the anxiety of inevitability. Somehow, these sensations were almost close enough to be mistaken for one another.

"So how do you deal with it?" Laz asked. "Beyond the booze, I mean. You've got to have a trick or something. It can't be as simple as trying not to think about it."

"Mostly it is," Brian said. "If anything, the drinking just makes it easier for me to bring it back up. It doesn't really help. Shit, remember when I told you about it?"

"Yeah."

"I was almost too drunk to stand, wasn't I?"

"You were actually lying down," Laz said. "For all I know, you—"

"I might have actually been too drunk to stand," Brian said, and laughed like they weren't discussing murder.

Laz's guts twisted in a different direction, and he shut his eyes briefly to focus on not throwing up.

When Brian had confessed to him, years ago, Laz had experienced the same sensation he felt now and had almost been grateful for it. Brian had shared his secret to help alleviate Laz's remorse over Harper.

You feel bad about what you did? That was nothing. You're a saint compared to me.

They'd had a mutual friend, Jack "Bigfoot" Lucas. A lumbering heavyweight who didn't quite have the chin necessary to be more than a step-up for better prospects. He had power, though, and a strong fighting will, and, outside of the ring, the financial acumen of someone who couldn't spell *money*. A lot of guys like Jack—and like Brian, for that matter—blew through whatever they earned in the ring and ended up selling their training and muscle independently to whoever needed it, often on short notice, at a bargain, or both.

Brian's ultimate sin came at the cost of five hundred dollars. To be fair to him, it was only supposed to be show work. All about the look, zero action required. Jack had a cousin he treated like a little sister. Her boss at a mom-and-pop boutique had knocked her up, then pretended to have never had a relationship with her and fired her when she confronted him about it. She asked Jack to help her out, gave him a grand to put the fear of responsible parenting into this aspiring deadbeat dad. Jack agreed, then approached Brian about the job, saying they could split the money.

He thought there'd be less chance of a fight if there were two of us. Swear to God, we thought we'd just scare this asshole. Between Bigfoot and me, who wouldn't be scared? I didn't know what would happen.

"I sometimes feel bad about the girl," Brian said now. "The guy, to hell with him. You get a girl pregnant and try to act like it's not yours, leave her to have the baby and deal with all of that, you should burn for it. Devil himself should show up to take you out. I don't know how a man like that lives with himself. But his daughter. Shit. *Shit.* We just didn't know. How could we know?"

How could they know the guy would fight back despite being outnumbered and untrained? How could they know this was his weekend with his daughter, all of fifteen? How could they know she'd wake up, come out of her room, and come at them with a kitchen knife to save her idiot father (who was already dead because of one punch from Bigfoot—with an assist from the corner of the coffee table he fell into)?

How could Brian know Bigfoot would fly into a rage after getting cut by the girl, and smash her head into the tile floor one too many times, cracking her skull? *Sounded like somebody dropped an egg on a brick*, Brian had said from Laz's couch, so drunk Laz had left an empty paint bucket beside him overnight.

Now, Laz watched Brian finish the back half of his whiskey. "Look, man, I just live with it and try not to think about it," Brian said. "There's no trick or secret. If it wasn't me, it would've been somebody else there. If it hadn't happened that night, it would have happened to that guy sooner or later. The girl was a mistake, but I was just there for that. I didn't *do* it. There's a reason Bigfoot shot himself, right? He knew that was more on him than me. What'd I do, really? I helped him clean up. I was … I was *there*, sure. Okay. I, you know … she went for him with the knife and I helped my friend out. I stopped her. I didn't know what he'd do after. I didn't think that would happen. Shit, all I was supposed to do was be there, you know?"

Laz nodded. "Why did you say dying sober is better than drunk?"

"What? I don't know. Because you made me pick one."

"But why that one?"

Brian shook his head. "Just seemed like the right answer. I don't know. I didn't really think about it, man."

You should try thinking for once, Laz thought. *It could save your life.*

The gun holstered under his jacket seemed to grow against his ribs, wanting to remind him it was there, knowing that he'd decided close to an hour ago not to go for it unless he had to. He didn't have to now and didn't want to. What he wanted was to get his hands muddy. Get his heart pumping. Feel sore in the morning. Endure the difficulty of the task.

He looked over Brian's shoulder and watched the bartender go to the front door, lock it, turn off the open sign, draw the window shades down, then turn back to Laz and nod.

"Closing time," Laz said. "Time to settle up."

"Oh shit," Brian said, looking back in time to see the bartender returning to the bar. "Should have got a drink for the road."

Laz stood, moved beside Brian, gave him his own drink. "Have mine. I'm done with it."

"You sure? Thanks." Brian threw the clear drink back, then almost coughed it back up. He held the glass just below his face and at an angle, inspecting it. "Jesus, what is this? Tastes like water."

"Yeah," Laz said, then grabbed the back of Brian's head and slammed him face-first through the glass and into the hardwood table. The glass broke on impact. Brian's scream was delayed, the liquor slowing his capacity to register that his nose was busted and bits of broken glass were lodged in his lips, gums, and cheeks.

Laz dragged Brian onto the stone-tile floor, held him face down, straddled his upper back, both hands now gripping his head.

"Laz? Laz, what the sh—"

Laz crushed Brian's face into the floor, then cried out as he did it a second and third time.

There are people far more deserving. I'm sure you know someone, the "hit man"—the man with frightening eyes and almost burned skin—had told him. *In fact, I know that you know someone.* Then he offered Laz a job that he said he couldn't take because the woman looking to hire him—the relative of another man who'd worked for him—couldn't offer appropriate payment. *Again, I have a reputation. Fuckups work cheap. Like your friend, Brian. That's why I'm paying you what you paid me. I'll set you up with the place and someone to help in case you need it, so you don't have any excuses. Don't be a fuckup. Don't be like him.*

"I'm not," Laz eked out as he lifted and smashed Brian's face into the floor again, barely noticing the three teeth that skittered across the tile.

This was the way it had to be, the imperfect rhyme of past and present that Brian had earned. The work that Laz had long neglected.

This is the "favor" you want me to do? he'd asked the man, and the man had scoffed.

No, this is a favor I'm doing for you. Help you pay back what you owe the world. You thought you could leave without settling up. You should know better, Laz. You're the wrong man to judge when it's time to say it's over.

Beneath him, Brian no longer struggled or convulsed. Laz ignored this and kept on, unsure of when to stop.

XII
יב
ΔΙΙ
12
١٢
十二

DOCTOR BAD EYES IS AT THE TOP OF THE STAIRS AGAIN

Kelly hustled the kids out of the house and into the car, then drove seven minutes to her sister Roxy's house before she parked, turned to her daughter, and said, "Now tell me again who you saw on the stairs?"

"Doctor Bad Eyes," Deena said.

Kelly looked at Ryan, her son, who was thirteen but looked like he'd hide behind his three-year-old sister if "Doctor Bad Eyes" appeared in the street. Maybe the degree of his fear was a product of being so close to his mother's fear, which was easily large enough to swallow two people and could choke down a third if necessary. The only one immune to it was Deena, who also happened to be the only one who had seen the man at the top of the stairs. Kelly could either take that as reassurance that there was little to be afraid of or as a warning that her daughter might turn out to be more threatening than the ghost she claimed to see.

I can still love her as much as ever, even if that's the case, Kelly thought. *Who says you can't love your kid to pieces and still be a little nervous around her? Those things aren't mutually exclusive under the circumstances.*

"The circumstances" being that they lived in a haunted house. They'd known it was haunted for two years. Kelly had suspected something was off about the place even before closing on the purchase and signing her mortgage. The list price was too low, the Realtor too fidgety and eager and willing to appease, and the place just *looked* like it had a ghost in every window. It even had a widow's walk and a tower with a conical roof. The first time she saw it at night Kelly swore she heard a pipe organ playing in the distance. But at a third of what its listing price should have been, who could resist that bargain?

Within a few months, whatever spirits roamed the house got comfortable enough with the family to move past generating cold spots and the vague sense of being watched. The family started to hear footsteps, knocks, whispers, and, deep in the night, a feverish grunting that sounded to Kelly like an older man suffering a heart attack mid-coitus. She had an idea of what that sounded like thanks to a brief obsession she'd once had with the fetish website CardiacDaddies.com.

When she first told her sister about the haunting, Roxy said, "Why don't you just leave?"

"You mean why don't I just screw up my credit for the next ten years?" Kelly said. "What do you think scares me more, some knocking and breathing I can't account for, or having to move my kids to the shittiest school district in the city? They're stabbing substitutes on the North Side."

"That's a rumor," Roxy said.

"A *plausible* rumor. I'd rather not have to send my kids to a school where 'Teachers get shanked out here' doesn't sound like complete bullshit."

"How are you going to keep a new boyfriend if the first time he sleeps over, he wakes up at midnight to the sound of Hugh Hefner's ghost fucking himself to death in the next room?"

"I'll expect him to be a man about it. And if he can't do that, then I guess he won't be the right guy for my situation. Look, regardless of who lived there before and is trying to stick around, that's *our* house now, and I'm not moving us out unless something really messed up happens. And you'll know if it does because I'll be at your door in the dead of night with the kids in tow."

So here she was, ten thirty at night, ringing the doorbell at her sister and brother-in-law's house. As soon as Roxy opened the door and saw Kelly's face, she knew.

"Come in," she said. Once she got the kids comfortable in the upstairs bedroom, out of earshot, she asked, "Are you hurt?"

"No," Kelly said, seated at the kitchen counter. Her hands weren't shaking anymore, but her voice was still unsteady, and she had to concentrate to keep from speaking too fast. "Nothing like that. Me and Ryan were in the living room, about to go to bed, when Deena walked in and said she saw … something."

"She's told you that before, though, hasn't she?" said Roxy's husband, Henderson. He had his glasses on, and his bottom lip was encroaching upon his upper lip in a way that made him look like he was always ready to ask, "But what about … ?" Even in his T-shirt and pajama bottoms, his expression and eyewear gave him the air of an aspiring detective unevenly balancing skepticism with a willingness to entertain all possibilities.

"Well, when we first moved in, she didn't 'say' much of anything," Kelly said. "She'd babble and gesture at something that wasn't there or try to hug something me and Ryan couldn't see. Then she started getting a word or two out to describe whatever she was looking at, but it was simple stuff. 'Man.' 'Lady.' 'Rabbit.'"

"Rabbit?" Henderson said.

"The house has a weird history," Kelly said. "An old lady who kept a couple of pet rabbits died there. So maybe that's it. Or it could be the guy who wore a bunny costume to a Halloween party at the house in 1952 and died during the 'Costume Party Massacre.'"

"Jesus Christ, you never told me about that," Roxy said.

Kelly shrugged. "I just read about it a few weeks ago. And anyway, I think the papers were overstating it a bit. Only three people died that night, and it might have just been an accident. That's half as many as were killed in the 'Bludgeoning Event of '33.' If anything warrants the term 'massacre'—"

"Bludgeoning Event? Holy shit, Kelly. You should've gotten out of there a while ago."

"I'm not rehashing that argument with you," Kelly said.

"What happened tonight?" Henderson asked. "What did Deena see?"

Kelly took a deep breath. "Something she called 'Doctor Bad Eyes.'"

Roxy and Henderson each flinched subtly like they'd heard a neighbor scream. The couple looked at each other for an answer to a question neither asked, then looked back to Kelly.

"Well," Roxy said, "that doesn't sound good at all."

"Right? I thought I might be overreacting but … you know, it was different when her vocabulary was limited and she couldn't get so descriptive. But 'Doctor Bad Eyes'? Fuck that. And she said she saw him at the top of the stairs. *Again*. 'Doctor Bad Eyes is at the top of the stairs again.' That's the exact quote. That's scary as hell, right? I'm not overreacting?"

"The top of the stairs is one of the creepiest places a ghost could hang out," Roxy said.

"A ghost doctor that she called *Bad Eyes*. What does that even mean? Are they blacked out or something? Are they bleeding? Are they fire red? *What does that mean?*"

"Well, let's consider some other questions that may be more pertinent," Henderson said, his thinking cap now on, evidently. "First, what kind of doctor are we talking about? Did Deena say?"

Kelly and Roxy stared at him a moment, eyebrows furrowed, looking more like sisters in their united bemusement than they ever would otherwise. Henderson went on. "Well, if it's a surgeon, let's say, or really any type of physician, then I agree that their presence is alarming, presuming they're malevolent. But if it's just someone who had a PhD, for instance—"

"A PhD?" Kelly said.

Roxy said, "Babe, how would the kid know that? Do you think this person was standing there holding a copy of their degree?"

"Who knows?" Henderson said. "We're talking about the supernatural, after all. We can't be sure of what a spirit would or wouldn't do. All I'm trying to say is that the spirit of an actual medical practitioner is probably more threatening than one of someone who earned an academic doctorate, particularly if it was just an honorary—"

"Stop, please," Kelly said. "I know you're just trying to make sense of this, but I'm ninety-nine percent sure my daughter didn't see some spectral, tweed-jacketed professor handing out business cards hoping to book a speaking engagement. I'm picturing something more like a man wearing—"

"Or woman," Roxy said.

"Or woman—dammit, Roxy—man *or woman* wearing full scrubs and maybe a white coat, probably holding a scalpel and wearing gloves, and wearing a surgical mask so all you can see are their eyes, which are bad enough that Deena felt like pointing it out and … oh my God, I really think I'm going to be sick. I mean how many times has this asshole been hanging out at the top of our staircase waiting for one of us to pass by so he can get to cutting and digging around inside—"

"All right, all right," Roxy said. "Just try to relax for a second."

"Relax? My youngest just told me she saw Doctor Bloody Eyes Cut-'em-Up-and-Gut-'em posted up at his favorite murder spot in my house, and you think I should relax?"

"Sis, take a breath. It's scary enough. No need to embellish."

Describing what she imagined her daughter had seen returned Kelly's terror to its initial outsized dimensions, and she felt the urge to scream before her head exploded, but she squelched this desire and reined in her fear. Screaming would just bring the children downstairs, and if nothing else, she needed to keep calm for them. Not just for the moment either. There were long-term ramifications to consider.

She had meant it when she'd said she didn't want to move the kids out of their school district. On one side of town, you had persistent rumors of fights, stabbings, and more, and on the other, "best" side of town, you had the recent front-page story of a teacher giving ninth graders an assignment asking them to write "5 Ways Slavery Could Have Been Good." One half-assed, "Sorry if you were offended, but I didn't mean it that way" apology later, the school district was content to punish the teacher with a two-week suspension. Even if, by some miracle, Kelly was able to find an apartment on that side of the city after defaulting on her mortgage, she'd just be subjecting her children to a different kind of unhealthy environment.

She liked where they were now. She didn't worry that Deena would come home crying from day care one day because some vile person's offspring had teased her about her hair. She never worried that Ryan would spend years showing more concern or compassion than some of his teachers. They lived in a perfectly normal, attainably comfortable part of town where neighbors waved hello but didn't come over to interrupt your yard work, and where cops miraculously didn't harass anyone unless they were speeding in a neighborhood or past an elementary school, which was fine by Kelly as she thought people who did thirty in a school zone should have a finger sliced off. The one true drawback to living where they did was that they shared their house with an unknown number of ghosts, who had always been fairly innocuous, all things considered.

That was before you heard about Doctor Bad Eyes, she thought.

Kelly shook her head. Following a deep breath, she said to Roxy and Henderson, "Listen, I hate to ask this, but I need a favor. I have to go back to the house. I owe it to myself and the kids to be sure about what's there—whether it's a threat or not—before

I decide to pack everything and leave. And I need one of you to stay here with the kids, and the other to come with me."

Roxy and Henderson looked at each other. "Well," Henderson said, "I already went out once tonight. To get the milk, remember? So, I feel like maybe it's your turn—"

"This is *not* the same thing!" Roxy said.

Kelly took Roxy's hand. "Come on. This can be the big-sister hero moment you never wanted."

Roxy followed Kelly to the front door but kept staring at her husband as she left, ensuring that he would see at least one baleful-eyed being before the night was through.

Had a future version of herself come back in time to tell her, "Your knowledge of old movies will be an unexpected benefit one day," Kelly might have thought she'd win a little money at bar trivia, or at best would meet her soulmate at a showing of *It Happened One Night*. She could never have predicted it would come in handy when trying to identify the unwelcome ghost inhabiting her home.

That she could see the ghost at all was something of a blessing. She had doubted that the spirit would make itself visible to anyone but Deena, who might be one of those ghost-spotting little kids that the movies are always trying to creep out parents with. But here it was, a translucent specter that Kelly had never seen before, but now could, perhaps because she was looking for it, or because it wanted to be seen. She stood at the midpoint of the stairway and examined the misty figure ahead of her.

Where her daughter got the "doctor" part of her description was evident. The ghost wore a surgical apron over a short-sleeved shirt and tie and had a stethoscope draped around his neck. The "bad eyes" part was a bit more curious at first. The ghost had on a pair of Groucho Marx glasses. He was dressed as the character Doctor Hackenbush from the film *A Day at the Races*.

Kelly realized that Deena had meant "bad eyes" in the sense of someone with bad vision. It was terminology she'd probably picked up from her grandmother, who would adjust her glasses and say, "Oh, my eyes have gotten so bad," any time she had to read anything. Kelly would have to talk to Deena later about using kinder language to identify the bespectacled.

The ghost was, Kelly surmised, one of the attendees of the 1952 costume party held at the house. In fact, he appeared to be the man behind the Costume Party Massacre, judging by the shimmering, decorative knife in his right hand.

The blade was long and serpentine, almost a dagger. The hilt was bejeweled, and so was what she could see of the handle. Without it, the man would not have appeared menacing, despite being long dead. She might have dismissed him as a threat without needing to speak to him, now that she recognized who he was dressed up as. But he had the knife, and the sight of it froze something inside of her. Her heart rate must have been setting a personal record, but she couldn't quite feel it.

Without looking back at Roxy, who stayed at the bottom of the stairs, Kelly asked, "Do you see him?"

Roxy nodded, not realizing Kelly hadn't looked back to see her for several seconds before answering, "Yes. Yes. I do."

Kelly swallowed, then pointed at Doctor Bad Eyes. "All right," she said, finding strength by thinking of her children, and of all the bullshit she didn't want to deal with if she and the kids had to move out. "Whatever you are, whatever you think you're doing here, you need to get out of my house. I live here now, me and my kids, and you ... you're dead. You need to accept that and move on. If you think you can scare us away, you're wrong. You don't scare me with your stupid costume and probably shitty Groucho impression. And if you try to scare my kids, if you try *anything* with my kids, I will take that knife and ... you don't even want to know what I'll—"

"Ma'am," the specter said, "why do you think I'm trying to scare anyone? I'm not."

It took Kelly a second to recover from hearing the ghost speak. The fact that it could hear her and had responded put her back on her heels, and she might have fallen down the stairs had she not grabbed the handrail. "Then what's the knife for, if you're not trying to scare anyone?"

Doctor Bad Eyes looked at the blade in his hand. "This? I have this because she asked me to get it."

"Who?" Kelly said, fearing he would say Deena. *Dammit, my kid better not turn out to have been the creepy one all along ...*

"Lacey. Lacey asked me, so I did it. If you could see her, you'd understand why. I always did what she asked, even when I knew better. She asked to see my father's prized knife, a gift from a man he'd known in Borneo. I don't think she even really wanted to see it. She just wanted to see if I was more afraid of disappointing her than I was of breaking into my father's trophy case and dealing with the consequences later."

"Oh," Kelly said, no longer numb. She instead felt an infectious sympathy for the stranger at the top of the stairs, something that she knew emanated from the specter itself and that possessed her, but that she did not try to resist. "You know, if that's really all she was going for, then you should have just told her no. Most women respect someone with some common sense and respect for other people's belongings. And a woman who wouldn't respect that isn't one you should be messing with anyway."

"I'll ... keep that in mind," Doctor Bad Eyes said. "I *do* understand that I'm dead, by the way. I have accepted it."

"But you're still here," Roxy said, startling Kelly, who'd forgotten her sister was there.

"I'm stuck here," the young man said. "I've tried to leave, but I can't. I think if I can just get to the bottom of the stairs ... *walk* down this time, not fall." He sighed. "I was always clumsy. And a fool. And this damn knife. Why would a trophy knife need to be so sharp? Why did I take it out? Why did there have to be anyone else on the stairs?"

"The massacre," Kelly said, covering her mouth after the words slipped out.

"*Accident*," Doctor Bad Eyes said. "It wasn't on purpose. Why would I want to hurt anyone? I didn't mean to."

Kelly started up the stairs. This could be a trick, she knew. Her sympathy for him was artificial. Some manner of spectral mesmerism, perhaps employed to draw her close where he could reach her with the blade. Maybe he truly was stuck at the top of the stairs, and this was the only way to ensnare fresh prey. Maybe the papers hadn't embellished at all when they'd written of the Costume Party Massacre of 1952.

Unable to stop herself, Kelly came to within arm's reach of him and extended her hand. "What if I help you walk down?"

She held her breath as he stared at her. She waited to see which hand he raised.

He held out his empty hand and his voice cracked as he said, "Thank you."

His grip was icy and surprisingly firm. She almost pulled away but managed not to. Kelly could suppress her queasiness long enough to walk this man down the stairs to exorcise him from her home.

They made it two steps before he pitched forward, letting out a surprised little, "Oh." As he cartwheeled past her, Kelly's first impulse was to laugh. This was a man dressed as Doctor Hackenbush falling down a staircase, after all. It was not a semidignified, gliding type of fall either, but a full-on flailing tumble that made him look like he had three extra limbs. Any notion of laughter vanished, however, when she heard the screams.

Disembodied voices cried out in pain, in surprise, in terror.

"I've been cut," an invisible man shouted.

"Mercy! You're bleeding," a woman said.

"Motherfucker stabbed me," another phantom woman said.

More voices joined in, some using their words, others yelling, others crying. A steady dripping sound grew into a minor cascade, and Kelly smelled the blood like a red-soaked rag was under her nose.

Doctor Bad Eyes came to a stop at the bottom of the stairs, at Roxy's feet. Somehow, in his clumsiness, he had punched the knife through his own throat up to the hilt. The blade had entered upright, not flat, and had apparently missed his cervical spine, as he could still move. Kelly wished he couldn't. He got to his knees, propping himself up with one hand while he tugged at the knife with the other. The blade was too stubborn, however, or he'd been too weakened by his injury, or both, so Kelly and Roxy witnessed the replay of a mortally wounded man struggling in vain not to die young.

A wave of sorrow slammed into Kelly and she had to sit down. She wanted to turn away, as Roxy had already, but forced herself not to. She needed to see if this was the worst of it.

Less than a minute later, when the young man ceased moving and his form evaporated into the floor, she knew that it was.

In the seven months since she'd first encountered him, with ample practice, Kelly had managed to escort Doctor Hackenbush down four steps before he fell to relive his death. Only eighteen more steps to go. At this rate, he'd find peace by the time Ryan was out of college and Deena was just getting old enough to be a pain in the ass.

Deena had initially found it difficult to pronounce the word "Hackenbush" and wanted to keep calling the young man Doctor Bad Eyes, but Kelly insisted and eventually got her daughter on board with the new name. She hadn't asked the young man his name yet and didn't plan to look it up. She thought of it as akin to naming a pet that you couldn't keep, which would only make you sadder when you had to part ways with it.

She did not meet with Doctor Hackenbush every night. It would have put too much strain on her. It never got easier, suffering the revulsion of touching his hand, seeing him roll down the stairs, hearing the screams, seeing his throat impaled by his father's knife, and dealing with the crushing wave of sadness as he struggled and failed to survive. Each time was very close to feeling like the first time. Still, she suffered through it, for her sake and her children's more than the doctor's.

She didn't want to move.

She still liked the school district.

She found the neighborhood pleasant, haunted house notwithstanding.

And, so far, she still found nothing in the house scarier than the prospect of ruining her credit.

EVERYWHEREVER

Originally published in *Obsolescence: A Dark Sci-Fi, Fantasy, and Horror Anthology* (May 2023)

The car was black from tires to glass. So dark that looking at it made Kevin feel it was sucking light from his eyes, trying to blind him.

The beer and "lean"—a codeine and promethazine cocktail cut with soda—might have contributed to his perception of the car. It had rendered him too drunk and too high to drive, as well as inebriated enough to take the latest piece of internet lore seriously for a moment. As a joke, he told himself, although a modicum of hopefulness had also motivated him.

The haze and distant droning that enveloped his head after hours of drinking didn't give him the deeper escape he sought. It never did. What better alternative escape could there be than the one offered by this car, which his nephew, Micah, had told him about yesterday?

"When you book a ride in the Wherever app," Micah had said, "in the Location box, you gotta type 'EveryWhereEver.' All run together like one word, but you capitalize the first letter of each word, do you know what I mean?"

Since the accident, Micah always spoke like he was younger than he was. As though he were twelve or thirteen, clinging to boyishness, rather than twenty-one. He explained things with the expectation that he would need to say them twice. Not as much for the benefit of the person he spoke to, but for himself, to feel certain he would be understood.

"If you do it, and it's the right time and place, or if the all-black car just chooses you—and really, nobody knows how that works—then it shows up. You can't see in through the windows or windshield, and when you get inside, it's uh … it's … what's the word? There's no one inside. It's …"

"Driverless," Kevin said.

"Yeah. Driverless. The only way to tell it where you want to go next is to type it in the app. But it's supposed to be able to take you anywhere you want to go. Literally *anywhere*. Crazy, right?"

Yes, Kevin thought as the car materialized from the night like spilled ink reversing into a tipped container, regaining its shape. *Yes, so crazy that if you saw it, it would be proof you've lost your mind.*

He stared at the almost metallic black windows, waiting for one to roll down and reveal Micah, laughing so hard he could barely get out the words "Got you." Then they'd laugh together, Kevin lying and saying that he was never scared, and Micah saying, "You're lying, Unc. You were shook as hell."

How would Micah even know where he was, though? How would he have known when Kevin was going to leave the bar, order a ride home? How could he even know Kevin would use the Wherever app, trusting this upstart rideshare company over one of its established competitors?

Even if Micah had a friend with a car perfectly matching the one from the images making the rounds in social media memes, he wouldn't have been able to orchestrate this. Who could?

Kevin looked down the street to his left, then to his right. No cars coming, no one walking. It was Tuesday night. No, it was past midnight, so technically it was Wednesday already. It wasn't impossible, or even unlikely, for there to be no one else in sight, but the surroundings held a distinct desertedness, like they hadn't seen a motorist or pedestrian in days and wouldn't see another for months.

This all had to be a product of the lean hitting him harder than it had before. The moment comes for most, the day they realize their tolerance has shrunk without them realizing. Too much beer never made anyone hallucinate, to his knowledge, and it might slow the drinker's mind and movements some, but it never made time drag its feet in ankle-deep mud the way lean did. And though he'd never seen things that weren't there before, some of his old friends who used to drink lean with him said it happened to them on occasion. Small discrepancies or impossibilities that seemed more like jumbled memories when described. A small dog or cat in a house where there were no pets. A tattoo or picture that changed color, size, or other features when stared at for too long. Nothing as large, complex, or persistently present as the black car.

Kevin heard its engine, thought he smelled its exhaust, waved his hand in front of its high beams to see the shadow it pitched down the road. He tried to open the front passenger door, found it locked. Touching the handle, however, confirmed for him that this was less hallucination than manifestation.

The back passenger-side door opened. Kevin looked inside. The upholstery was as black as the exterior. There was no driver in the car, just as Micah said, and Kevin was minimally aware of how hard his heart should be beating compared to how steady it still was.

What would you do if you were perfectly sober? He had trained himself to ask this question several times per night so that it became habitual, and he didn't have to depend on remembering to ask it. He knew that he would not get in the car if this were one of the five nights a week he dedicated to staying clean. If he was sober, he'd have never been in this position at all, and he would have missed out on a minor phenomenon.

Not everything he had done under the influence had been regrettable. He'd experienced friendships, memorable flings, and trips to amazing places while inspired by alcohol and illegal medicine. None of these things outweighed his greatest mistake, but that hadn't occurred *while* he was intoxicated. That had come in the aftermath of a particularly long night. It was one of those things that didn't get talked about enough, he believed. How a hangover can be more than just its symptoms. Headache, nausea, fatigue. It was one thing to suffer those things alone, another to make decisions that impacted others while you were sleepier, more distracted, and less clearheaded than you otherwise would be. Technically sober, but not truly sober.

If this was another mistake in the making, at least it would only hurt him, no one else. A part of him might have wanted that. The rest of him, however, could foresee the regret he would carry the moment he backed away from this. The stories he wouldn't get to tell. What did he have to worry about anyway? With the likelihood of this being a hallucination removed—at least for the most part—the remaining, grounded explanation for the car was that it was a publicity stunt concocted by the Wherever rideshare team. Something they did to random people who took the bait of their viral phantom car story.

Before he could repeat the sobriety question again, and give himself a chance to make the wiser, less interesting decision, Kevin got into the car, shut the door, and was encased in almost total darkness, save for the light from his phone's screen. He may as well have been in a cave or a tomb. The windows were as impenetrable from the inside as they were from the outside.

When he looked down at his phone, he saw only a single text field with "Location" stamped above it in red. Hadn't there been more to the app earlier? The usual features? Different graphics, maybe a background watermark, a logo, a menu, a profile icon? Something to scroll down to, at least. A link to contact information in case you had a complaint, for instance.

The screen consisted of whiteness as stark as the car's darkness, save for the single word and text field below it.

Location.

Kevin reached for a door handle he could not see, felt high and low for it along the smooth, fabric interior of the car door, and found nothing.

Now, at last, apprehension sizzled within him, centered right between his gut and groin, and he had to fight not to enjoy it, not transform its energy into euphoria. It was as if an alarm were blaring, but his inebriated mind wanted to turn it into a sound effect a DJ would use to enliven a party. This was serious. Hadn't he pulled the door closed by a handle? Now it had disappeared. He couldn't get out of the car. How was that possible? Had he drunk so much he couldn't tell what was real and what wasn't?

He made a point of setting a limit on his consumption before going out but sometimes let one or two or four more drinks slide by if he was feeling right. Had that been the case tonight? He couldn't remember. Maybe he was still at his preferred little booth in the bar, passed out, the bartender having already called his sister, Minerva, who would come get him when her shift was over, and this was all a dream. It felt too real to be a dream, but didn't all dreams feel that way?

Point the phone at the door, he thought, then responded aloud, "What?"

Turn the light of the phone—

"Right, right," Kevin said and flushed with embarrassment. He shined the phone screen onto the door and confirmed it was a smooth surface.

The phone has a flashlight, it's brighter—

"I know," he said to himself, then swiped down on the screen to get to his phone's shortcuts menu and turn on the flashlight feature. When this did nothing, he swiped left to get away from the Wherever app to try again. The screen went black, leaving Kevin in complete darkness. He swiped left again, an automatic, unthinking movement, programmed into him—as it was into most people—by a lifetime of such responses to defective technology. The elevator button doesn't light up when you press it? Press it again. Your car makes a weird noise and doesn't start when you turn the key? Turn it again. The touchscreen does something unexpected when you swipe your thumb? Swipe again.

The screen stayed blank, and Kevin swiped right twice, hoping to get back to the Wherever app, exhaling when the light it proffered returned.

If this was a trick, the mechanics of it escaped him. If it was a dream, a lean-induced one at that, what could he do other than wait to wake up?

Steer into it, he thought, then felt sadness clawing at him like hands emerging from the seatback. The metaphor might have pained him, but the advice struck him as reasonable. Go with it. That made sense. More sense than trying to punch through a window, breaking his hand and probably slicing his arm up if he was successful. Screaming for help from within a space where light couldn't escape didn't make sense to him either, and he didn't feel he had the energy to scream, besides.

But what would "steering into it" entail?

"It can take you anywhere you want to go. Literally *anywhere,*" Micah had said.

"So if I wrote 'Paris' as my destination, the car would drive me there, across the ocean?" Kevin had said, not out of sincere interest, but because Micah liked and needed the engagement.

"That's what they say," Micah said. "Literally anywhere."

"What about if I wrote 'the bottom of the ocean'? Or 'the moon'?"

"Unc, literally means … wait, I'm using that word right, right?"

"Yes," Kevin said.

"Okay, well it means what it means."

Kevin had sensed slight agitation entering Micah's tone, so he ceased with questions he thought were playful. He'd had more in mind, however, and they came to him now.

What if I put in something like 'my happy place'? Could the black car read someone's mind, know where to take them then? What if you didn't even know where your happy place was? Could it decide for you? What if you wrote "the saddest place in the world"? Was there an objective truth for such a location? Might the car have its own destination in mind?

In mind.

He wished he could scoff at himself for giving the car the capacity to think and make decisions but thought it sillier to dismiss any strangeness related to the situation, considering where he was. If he was stuck in his own nightmare, then there were no limits to what his imagination could conjure. If this was reality, then he no longer had any grasp of the shape of it, or what it could become.

He thought of testing the app and the car with something small and plausible. Typing "Home" or "Library" into the Location field. What good would that do, though? If it could take him someplace ordinary, that didn't preclude it from taking him somewhere extraordinary. If it could bring him somewhere that shouldn't be possible, however, then it might indeed be able to take him anywhere. And wherever it took him, it would have to show him that it had brought him there, wouldn't it? It would have to open the door, or at least lower the window, to prove itself. Otherwise, what would be the point?

A place popped into his head, something inaccessible that he couldn't even name. *The bridge in Brazil I heard about*, he typed into the field, then hit the Enter key. The engine hummed, the black car moved. As it picked up speed, Kevin felt and searched for a seat belt that wasn't present. The tingling under his stomach, which felt like a previously unknown part of him forever dissolving, spread everywhere from his toes to his fingertips. He became a conscious vapor held in a human form by the memory of being human. The only thing belying this sensation was that he still held his phone.

He concentrated on the bridge in Brazil to stave off insanity. It was something else he had heard about from Micah, on a different occasion. Something real and verifiable that his nephew had seen in a documentary and was excited to talk about. A bridge unfinished and abandoned to the jungle, disconnected from any roads.

The car decelerated and Kevin gradually felt whole and solid once more. The car eased to a stop as if cognizant of his lack of a safety belt, careful to keep him from lurching forward when it parked. After it stopped, it opened the back passenger door, and Kevin fell out in his eagerness to get outside.

The night was warm and lit by a full moon. The wind rolled down the mountain above him, making the rainforest sound like it was alive, its trees swaying and talking with each other over the sound of insects chittering and buzzing, night birds calling, all spreading word of the intruder on the bridge.

Kevin *was* on the unfinished bridge. He stood and staggered away from the railing, almost backing into the open car before remembering what was behind him. He had heard of people being scared sober before, but he had never experienced it. Not even when he'd been threatened by a man waving a knife at a bar, or when the sound of gunshots had cleared a nightclub parking lot after closing time. Being where he was, however, brewed a fear that gave him a distinct, unwanted level of clarity he hadn't felt since the night he'd pulled Micah from the wreck.

Pain compressed his stomach, squeezed everything undigested out of it, up through his throat. He threw up, wiped his mouth, glanced at the forest canopy spread farther than he could see in the valley beneath the bridge, and felt the urge to vomit again.

He had to get away. Not just from the bridge, from himself. He missed the insubstantiality he felt a moment ago. Someone so close to nonexistence couldn't get sick all over themselves, or feel any other physical pain or discomfort, could they? The answer had to be no. And the darkness appealed to him now, too, seeming more merciful than dreadful. In the dark, there were no sights that could even indirectly dredge up bad memories.

After he got back into the car and the door shut on its own, he realized how stupid he'd been to consider it a haven. The vaporous state he thought he entered before—and wanted now—had only come when the car was moving. The blackness likewise didn't give him any relief. No, it didn't bring to mind the night of the accident and all that came with it—the loneliness of the road, the flames, the blood on the asphalt—but it also could not displace these things either, and they were already alive in his head.

An acrid belch preceded another tightening of his stomach. Kevin choked down everything trying to come back up. The smell of it burned his nostrils and brought tears to his eyes. Through blurred vision, he looked at his phone, started to type the word "Home." That wasn't where he wanted to be, however. Alone in his apartment, too sick to fall asleep, waiting for the additional misery of a hangover that would feel like he'd taken a beating …

Or crawled out of a car wreck.

He shook the thought from his head and felt dizzy. Instead of entering "Home" in the location, he typed, "Happiness."

The car moved forward. This time, the ethereal sensation did not come.

When the car stopped and the door opened, Kevin's first instinct was to shut his eyes. This would be a cruel trick, he was sure. The app had taken what he wanted and twisted it in some way he couldn't have anticipated, like he'd wished upon the monkey's paw from that old, famous story. But he did not shut his eyes in time to avoid seeing the park, the outdoor basketball court. And there was no way to close his ears anyway, so he heard the distinct sound of sneakers squeaking, players calling for the ball, others calling out defensive assignments, and spectators cheering and heckling. Cheering primarily. Much of it regarding the kid.

This couldn't be any other moment. There were other happy days, other games and events Kevin had taken his nephew to in lieu of his departed brother-in-law and Minerva, an ER nurse. But only one occasion could define happiness for him.

Micah had just turned fifteen a week before they went to the park. All he'd wanted for his birthday was to come to the court on the day a semipro internet star who made his living touring the country was arriving to play. There would be cameras, there would be fans, there would be serious ballers who had played in college, or played in overseas leagues, or had a drink of water in the NBA, or all of the above, present. And then there'd be the kid. Still a freshman in high school and a natural on the court.

He hadn't even played his best ball that day and was outplayed by a few other guys, but given how much older, bigger, and stronger they all were, to outplay the majority of them was remarkable, and people had noticed. He finished the day with several highlights and an immediate online buzz, his highlights even getting a few comments and likes from pros on social media.

It took them almost an hour to leave after the last game because children were asking Micah to sign their shoes or sign the ball they had brought with them that day; a few bloggers asked for, and received, short interviews with him, and several other players asked him to pose with them in pictures, all while telling him how impressed they were.

"Was I really that good out there, Unc?" Micah had said when they made it to Kevin's car, and for the first time, Kevin realized his nephew always said "Unc" the way other kids said "Pop" or "Dad."

"You were awesome," Kevin said. "You belonged out there. Don't ever question that."

He could have stepped out of the black car now and relived every part of that day. His best day. The perfect moment when Micah's work—and Kevin's contribution to that work—made a broken promise that would pay off in the best way possible. The moment his future seemed brightest, even in light of the scholarship offers and more to come later.

Kevin pulled the door closed, then shuddered in the dark, thinking of all the things the kid had earned and never seen. The moments robbed of him. Making it to the pros. Buying his mother a house with his first big check. Hoisting trophies. Becoming a hero and inspiration to others. So much more, none of it guaranteed, but much of it paid for in advance.

The kid had done more than worked, he'd sacrificed. So many people didn't understand that or didn't want to hear it. They just saw Micah as a boy born with gifts, who only had to stay out of his own way to live a spoiled, rich life. There was far more to it than that, but Kevin understood that line of thought. He'd had to fight against it at times himself when watching Micah glide past, or rise above, defenders on the court.

Anyone could be a pro if they could do that, he sometimes thought. Yes, Micah had given up certain things others his age enjoyed to maximize his talent—late nights, lazy weekends, girlfriends, junk foods—but it was still less than a lot of other people, younger and older, had to give up to have even a fraction of the chance at a good life that he had. Kevin himself, for instance. How much of his time and energy had he given up to help his nephew fulfill his potential and pursue his dream?

"Not enough," Kevin whispered, and could almost imagine seeing a distant, flickering light, flames surrounded by so much night it should have been impossible to see the fire through it. Enough darkness to make you think you were alone in the universe. The depth of night he'd felt while pulling Micah away from the wreck, the feeling that somehow, even though his car was overturned and ablaze on the side of a commonly used road, their isolation in the seconds immediately after the accident would last forever, and nobody would find them.

Micah had needed help. His left leg—the one he would eventually lose after a dozen surgeries—was shattered in several places, and looked like something haphazardly grafted onto his body, never meant to be part of him. He'd have been shrieking in pain were he not unconscious. Bleeding and swelling in his forehead hid a small dent in his skull, and a brain bruise underneath that. He needed someone to get him to a hospital, but nothing existed in all of reality other than the wreck and his uncle. There were no hospitals. There were no paramedics. There was no help coming.

A call for far more ordinary help had brought them here. "Unc, I came out to this party for a bit, and my boy who drove me started drinking. Can you come get me?"

Kevin had put it in Micah's head not to trust rideshare services. "You've got to be careful. You never know who might be picking you up." Had he any capacity to laugh about that now, he would have.

Looking back, even with the knowledge of what had happened, Kevin struggled to accept he shouldn't have gotten behind the wheel. He hadn't had a drink since leaving a house party just before dawn, close to sixteen hours prior. His headache was still sharp and heavy, forcing him to squint through the pain of it intermittently, but he'd functioned through worse, he thought.

Yes, he was tired—he'd slept little in the past week while catching up with friends back in town—but not too tired to come through for his nephew and make sure the kid got home safely while his mother worked a double shift.

Certainly not so tired he'd pass out on the drive home, jerking awake as Micah tried to reach over from the passenger side to steer the car left, back onto the street, only to clip the roadside barrier and send the car tumbling.

Kevin stared at the phone. The cursor blinked in the blank field. Where to next?

He heard Micah's voice. *Literally anywhere …*

What if that wasn't limited to anywhere in the world, but anywhere that *could* be?

He typed, *Where the accident never happened*, but did not push the Enter key.

If the car could take him to such a place, he didn't deserve to go there any more than he deserved to relive that perfect day at the outdoor court. Micah deserved it. Or, no, that might be the worst thing for the kid. The car could only take him to such a place—it couldn't transform him into the version of himself that existed there, could it? Even if it could, was that fair to him, to who he was now? Since the accident, Micah had worked harder than before, albeit to a different end. Instead of working to become the best athlete he was capable of being, he worked to fend off short-term memory loss; he worked to control mood swings born from frustration with sometimes not finding the right word, or not finding it quickly enough. He fought with the knowledge of who he used to be, the knowledge that he'd never be that person again, and the need to accept it. He worked hard simply to be decent.

"I just want to be good," he'd told Kevin during a quiet moment less than a month ago. "Just good, you know what I mean?"

Kevin had known exactly what the kid meant but didn't know how to tell Micah he was already there without patronizing him. The kid wanted to earn it, even if he already had it. Maybe because some things in his possession weren't easy to keep. The peace he felt from forgiving his uncle, for instance. Micah made it look easy, the way he used to make it look easy when he was toying with opponents on the court, but Kevin knew well that forgiveness took effort. A certain kind of strength. Micah had it. Kevin wondered if he could have found it, too, if he hadn't spent so much time searching for an escape from his guilt.

He closed his eyes to get away from the light of the phone. Maybe he didn't have to go anywhere else. Why couldn't he stay here until, one way or another, the darkness took him?

Because this isn't where it ends, he thought. Something else had to be waiting. Call it heaven, call it hell. Paradise or the abyss. Names didn't matter. *Location*. Destination. That mattered. Where are you going? Where do you deserve to go?

People described heaven as though it were made of joy and love. He'd been taken to the place that defined happiness for him and sensed a grief waiting for him within it that scared him into hiding in the dark.

Hell, meanwhile, was supposedly built of pain and misery. And fire. He knew what his hell would be.

He opened his eyes, stared at the phone.

Location.

He typed, *Wherever,* and almost hit the Enter key, but took a breath and a moment instead, and summoned the nerve to type the rest.

Wherever I deserve to go.

The engine revved, the car carried him off, and Kevin thought of Micah and the many others like him who never made it to the places they deserved to go. He thought of how such a fate was a tragedy for some, while for others it would be the ultimate blessing.

CHARAKAKON

Originally published in *Weird Tales*
(December 2024, Issue 370)

"Tell me something about yourself you thought you'd never tell anyone."

Only one of Carter's prior boyfriends had refused this request. Most had shared stories that, while personal, did not feel confidential. He surmised their reluctance stemmed from distrust. Why was he asking this? What would he do with the information? Use it against them later? Ridicule them for it? He understood their misgivings, but they always disappointed him.

"My family is cursed," Ivan told him, liquor lubricating his candidness. "Legitimately cursed, not a metaphorical thing. We don't know why, just who it started with. My great-grandfather, Abram. He was the first in the family to feel the curse. He was a rich man, and none of us knows exactly how he built his fortune, so I think our curse is probably owed to something terrible he did."

"My God, you're serious," Carter said. "You're not nearly creative enough to spin this out of thin air."

"You want to hear this or not?"

"I do."

"Then hush." He finished his sixth Gibson of the night, then continued. "The things that haunt us are called *charakakon*. That's what my grandmother said they're called, anyway."

"Chaka-what?"

"I said to hush, didn't I?"

"I'm sorry. I promise to shut up now."

"Thank you. I've tried to look that name up to see what old-world lore might exist about these things, but when I type *charakakon* in a search engine I get nothing. Everything I know about this comes from our family record.

"My grandmother was there when the first one approached Abram. She said that the thing looked like a creature pretending to be a man. It walked with a weird lean and wore strange clothes that didn't fit well and smelled … off. She said the smell reminded her of food right before it goes bad, when it still might smell good enough for you to eat it, but wrong enough for you to know you shouldn't. Strangest of all was that her father didn't seem to notice the thing until it got close. Like it was any other ordinary pedestrian passing them by.

"When the charakakon got close, it told Abram, 'You will die in poverty, your fortune squandered.' Then it walked away. My grandmother said its smile was too wide to fit through a door."

Ivan took a drink, shut his eyes, and exhaled gently through his nostrils as the liquor went down, like he was savoring hot soup. He did this, Carter knew, when he was anxious. He'd done it at this very bar last month before unsuccessfully trying to convince Carter they should stop seeing each other.

"And did your great-grandfather actually lose his money?" Carter asked.

"Oh yes, after a few years of disastrous decisions. When it got bad enough, he finally told the rest of the family about the stranger who'd cursed him. And that's when some of his siblings told him of similar encounters they'd had with someone who approached them and cursed them with future misfortune.

"Except, misfortune isn't really the curse. My grandmother was the first to figure this out, after hearing some of the stories from her aunts and uncles. The strangers don't curse us with the event, they curse us with the knowledge. That first charakakon didn't make Abram lose his money. It put the knowledge of this future in his mind. Which might have scared him into making it a self-fulfilling prophecy. Or maybe not. We can't know for sure. I have a large family, and we've all had different experiences. I've had uncles, aunts, and cousins who lived their entire lives without letting their charakakon catch up to them or corner them to give them the bad news. I can't say that any of them lived perfect lives. They've all had issues, some worse than others. A couple even said they wished they had let their charakakon tell them about what was coming because maybe if they had known in advance … who knows? I don't agree with that, though. I've avoided mine since I was sixteen. I've never once thought I think I'd be better off knowing."

"But you won't know if you'd have been better off knowing until after whatever's meant to happen happens," Carter said. He couldn't keep his glee buried. At the edge of his mind, it occurred to him that he didn't believe a word of what Ivan had said. Ivan clearly believed in it, though, and that made the story compelling. "Maybe those relatives had a point."

Ivan nodded to the bartender, who brought him another drink. Carter got around to finishing off the rum and Coke he'd been nursing. He was, by his count, six drinks behind Ivan and had no interest in shrinking the gap.

"That could be. One of my cousins met hers not long after she got married. It told her that she was destined to miscarry. That probably would have discouraged some people from even trying to have a child, but she and her husband had originally planned to wait a few years before having a baby. Instead, she told him she'd changed her mind and that they should try for it sooner. She didn't tell him anything about the curse, though. Sure enough, she miscarried. But a few years later, back on their original schedule, she had a perfectly healthy baby girl."

"She gamed the curse," Carter said, his volume betraying his excitement.

"That's a way of putting it," Ivan said.

"It's brilliant."

"It's something. She seems to be at peace with the outcome, and I'm not the one to press her on it. Doesn't always work out so well, though. An uncle of mine was told he'd spend the worst year of his life in prison. He somehow took that to mean he'd only be sentenced to a year for any crime he might be caught doing."

"Oh no …"

"Yeah. He did manage get through a couple of bank robberies before he was arrested. I guess he thought he'd have some money waiting for him on the outside after his year in. I don't know. Anyway, he was sentenced to twelve years. He's about halfway through his time right now. Don't know if he's lived through that worst year yet."

Carter chuckled. "Forgive me. I shouldn't laugh."

"It's pretty funny."

After knocking back his last drink, Ivan pulled five twenties from his wallet and left them on the counter. "For both of us. No change," he said to the bartender. "Thanks for putting up with us."

The bartender nodded and swept the money toward the register. Carter held Ivan lightly by the crook of his arm as Ivan slid off the stool. Ivan was in no danger of falling or stumbling, but Carter felt compelled to steady him all the same. With his free hand, he used an application on his phone to summon a driver to take them away.

"I have an untouched bottle back at my place, if you're interested," Ivan said.

"Am I ever not?" Carter responded.

In hindsight, moving in together had been a life preserver thrown to a body too deep under the waves to reach it. But it wasn't the small epiphanies of aggravation that arose from cohabitation that killed their relationship. It wasn't Ivan's drinking, either, nor was it Carter's half-in-half-out support peppered with equal amounts of scorn and enablement.

It was what Carter saw on a night in April, during San Antonio's annual weeklong fiesta, that killed them as a couple and changed Carter's life.

"Can I show you something if you promise not to be upset?" Ivan said. Carter tried not to admire how well Ivan literally and figuratively held his alcohol. Amid the thick, jostling tides of people pushing their way to booths or stages or bathrooms at the Night in Old San Antonio festival, Ivan's cup of sangria never tipped, and he never swayed. People parted around him like he was an old stone fixture.

"What? I can't promise that," Carter said.

"Come on."

"No. What if … what if you showed me some horrible video of a dog being abused?"

"Oh my God. Why would I show you that? *I* wouldn't want to see that."

"Well, that's just an example of one thing that would upset me. I'm just saying, without knowing what you'll show me, I can't well promise—"

"Okay, okay. Point taken. Just look over there, would you? See the guy with the guitar under that tree?"

Carter's eyes followed Ivan's pointing finger. There was indeed a man under a tree. He was spindly, wore a low-brimmed straw hat, and strummed an old, fat guitar that looked big enough for him to sleep in. He had oddly shaded skin, as if he'd walked past a bonfire, absorbed some of the smoke, more of the ash, and the two were fighting over whether to darken or lighten his complexion. Carter was not sure, but he thought that the thin guitarist had looked down at his instrument just as Carter turned to him, as if to not be caught peeping.

"What of him?" Carter said.

"That jacket's a little small on him, isn't it?"

"A little," Carter said, noticing now how the cuffs of the man's snug, barn-red suit jacket stopped well short of his wrists.

"And those pants," Ivan said, "it's like he got them tailored to keep him from being able to bend at the knees."

"Are we really just having a go at this poor guy's clothes? He's just out here trying to earn a few tips."

"It's almost like he's not sure how real people are supposed to dress themselves. Or like he's trying to make a joke of it."

Carter frowned at Ivan. "I've never thought of you as a mean drunk before, but—"

Something in Ivan's smile made Carter pause. A second later he realized that it was what lay behind Ivan's smile that seized him, and another second later he felt like he could overload every outlet in a building with the wattage running through him.

Ivan nodded before the question came.

"You're saying that man's your … your demon? Your follower who knows about your future? Oh, what's the damn word?"

"Charakakon," Ivan said gently, like a language instructor.

"Charakakon," Carter repeated. "That's him? How can you tell?" Even as he said this, however, he knew that the answer must be, *You just can. He* could tell now, after all. A moment before, he wouldn't have looked twice at the guitarist. Now he noticed the spidery, unnatural movements of the man's fingers on the guitar strings, not quite in proper concert with one another. He saw that the man's clothes were not merely ill-fitting, but a costume and impulsive insult. A mockery of the silly threads humans hid behind to conceal the fragile shame they dwelled on within and barely understood.

When the man sneaked another glance in their direction, Carter could see the burnt, fool's-gold tint of his eyes.

"Like my grandmother said, they look like something pretending to be human. Something that *hates* people. They're easy enough to miss until the first time you recognize one. Once you do, then it's harder for you *not* to see it."

Carter took a step closer to the guitarist, bumping into a woman passing by and causing her to spill some of her beer. The woman and her boyfriend cursed at Carter but kept walking when they saw how oblivious he was to them.

The guitarist lifted his head slowly and glanced past Carter to look at Ivan, who waved back. The charakakon looked down again at the guitar strings and plucked at them, tuning up for a song never to be played.

"Has he … has *it* been following us since we got here?" Carter asked.

"Maybe. Doesn't really matter. Only important thing is that I spotted it, yet again. Just like I've been doing since I—"

"Since you were sixteen."

A clipped hiccup of startled laughter escaped Ivan. "You remember."

Carter twisted and glared at Ivan, offended by the surprise in his tone. "Of course I do. Ivan, aren't you afraid? What if it knows where we live? What if it follows us home?"

Ivan shrugged. "Then it'll just wait outside, I guess. They can only approach freely in public. They can't come into any place where you're resting your head unless you welcome them in. Like the old stories about vampires. That's another one my wonderful grandmother figured out."

"You never mentioned that before," Carter said, the tightness at the base of his spine abating with the news that the charakakon could not invade his house uninvited.

"Well, I was confident you didn't believe in the curse anyway. But even assuming you did, it was never your issue before. Now we're living together. Why do you think I bothered pointing it out? You think it's the first time we've been out and I've seen it?" Ivan caressed Carter's face with his thumb, then playfully patted his cheek with his fingertips. "I pointed it out so that now you won't mistake it for a salesman or one of my coworkers or something and invite it in."

"You're sure about all of that? It can't disguise itself again, or—"

"Oh, it can try, and it definitely will. But like I said, once you've really seen the thing for what it is, you'll always be able to see it. Trust me." He took Carter's hand. "Hey. You trust me, right?"

"I … sure. Yes."

"We're going to be fine. I've been fine all this time, and now I've even got you to help me look out for it. I think we've got this, don't you?"

Carter nodded and exhaled, allowing himself to smile. "I do."

"Okay. Now let's go find some elotes. Somebody just walked by with one and it looked like heaven."

As he followed behind Ivan, who continued to effortlessly part groups ahead of him, Carter felt a prickly heat on the back of his neck that made him lift his shoulders and tilt his head back to shed it. He was tempted to turn around to see who might have grazed him with the hot needle that must have been the source of the sensation, but he resisted the impulse. He knew that what he felt was the glare of the stranger beneath the tree. The man who was not a man.

Charakakon.

To his surprise, the thought of hearing every dark secret the monster wanted to free from its tongue gave Carter a propellant high, like he'd been vaulted into the stars and could see more than was meant to be seen.

When he thought of leaving a note, he thought of it being succinct, if not entirely open. *I was never depressed. I chose to do this*

because I am impatient, adventurous, and curious. Not because I was sad.

Prior to seeing the charakakon, Carter had been an ardent skeptic. Seeing the thing unmasked had flipped him to the opposite end of the spectrum, certain that there was a life beyond the physical death that marked one's departure from this world.

All that kept Carter from ending his own life was the fear of going alone and uninformed. He resented this fear, this confining instinct that warned him of undiscovered dangers he would encounter once this life stopped. It was impossible to know what these dangers could be, or if they were threats worthy of making him dither. They had to exist, that much he was sure of. No journey came without risk. He couldn't possibly prepare for these unknowns, however, so what good did it do him to delay moving onward? It would happen to him one day, regardless of whether he had a hand in it or not. Why not take charge of his departure?

He did some cursory reading regarding the "afterlife," a term he despised. You didn't call your actual life the "post-non-existence." "Afterlife" elevated an apparent preamble to the core story, and reduced what he believed must be a truer, freer state of being to an epilogue. His aversion to the term and loathing for authors passing off their best guesses as expertise killed his interest in any literature on the subject. It was for the best. Any time spent consulting the uninformed notions and self-gratifying dogmas of human beings was time better spent pursuing answers from something with more intimate knowledge of things that escaped man's observation.

Perhaps Ivan had sensed something was amiss, and that the temptation to welcome the charakakon in for a sit-down to pick its brain might prove too alluring to Carter. Or maybe Ivan hadn't simply been trying to hurt Carter's feelings when he said that Carter was no good for him, that Carter exploited and even nurtured Ivan's alcoholism to keep him dependent. It was possible that Ivan truly believed those things. Carter supposed it didn't matter one way or the other. For whatever reason, Ivan chose to leave him, and on the day he left, Carter felt shame when he realized he would regret never speaking to the charakakon at least as much as he would miss the man he loved.

Soon after their separation, Carter began following Ivan to and from his rehab meetings, then to and from his office downtown.

It wasn't stalking, Carter assured himself, if the person he was tracking wasn't the true target.

At first, he thought Ivan had been mistaken about identifying the charakakon. He followed Ivan's comings and goings for two months without seeing the creature again, and he was sure that it had switched its guise to become unnoticeable. Maybe Ivan could identify it more easily because it was his curse, and because he had something to fear if he let it trick him. Carter's concerns tied to misidentifying the charakakon weren't nearly as urgent as Ivan's. Worst-case scenario, Carter's worry of moving on without advanced knowledge of what was to come would paralyze him and condemn him to an ordinary life that would eventually end, nonetheless. He'd be ushered onto the next stage as blind as the billions who'd passed before him. It wasn't ideal, but Ivan had far more at stake. Carter couldn't imagine finding out the worst thing that was destined to happen to him. Living with that poisonous information in his head at all hours. How awful must that be?

He did not, at first, intend to betray Ivan, whom he was obliged to love above any other lover he'd had, if for no other reason than because Ivan had opened his eyes to things beyond human understanding. Had Carter found the charakakon during one of his many stakeouts, instead of it finding him, the idea of betraying Ivan might never have come to him. He'd have had more time to map his approach and plot the conversation.

But the charakakon found him first, in the back row of the parking lot of a dance club he had followed Ivan to. When it appeared in the side mirror of his car, staring at Carter with those jaundiced, molten eyes, his first instinct was to start the car and drive away. It approached the car and Carter was, for a moment, sure that Ivan had found a way to transfer the curse onto him. Ivan had known Carter had been following him, had grown sick of it, and instead of calling the police he had cut a deal with his devil to feed his ex to it.

Too afraid to move or start the engine, as though any movement or noise might rouse it to strike, Carter remained still and allowed the charakakon to approach the driver's-side window. It peered inside, grinning like a horrible child looking into a small aquarium, contemplating how to torment the fish. It even tapped the glass. When it did so again, Carter understood that it wanted him to roll the window down. He acted as though he could not see it. The charakakon put its hands together as if to pray, held its long fingers to its lips. "Please," it said to Carter. He barely heard this, transfixed by fingers that either had two too many knuckles apiece or were so broken and knotted it was impossible to tell the difference.

It tapped the glass again and said, "I can give him to you if you will give him to me." Its voice sounded like sailing stones sliding over the desert.

Talk to him, damn it, Carter thought. *Isn't this the point of all of this? You finally have him here and he wants to talk to you. Do it, for Christ's sake, before you lose your chance.*

He cracked the window, his rationale barely overriding his trepidation. A warm aroma drifted through the gap, the smell of something venomous roasting over a flame.

"What do you mean?" Carter said.

"What I said."

"I don't … I don't want him. And I don't want you to hurt him. I just want to ask you some things."

The creature slipped its fingers in the gap between the window and the door and flattened its nose against the glass. "Ah, the lies. The denials. Never failing to appear. Do they cure your conscience? Is that why you tell them? Does it make it well with you, what you know you intend to do, as long as you can bring yourself to say you don't intend it? Is that it?"

Carter's abrupt contempt for the creature rose almost to the height of his apprehension. Once again he was inclined to start his car and drive off, and once again the steady, rational voice only he could hear reached him.

You are having a conversation with something that isn't supposed to be real. It's offering you a quid pro quo deal. You are on the cusp of being a pioneer without peer, and you're going to blow it because you don't like the way you're being spoken to? You're going to pout and run off like a child? Grow the fuck up.

"Get in," he said to the charakakon. "Let's talk about how we can help each other."

"Why did you call me, Carter?"

Carter took a moment to visualize the words he'd rehearsed. It was important not to misspeak. "I believe that it would be best for us to see each other one more time."

A long silence, and then Ivan told him, "No."

His counterargument to the anticipated response of "Why?" was already halfway up before Carter realized he needed to recalculate the course of the conversation.

"Okay, that's … I think that's a rash response."

"It's the one I'm giving you," Ivan said. "Goodbye."

"Wait, please. Look … I still love you." This declaration rushed past his lips like it was racing to reach Ivan's ears before something else did. He repeated himself, more deliberately this time. "I still love you."

"I'm sure you do. But you're bad for me, all around, and you always were."

"I've changed," Carter said. He smiled with pride at the restraint he exhibited by not blurting out, *No I'm not* and *No I wasn't*. "I've even been to rehab."

"Really?" Ivan said. "What happened to it only being for weak people?"

"I was wrong. And once again, just for the record, I wasn't talking about you when I said that. But I was still wrong to say it. I was wrong about a hundred different things, and I owe you an apology for each one. I'd like to apologize face-to-face if you'd please agree to see me. I think that would be best for both of us. And after that, if you want to tell me to go to hell, or just never see me again, then I'll be at peace with that. But I think it's important that we at least see each other this last time, if it *is* the last time."

"Where at?" Ivan said.

"Cassy's."

"I'm not trying to make this a whole lunch date with you."

"We can just have coffee or tea. Or nothing, if you prefer."

"When?" Ivan said.

"Tomorrow, if you're free," Carter said. "About noon?"

"Fine."

"Thank you."

"Yeah. Look, I have to go."

"Okay. I'll see you tomorrow," Carter said.

"Yeah."

The phone beeped as Ivan hung up. Carter set the phone down, stood from his chair at his dining-room table, and approached the charakakon, which waited in a corner of the room. "He agreed to meet—"

"I am aware," it said. "And now I'm curious to know how you feel. Is it well with you to have it done with?"

Carter's queasiness made the floor feel fluid beneath him.

"I can't say, because it's not done with, now is it?" he said. "I could change my mind and not go through with this."

It chuckled. "But you won't. You surely won't. And therein lies much of the joy of this, as always."

An impulse to strike the demon, smack the arrogance out of it, made Carter stretch his fingers, but he thought better of it. At best it would be pointless. At worst ... he was unsure and uneager to find out.

"If you're done here," Carter said, "you can now consider yourself officially uninvited. Just make sure you're there tomorr—"

The charakakon vanished. A fast-fading visual residue, like evaporating ink, held the space it had occupied a fraction of a second before. Carter's surprise at this evolved into steady nervousness that lived within him like an eel swimming between his ribs.

Even with his invitation rescinded and his unholy guest banished, he no longer felt comfortable in his house. He soon departed to check into a hotel room.

After the waitress delivered their coffees and left, Ivan said, "You could have added your spike if you wanted to. I wouldn't have minded."

"I went to rehab. I told you," Carter said, recalling his lie from their earlier conversation before he could say something that might trip him up.

"Oh, that's right."

"I haven't even wanted a drink in twelve weeks."

"No shit?" Ivan said. "What inspired that, anyway? It's not like you ever knocked down bottles how I used to."

"True," Carter said, "but I had started to do too much. Rum in my coffee every morning. A drink or two with lunch. Wine for dinner on an easy night, and harder stuff if I was going out. I wasn't even enjoying it. I just did it because I thought it was cute. It made me feel like a kind of classical man from a bygone era. Stupid, really."

The details of the improvised lie flowed from him so smoothly he decided to abandon his original script. Better to be natural and to accept that being casually manipulative and loose with the truth came easy to him. He had only one chance at this. Between that fact and the echo of what the charakakon had shared with him—Ivan's fate—he was struggling to keep any other thoughts in order.

"I have to tell you something, Ivan. You probably know this, or guessed it, but I didn't ask to meet you here just to apologize. I do *want* to apologize. I *do* apologize, for everything I put you through. I'd list it all, but I think you'd find it tedious."

"Never know until you try," Ivan said. "And I believe I was promised a hundred apologies yesterday."

Carter acknowledged this with a weak smile but continued as though uninterrupted. "I meant it when I said I still love you."

"I believed you."

"And it's hard for me to believe you don't love me still."

"I believe that too."

Carter sighed. "Please, Ivan. I'm being as honest as I've ever been with you. I miss you."

"I didn't come here for this."

"But you had to know this is where I was going to take this. And you came here anyway. That means something. Tell me it doesn't."

Ivan opened his mouth to respond, then shut it, along with his eyes, as he exhaled through his nostrils, and with that Carter knew he was on the right path.

"All it means," Ivan said, glaring at Carter now, "is that I trust myself, even if I know I can't trust you. I knew I could come here, hear whatever you had to say, and then never speak to you again."

"I have no doubt that you could. But I don't think that's what you want to do."

"You don't know anything."

"I don't. You're right. I never did. So I'm asking you, please, tell me what to do. All I want is to try to fix everything that I fucked up. Tell me where to start."

Ivan's jaw tightened as he chewed on what he was reluctant to say. Carter had to fight the joy that bubbled through him as he realized his pleas had the desired effect.

"I'll tell you this," Ivan said, "we need to order some food if we're going to be here for as long as I think we will."

Carter laughed so hard with relief his voice cracked. He immediately flushed red, and at this, a smile broke Ivan's hard grimace.

It's going to be okay, Carter thought. *He's going to hate me soon, but not for long. When it's all done and he understands what I understand, he'll forgive me. He'll show me how much he still loves me, and we'll make this great discovery together.*

Carter had chosen Cassy's Bistro as the meeting place because it was next door to La Habana, a boutique hotel he and Ivan went to for "staycations" when they were together. It had taken almost three hours of talking, laughing, and flirting to pull down enough of Ivan's barriers to make him join Carter at La Habana. Thankfully, no alcohol had been needed. Ivan deserved to approach his new beginning with a clear mind.

The sex was decent under the circumstances, but clumsier than Carter had envisioned. The graceless fumbling had been fun and cute at first, when trying to work through belt buckles and shirt buttons. Failing to find their rhythm and synchronicity even an hour later, however, and then through the encore, belied any idea of the eternal, effortless physical chemistry Carter wanted them to have. He knew it was his fault. He hadn't been able to overcome seeing all of this as a means to an end.

Half an hour after they finished, Ivan was asleep, as Carter knew he would be. Carter carefully slipped out of bed, went to the bathroom, and waited with the lights off and door closed. He sat on the tiled floor in silence, forcing himself not to count the seconds. He had practiced being indifferent to time. He imagined he could free himself from chronological constraints once he entered the next plane, as long as he trained himself.

He was so focused on this exercise that he did not hear the charakakon enter the room, which Carter had checked into the night before so he could invite the demon inside. Carter did not hear the creature speak, but he heard Ivan gasp, heard his heels slam on the wood floorboards as he sprung from the bed. Carter heard movement. Footsteps moving back and forth. Was Ivan trying to evade the charakakon? Was he pacing? Had he already heard his fate and was pondering whether to act on it immediately?

Stillness returned to the room. Carter felt a rush of energy. It was done. Ivan had learned his destiny and was coming to terms with it. Should Carter step out now, encourage Ivan to do what he must? Or would that be moving too fast? Ivan would need a moment, surely. After luring him into this trap, the least Carter could do was give him sufficient time to collect his thoughts. Ready himself.

At the sound of a door creaking, Carter shuddered with nervous elation. It was happening. He could sense a beautiful brightness that he could not yet see. He turned, started to speak, eager to explain himself, then saw that the bathroom door was still closed. The imaginary light of his anticipation collapsed into the true darkness that still surrounded him. The door he'd heard had been the door to the hotel room.

He left the bathroom and looked around in the futile hope that Ivan might be hiding, that he hadn't actually left. He felt foolish looking under the bed, then in the closet, and then under the bed again before stepping into the hallway to see if Ivan might be waiting for him there. He was not. If Carter ran now, he might be able to catch up to Ivan in the lobby or the parking lot, but what good would that do? If Ivan had left, that meant he didn't want to see things through, at least not now. Carter could only arrange so much. He could not force Ivan's hand.

He returned to the room and sat still at the foot of the bed. He had accounted for the possibility of being wrong about his place in Ivan's destiny the way you might account for the possibility of the plane you're boarding falling out of the sky. He was vaguely aware that it could happen but had wholeheartedly believed it wouldn't and had no recourse should it come to pass.

Behind him, from a corner of the room, he heard a strange sound, like laughter trying to burble up through the throat of something headless.

"Is it well with you, now that it is done?" the charakakon said.

"It's not over," Carter said, then repeated it in a whisper to show that he was still in control of something.

On his way home, after staying in the hotel until dawn, Carter convinced himself that this setback would be brief. He had counted on Ivan's anger overriding his composure, and their love then guiding him downstream, showing him how counterproductive resistance would be. He had underestimated Ivan, something he'd made a habit of when they were together, though this time he could honestly say he'd tried not to repeat past mistakes. Still, he hadn't given enough weight to Ivan's pride. It was clear to him now, so clear it embarrassed him to have missed it earlier, that Ivan's initial response—almost a reflex—would be to deny his fate.

Carter parked in his driveway, stepped out of his car, and approached his front door. He had his key out by the time he noticed the door was cracked open. His breath caught in his chest and delight turned the world a color he'd never seen before. He pushed the door open and rushed inside. He was in such a hurry to look for Ivan that he didn't see him sitting in the largest chair of his living room until his second scan of the room.

Ivan looked surprisingly comfortable in the cushioned chair. A large chef's knife lay on the armrest, and his gloved hand rested on the knife's handle like he'd forgotten it was there. Carter did not speak until the silence between them became more unbearable than the threat of saying the wrong thing.

"You never got rid of your key," Carter said.

"Just never got around to it."

"Right. Are you upset with me?"

"What a stupid fucking question," Ivan said.

After a deep breath, Carter tried again. "Did the charakakon say anything to you?"

"You know it did."

"What did it say?"

"You know."

"Tell me, please."

Ivan waited, and Carter could tell it was deliberate. A tease. Then Ivan finally confirmed what Carter knew. "It told me that I would kill my one true love and then kill myself."

Carter shuddered. He wanted to drop to the floor and shout that he was ready but thought he owed this moment, and their love, a little more dignity than that.

"And that's for me?" Carter said, nodding at the knife.

"It is," Ivan said.

"And then for you," Carter said, unable to stop himself, his exaltation floating the words out of the room almost before he could hear them. "Listen, I understand you're upset, but it's going to be okay. You have to know that I only did this because—"

"Stop." Ivan stood and grabbed the knife. "Whatever you're about to say, I don't need to hear it. It doesn't matter. I'm not going to kill myself."

Indignant laughter shot up from Carter's chest. He swallowed, held up his hands as an apology, but now understood Ivan still needed guidance. "Come on. You're standing at the doorstep of your calling, with something even greater on the other side. There's no sense in denying or delaying it, now that you know what's meant for you. That's why I—"

"I'm not killing myself over you, Carter."

"No? Then what's that knife for? You just said it's for me."

"It is."

"Well, then what else—"

Ivan moved forward, leveled the knife with Carter's stomach, and gave him the blade until it disappeared. The initial shock of pain made Carter's legs wobble, but the voracity of it robbed him of the strength to stand. The pain wasn't content to confine itself to the thin space the blade had carved out. It expanded and explored like the roots of an unquenchable weed. It stretched up to the center of his chest and down through his pelvis. Carter had mentally prepared for the pain as well as he could, for several days, but imagining it could not compare to experiencing it.

Ivan withdrew the blade and stabbed Carter three more times. Carter found himself on the floor, not having felt his fall. He forced a smile through gritted teeth and watched his lover through tear-blurred vision. "I'm ready. Finish it."

"You know, when it first walked into the room, I figured you set me up out of spite for our breakup," Ivan said. "That didn't add up, though. That was never you, but it was all I could think of. Then it told me my future and I understood. It was half the side of you that thinks you're a romantic, and the other half that's so fucking selfish you can't imagine anyone else's feelings matter more than yours. That's what pushed you to do it."

"No. This … this is for us. You have to see that."

"When I left the room, I was sure of two things: One, I never loved you enough to give you the satisfaction of killing you. And two, I was going to leave you there, never answer your calls or messages, never give you another thought. But then it hit me on the way home. I'd been focused on what the charakakon said, not what it didn't say. I'm supposed to kill my one true love and then myself. It didn't say I would never kill anyone else."

Ivan pulled the knife from Carter and smiled, his flat expression breaking at last. Carter felt his vision widening even as his eyes squinted at the wild pain housed in his torso.

"You get it, don't you?" Ivan said. "All you are is someone else."

"No. I'm the one. I'm yours and you're mine. We're meant to …"

The knife now went to the side of Carter's neck, but he was so focused on Ivan's knowing smile that he hardly noticed. The blade opened a vein, and the blood fled like it had waited an age to be free. Ivan stood and walked through the front door with no lingering look at what he'd left on the floor, no glance back to be sure his work was finished.

Carter watched Ivan leave, too weak to talk sense to him, to better explain why he'd done what he'd done, to beg him to come back. Fear drove his heart to beat harder, and he became stunningly conscious of how quickly it pumped the blood out of him, how ill-suited his hands were for closing the wound, and how awful and unrelenting time was. Seconds he could not afford to lose and could never regain were being spent with him on the floor, his tingling and blood-slicked fingers unable to secure the phone in his pocket to call 9-1-1.

Not like this, he thought. *Not alone*.

As if summoned by this thought, the charakakon walked through the open door. It stood above him, looked down for a few seconds, then stooped to get a closer view, tilted its head to match and mock Carter's position.

Its huge, thin-toothed grin made the rest of its face fade into an illusion, a blurred camouflage somehow worn under its real, translucent skin.

"Would you like to hear the worst thing that will ever happen to you?" it said.

This isn't it? Carter thought.

This isn't *it*, he knew.

XII
יב
١٢
十二
12

THE ONE

"When I was seventeen, this lady approached me with her baby after a game, and she asked me to put my hand on her son's forehead just for a second. She straight up said, 'Can you lay hands on him.' I knew what that meant. I've got a couple of uncles that are old-school Southern preachers. My first thought was that it was crazy, but I did it anyway, just put my hand on the kid's forehead, because I thought it would get her away from me faster. But you know what's crazier? Soon as I did it, the kid smiled. It was probably because my hands are pretty big, and I accidentally covered like half of his face. It was probably like peekaboo or something to him, but he really did smile, and that lady started crying and couldn't stop saying thank you. And I felt something new. All of the other shit felt smaller.

"You know, it was all cool, blowing up, all the attention, the girls, having millionaire coaches pretty much begging me to play for them. I had just had my back-to-back forty-point games against Highland and St. James. I was getting national press, and it really became real to me then that I could go pro. People were already saying I might be the first pick in the draft, and I was two years away from even being eligible. But I couldn't even enjoy half of that, you know, because everybody in my family taught me young to be careful who you trust, keep working, don't get into trouble, all of that. So I couldn't do the parties, and I didn't trust most of the girls trying to get to me, and I didn't trust most of those coaches saying they'd treat me like their son either. I just stayed in the gym and trusted my game.

"But what I felt with that lady and her baby was different. That was pure. People like her were the reason my fans were already calling me 'the One.' I even looked it up to see if anything like this had ever happened to Jordan. I found a video of his trainer saying it did, but after he was already *Jordan,* you know? I was way ahead of schedule. I feel like I still could be, I just … you know … nah, you *don't* know. Nobody knows but me."

Justin Bless let the silence linger, and as it stretched, he armored himself with it. He'd expected Doctor White to be stymied by this story. It had to be unlike anything her other clients had told her. Particularly Trae Walters, the man who had referred Justin to the therapist. He knew Trae's history well. Had analyzed him before they became teammates. Trae had been a good high school player and had grown into a better player through three years of college ball, but the fact that he had spent that much time in college said it all. The better prospects, the "chosen ones" these days did one year in college, two at most, and that was likely to be due to an injury or something. Justin could have made the leap from high school to the pros if they hadn't put in the rule forcing players to go spend a year at a university. Hell, he could have skipped his last year of high school were that permitted. Maybe he should have and gone overseas, where there were no such rules in place. He could have sharpened his game that much more against old, savvy pros in Europe.

Trae was good. Only forty-five hundred men had played in the NBA in the league's seventy-five-year history. The fewest number of professional athletes in the history of any other major team sport in America, and he was among them. Something to be proud of if you were a man like Trae. Justin was different, though. He wasn't meant to be just one of forty-five hundred. Since the age of fourteen, people had been calling him "the One," and since seventeen he had understood why. He had understood his eventual place in the history of the game even before he'd made it to the NBA. He was born to be an icon. The elitest of the elite. Even his name, he came to understand, foretold his future. Most of the greats had a perfect, memorable name, built for billboards and headlines, built to be its own nickname if needed.

Kareem Abdul-Jabbar. *Kareem.*

Larry Bird. *Bird.*

LeBron James. *Bron.*

Michael Jordan. *Mike. Jordan.*

If not that, then they were given a nickname so fitting and indelible it essentially became their first name.

Magic Johnson.

Doctor J.

And he was Justin Bless. *Bless.*

"The One" was almost a demotion.

"Do you remember the woman's name?" Doctor White said.

Justin stared at her like she'd asked, *Do you know the weight of sound?* or something similar.

"I never got her name," he said.

"I see. Do you remember what she looked like? Or her son?"

"She was … I don't know … she was white. And the kid was mixed, I think. Why are you asking that?"

"They just seemed like they were important to you, the way you spoke of them."

"*I* was important to *them.* That's the point. I'm talking about where I was and where I have to get back to. Do you get it?"

Doctor White nodded and said she understood before moving on to another question, but Justin knew that she didn't understand. Nobody else did. Nobody knew but him.

"She didn't want to hear what I was saying. I told you—nobody wants to hear about whatever anybody else is dealing with," Justin said. "Nobody cares."

"Bro, it takes time," Trae said. "I told you—you have to give it time."

"Nah. It ain't for me, man."

"It's good for everybody, bro. Everybody needs somebody to talk to sometimes."

"You sound like all these other new motherfuckers that think weird. That's weak talk."

"It's not weak, bro. Don't start that. And what are you talking about 'new'? You're twenty-four talking like you're forty."

"It ain't about the years, it's about the mindset," Justin said. "I appreciate you thinking you could help, but I'm just built different, Trae. You know what all those other dudes have in common? Talking about therapy and all that shit? Name one of them that's ever been *the one* on a winning team. Much less *the one* for the whole league. All of these dudes either got no rings, or they got one riding the back of the bus while someone else took them to the promised land. I'm not about that. I'm cut different, Trae. I'm—"

"You're not the fucking 'one' anymore, bro," Trae said.

Justin sat with the silence, knowing that it would injure Trae more than him, that Trae would speak up first if he stayed quiet for just a few seconds.

"Yo, I shouldn't have said that," Trae said. "That was … I apologize, bro. I just felt like you were maybe coming at me a little bit with what you were saying, because … You know what, no excuses. I'm sorry I said that, bro. We good?"

Justin smiled. He thought of a book he'd read last year: *Winners Win: The Traits That Manifest Victory*. The fourth chapter was titled "Winners Never Say They're Sorry." He'd spent a year developing that trait, practicing withholding apologies, starting at home with Cindy, even with his baby girl, Aurelia.

To break the slump he'd been in, he'd had to break his promise to be home more often after his daughter was born. Before reading the book, he'd sought Cindy's forgiveness for the late practices and predawn training that left her to fend for their child alone. After reading the book, applying its lessons to his life, he understood he had nothing to apologize for. Not to anyone, and not to Cindy and Aurelia perhaps most of all. How would it help him if he was just there, at the house or park or wherever, his mind elsewhere? He had to be in the gym, getting shots up, pushing weights, maximizing his game. When he got to where he needed to be—became who he was meant to be before five years of bad coaching, bad teammates, bad press, and bad management reduced him to half the player he should be—Cindy wouldn't think of him as absent or neglectful. They'd reap the rewards of being his, understand that anything he did to improve himself was inherently to their benefit as well.

There was no reason to apologize for that.

That's what separated him from guys who thought like Trae, who were quick with a "sorry," who thought they needed help. How the coaches couldn't see it and insisted on giving Trae more playing time than Justin baffled him. Justin would make them see it, though, and soon. He just had to put in the work.

No one else was in the gym, not even a ball boy or trainer to get the ball and pass it to him after each shot, but Justin wished there was a single spectator there. Just one person sitting courtside, close, laughing at him as he missed shots, pointing and heckling, calling him a loser, repeating the words Trae had told him earlier.

You're not the fucking 'one' anymore.

He wanted that person to be there because instead of taking another shot, he wanted to throw the ball at them as hard as he could, hit them square in the face, watch blood streak from their nose and a few teeth drop out of their mouth.

He imagined this and was sickened by what he saw because the bloodied person did not stop laughing.

How was it possible that he was playing this poorly when no one else was around? Against no defense? Against no one but himself? How was he ever going to be the player he needed to be in real games when he couldn't even play well one-on-none? If he couldn't even hit 80 percent of his goddamn free throws anymore?

It made no sense to him. Basketball struck him as different from most other sports in that once you became great at a certain element of it, nothing should have kept you from maintaining that greatness. His shot had been pure in high school and in his one year of college and had deteriorated inexplicably in his five years in the league, despite him spending more time practicing and perfecting it than he could have when he was younger.

Yes, the game was faster at this level, his opponents taller and stronger on average than what he'd faced in his teens, but he was three inches taller and fifteen pounds of muscle heavier as well. Besides, basketball wasn't like football or even hockey, collision sports where sheer physicality could sometimes overwhelm skill, pretty much by design. Basketball didn't reward contact and force the same way. It differed from baseball, as well, where the difference between the control and velocity employed by major-league pitchers compared to minor leaguers and below was what separated those who belong from those who would never make it.

Basketball was an indoor sport with a uniform playing surface. No alternate turfs to contend with, no windy or rainy conditions to adjust to. It wasn't like baseball where every field was built differently. There were no courts where the goal wasn't the same height it was everywhere else, where the court was wider or narrower, where there might be a retractable roof to let the sun beam down and get in your eyes when you were facing a certain direction.

The shots he'd made thirty feet away from the rim in high school would have been good in any NBA arena. The game was the game. A free throw in a field-house gym in the middle of Georgia was a free throw in a twenty-thousand-seat arena in New York City, for fuck's sake. An uncontested shot fifteen feet away from a ten-foot-high goal. He'd made these with his eyes literally closed when he was seventeen, made 91 percent of them in college, and felt like that figure was low. His first year in the pros he'd shot just 88 percent. Then a little worse each year after, until now he was at 71 percent. Almost in the sixties. How the hell was he averaging seventy-one out of a hundred midrange set shots with nobody playing defense on him? It was absurd.

Something was wrong with him, and he suspected it was the fact that he believed something was wrong with him.

The metal rim clanged as he missed yet another free throw. Justin almost hurled the next ball he took off the rack. He had told himself he couldn't go home until he'd made ten in a row. After topping out at seven consecutive makes over one hundred attempts, he amended the stipulation to the seemingly attainable eight consecutive makes. Another hundred shots later, he'd only managed six in a row.

That was proof that it was all in his head, wasn't it? Instead of seeking therapy, all he really needed to do was find the exit for this self-doubt. Get *out* of his head—not deeper into it—and return to what he once was. It wasn't too late. He had turned twenty-four two months ago. The greats could play at or near their peak into their late thirties these days. He had at least eight more years of his prime left, by his estimation. Plenty of time to make himself a legend. But he wasn't going to take a step toward that until he got out of the gym tonight, and he wasn't going to do that until he made eight straight free throws.

Fuck it, seven.

In his periphery he saw his phone, resting face up on a chair along the sidelines, light up. Cindy calling again. Shit. He'd bring it down to five in a row. He'd already made more than that a few times tonight. He should be able to do it again within the next ten shots or so, right?

The next shot fell at least half a foot short of even touching the front of the rim. He grabbed the next ball off the rack, squeezed it in his hands as though crushing it would cure all his problems, and screamed.

Someone behind him laughed, a deep, echoing sound that stumbled out of someone's mouth and then rolled down a rocky hill. It cut through Justin's scream and silenced him. He turned and saw someone standing at half-court, a tall man in a dark hoodie so long, baggy, and ragged it resembled a robe. Vestments of a holy man who'd spent years praying in the wilderness. His hood was up, obscuring his face, save for his jutting chin.

The man's hands were in the pockets of his hoodie. He stood with his legs close together, almost making him look like he had a single, centered leg, with his pants and shoes as dark as his hoodie. Justin narrowed his eyes at the man as if he was trying to remember where he might have seen him before. This had to be one of his teammates fucking around, playing a prank to spook him.

"Yo, who is that?" Justin said.

The laughter stopped, then started again, sharper and more deliberately mocking now. Not even truly the sound of laughter, but a mimicry of it, intentionally overpronouncing every "Ha."

None of his teammates were clever or weird enough to pull something like this. There were only one or two guys in the league who might think something like this was funny. The kind of guys who Justin thought probably needed help even Doctor White couldn't provide. Everyone else was content to fill your car with popcorn or get the team mascot to jump out from behind a corner to startle you. This was ... something else.

"Hey, who the fuck are you, man? You're not with the uh … the custodial staff, are you?"

The laughter ceased, though the grin remained fixed. The hooded figure shook their head quickly as if trying to dislodge their own jaw by whipping their head back and forth. Something about the movement froze Justin's breath in his chest for a moment. When that subsided, he made sure to raise his voice, summon an appropriate level of *I'm not scared, but* you *should be.*

"This isn't funny. You need to leave."

If this wasn't a teammate playing a practical joke, or somebody who worked at the gym completely misreading how they should interact with him, it had to be a crazed fan. One of those idiots from social media who made weird threats or even weirder proposals to players. People who got obsessed, and not in a complimentary way like the woman who asked him to bless her baby. She'd been an odd one, of course, but not threatening. In a perfect world, she'd have a healthier mindset than to believe a seventeen-year-old with a killer jump shot should be idolized, but in the imperfect world that was reality, she was a welcome balance to the maniacs who jumped on Twitter to say they were going to firebomb your house with your family in it because they thought you were lazy on defense. Or who said you should jump off a bridge because you lost them a bet when you missed a free throw.

It was sickening to read that kind of shit. Stressful, if he was honest about it. Cindy had told him to delete his social media altogether because of it, but he was holding on to every one of those comments to see which people would come crawling back, licking his feet online and swearing they always loved him when he turned it around. Won his first championship, his first MVP award, started stacking more trophies on top of those. Many of them—maybe most—would act like they had always loved him, then. Then he'd throw their threats back in their faces, share screenshots of comments they would have probably deleted by then. Sic all his followers and fans on them, watch when their employers caught word and fired them, read their weak-ass apologies, soak it in as they experienced the same sleepless nights he'd suffered because of the unforgivable things they'd said to him.

He always thought the ones who threatened him online were all talk, but a small part of him had to know there was a remote chance one or two of them might be legitimately deranged. That might be what he was dealing with here. Shit, that *had* to be it, right? He found it even harder to imagine it was a teammate now. No teammate would cross this line, do anything to make a fellow player believe they might be facing a dangerous fan.

"My man, I'm not playing with you. You need to get the fuck out. Now!"

At this, the man resumed his laughter, louder now, although his jaw—what Justin could see of it—looked more rigid. Not matching the sound he made, like the laughter was coming from a speaker hiding behind his teeth.

Justin decided to go on the offensive. He wasn't going to run. That would require turning his back, and this guy with his hands in his pockets could have a weapon on him. The way he was behaving, he probably hoped Justin would turn, and that's when he'd try to take advantage, when Justin wasn't facing him. Instead, Justin walked toward him.

"All right, I'm about to fuck you up. On God, I am *not* playing, bro."

The laughter stopped, and the hooded man's mouth still did not move as he stated, "Who do you think you are, Justin Bless? Who do you think you are? *Who do you think you are?*"

The taunt stabbed into a part of Justin's mind he didn't want to acknowledge was real. The part that tried to interject every time he spoke or thought of who he had been, and who he ought to be. It was either trying to persuade him to focus more on the present, who he was in the moment, or dissuade him from thinking he ever was or could be anything more.

The hooded man repeated those words while remaining stone-still as Justin marched toward him, adrenaline, fear, and anger combining to fuel him. When Justin got within a few feet of the man, he launched the ball he held at the hooded man's face and saw the ball pass through nothing. It took him an extra moment to realize no one was there.

He was alone in the gym. The only other thing with him was the echo of the ball he'd thrown bouncing at the other end of the court.

Justin caught his breath, choked down a sudden urge to vomit. He tried to force up a laugh of his own, one to counter the mocking humor of the man he had imagined, but this died before it passed his lips, and a shaky cry came out instead.

He shut his eyes to focus, gather himself, then felt an urge to reopen them, afraid that the man who couldn't have been there had returned while he wasn't looking. He looked around, confirmed that he was by himself. As he circled, he saw his phone flash again and thought that he should answer it this time. Tell Cindy he was on his way home. Ask if Aurelia was still up, and if she was, ask if he could speak to her, just to hear her voice. Tell her a silly joke about where he'd been to hear her laugh. Something to calm himself, plant him firmly back in reality, remind him of who he indeed was. Not the seventeen-year-old who once mimicked a faith healer for the benefit of an overzealous fan holding her son, nor the future version of himself that the seventeen-year-old dreamed of being. Right now, he was a guy on his way home, getting away from a scare, looking forward to the refuge of family. There were worse things he could be.

He struggled to sleep, and his restlessness awakened Cindy a few hours before sunrise. They spent some energy making love, trying to tire themselves out, but it was perfunctory for him. Something he was doing for her, not truly *with* her, and she noticed.

When they finished, she asked what was wrong. What could he tell her? That he had seen, heard, spoken to, and even attacked a dark figure who wasn't really there? That he then dreamed of that man as soon as he fell asleep in their bed, heard him laugh like he wanted to be heard from deep space, then pause to ask, "*Who do you think you are?*" Then repeat this, coming a little closer with each utterance, his smile unwavering, his hands in his pockets, his eyes and nose and forehead still shrouded, invisible.

How could he expect her to respond to that? She'd side-eye him at best. Hell, she might even leave him, at least for a little while, and could he blame her? Did a man who attacked hallucinations sound like someone she should keep her daughter around?

He told her nothing was wrong, kept it to himself, kissed her, then stayed awake until daybreak, listening to her breathe beside him, scared to close his eyes for too long, scared to think of someone being in the bedroom with them. Scared to look to his left or right and see the hooded man in one corner of the room, or standing in the open doorway, or standing outside a window, even though they were on the second floor.

Or in all of these places at once.

Can I call you real quick?

Trae had texted back faster than Justin expected him to. *Sure.*

Justin hesitated to call. He waited in his car in the parking lot of the team's practice facility. None of his teammates would be here for another hour, and even some of his coaches were at least twenty minutes away.

First one in, last one out. He was still living by that mantra, but today it served a different purpose. It got him out into the open, out of the house, out of his head a little bit, though not far enough. Once he arrived, he realized there was no way he was going inside to practice alone and put himself in the same position he'd been in last night.

The hooded man might be waiting for him inside.

"Hey, man, this may seem a little weird or random," Justin said after Trae answered his call, "but, um, what made you go see Doctor White in the first place? Like … you had a breakdown or something?"

"I wouldn't say all that. I mean, I was having some moments, for sure, but I don't know if I'd call it a breakdown. I don't know, man. I was just feeling more anxious, and I couldn't figure out why. And I heard more guys talking about mental health and all of that and thought I should try it out before it got worse, and it helped. Why?"

"I don't know. I, uh … You're sure it helped you?"

"Yeah, definitely," Trae said.

"But was there a point where it got worse first? Like did she have to dig into a bad memory or something or make you kind of bottom out first before it got better? I always figured it was supposed to be like that."

"It wasn't like that for me, man. She just helped me talk through things. Are you good?"

"I'm good," Justin said.

"I'm seriously asking," Trae said. "I'm not just saying it like saying 'hello.' Are you good?"

Justin sighed. He wasn't used to this, wasn't ready to be this open with anyone. If he couldn't open up about it to his wife, he damn sure couldn't go that far with Trae, a man who, regardless of their friendship, was ultimately his competition, just like everyone else in the league. Even as teammates, they had to compete for playing time, with Trae currently getting more game action than Justin did. Someday soon they might even be going head-to-head for a contract extension if the team had to decide which one of them to keep. Trae didn't seem the sort who thought this way, which Justin believed made Trae weaker, but how sure could he be that Trae wouldn't let some information slip to coaches and management to gain an edge when contract negotiations came up?

Hey, just between us, I don't know if Justin can handle being 'the one' for a team. You should've heard what he told me about this weird guy he thought he saw one time when no one was really there …

"Hey, man, are you there?" Trae said.

"Yeah, sorry. Um, listen, do you think Doctor White would fit me in again soon if you asked her for me? Like, this week? I know you already helped me out with this once. I hate to ask again."

"Hell, you didn't ask the first time. I pretty much had to beg you. If you need to see her that bad, I'll give her a call, see if … Oh, hey, one sec. Somebody's at the door. I probably need to sign for this."

If you need to see her that bad. Had Trae meant something by that? Shit, this had all been a mistake. He never should have accepted Trae's offer, never should have gone to Doctor White or succumbed to the notion that he needed help.

"Hey, whoa, who are—hey, *what the* FUC—"

Trae's desperate cries came through the phone along with the sound of his door opening. Justin called out Trae's name, felt his pulse hasten. Trae did not answer, only cried out more, saying no words, communicating only pain and terror.

Justin didn't know if he was supposed to hang up and call the police or stay on the line and try to get Trae to answer, explain what was happening. Shit, that couldn't be right. What good could he do for him over the phone? Just before he hung up to dial 9-1-1, he was frozen by an abrupt halt to Trae's screaming, followed by performative laughter. What chilled him more than the laughter itself was the familiarity of the voice behind it.

It wasn't the man he'd heard the night before. Trae was the one laughing.

A joke, Justin thought. *Just a joke.* But he didn't believe this. Trae wasn't the type to do something this mean-spirited.

"Trae … hey, bro, are you okay?"

Trae laughed for a few seconds more, then stopped.

"Trae?"

"Who do you think you are, Justin Bless?" Trae said. "*Who do you think you are?*"

Justin dropped his phone, started his car, and drove off, not knowing where he would go, feeling only that he had to get away.

He sat at the bar wearing the mask he'd kept in his glove compartment since the pandemic. A convenient way to go out in public and reduce the odds of being recognized. Even with that in mind, given the attention his car would bring, to say nothing of his height and general build, he'd driven two hours south, his phone off the entire time, until he found a small roadside bar that looked like a place where, even if anyone noticed him, they'd find staring into their noonday beer more interesting.

Justin looked at his phone and went through the messages and calls he'd missed while driving. Most from Cindy, which came after the coaches called her to check on him when they couldn't get ahold of him to see why he'd missed practice. Finally, he got a message from Trae saying he'd spoken to the coaches on Justin's behalf, explained that they'd had a conversation earlier, and that Justin expressed a need for a "mental health" day. He even indicated that he'd talked to Doctor White for him, and she'd agreed to grant him a short-notice appointment.

Cindy's messages kept coming even after Justin made it to the bar and responded to her with, *I'm okay. I just had to go somewhere.*

Where?! she texted back. *Talk to me please!*

Several more texts repeating and rewording this sentiment came through, but instead of replying with additional reassurance, or calling and talking to his wife, which he knew he should do, Justin dwelled on the link that Trae had forwarded to him in his message. From the URL, he could tell it was a video, and he was sure it was something he should be wary of watching, but he also could not avoid.

He opened the video, which was titled "Bless Absent from Practice?" As if whoever made this didn't already know the answer before posting the video. Making it a question somehow made the story more scandalous, however, and grabbed people's attention. Just one more thing to scrape under his skin like a jagged, bitten fingernail. Not enough to do damage on its own, but when joined by several others, all working to scratch and cut you multiple times per day, it was enough to make him want to scream.

He kept the volume low and watched the video with captions on. An unseen narrator explained that Justin was missing from the team's practice today, a day before a big road trip that might be their last chance to save the season. The standard footage of his teammates scrimmaging and putting up shots played behind the voice-over, but something soon jumped out at Justin as the video played. He thought it was some kind of glitch at first, something the production team at the station failed to fix in their rush to post the video. It quickly became evident that wasn't the case.

The black mass that obscured the top half of Trae's face—his alone—couldn't be an issue with the video. It didn't even feel like it was part of the video, but a blotch stuck in Justin's eye.

It looked like a childish god had tried to mark out Trae's face with black ink but got bored with the job half finished. Only the bottom half of Trae's face was visible. Just like the hooded man. His head shook bizarrely too. Nobody else on the court with him seemed to react to this, much less the black smudge enveloping everything past his upper lip.

As the clip continued, Trae appeared briefly front and center for an interview. The caption claimed that he said something about Justin being "one of our brothers," and how the team "is here for him if he needs us or just needs a little space." More than he should have been sharing with the media, but that wasn't what alarmed Justin. Trae's lips did not move as he spoke, although the reporter responded as though he was talking to her. His head shook occasionally, that shocking, violent spasm of side-to-side motion before going still again. As shady as Justin knew the sports media could be, it would be absurd to believe they'd resort to pretending he gave them a quote on camera when he wasn't even talking. Hell, it was absurd to think Trae would do something this odd. But here it was, on his screen.

Justin scrolled the video back to the beginning, watched it again. When he replayed it the second time, Trae was starting to smile, and when he watched the third time, Trae displayed a grin with more teeth than naturally fit in a human mouth.

Justin wanted to throw his phone down. He searched his teammate's name on the internet—Trae Walters—and then selected the Images option from the search results. A field of images appeared, some dating back to Trae's high school playing days, others showing him at charity events. One showed him in the bleachers at a baseball game. Most showed him on the court in the pros, wearing the uniform of one of the three teams he'd played for in his career.

In all of them, the black marker covered his forehead, eyes, and nose like an unfinished, ill-fitting mask, one wider than his skull and seemingly hovering a few inches in front of him.

In a few of the still images, he shook his head violently.

Concentrating to keep from hyperventilating, Justin looked up at the bartender, who was eyeing him cautiously, maybe trying to think of where he knew him from, maybe objecting to Justin's pandemic mask, or maybe just seeing the shock in Justin's eyes.

"Excuse me, I'm sorry, do you have NBA TV?" Justin asked the bartender, pointing at the television hanging over the top shelf of liquor.

The bartender nodded, checked to see if anyone else was watching what was currently on-screen, then changed the channel. Justin knew that the talking heads would be on now, discussing league stories, trying to fill time and find something to debate, and didn't expect he'd have to wait long to see the story about him come up. Nonetheless, it surprised him to see Trae on the television immediately, looking just as he did in every image on Justin's phone.

Justin looked at the bartender, who viewed the television with indifference but glanced at Justin with concern. He didn't see what Justin saw. Of course not. Nobody else could see it but him. He was alone in this. The only one.

"I can give you fifteen minutes, that's it," Doctor White said.

"Thank you. Thanks. I'm …" Justin almost apologized for showing up at her office unannounced, throwing her schedule off, surely inconveniencing her, her receptionist, and probably both of the clients in her waiting room who had gone through the proper method of scheduling. He didn't know where else to go, however. Doctor White was a professional. She was paid well to take care of things like this.

Maybe he should have run to Cindy about it. It might have put her at ease somewhat, seeing him, knowing he wasn't still just out there "somewhere," as he'd told her. Then again, he didn't want to bring whatever was happening to him home.

"I think … I'm *sure* I'm having some kind of breakdown," Justin said when he got into Doctor White's office.

"Okay, sit down. Just tell me—"

"No, no. Listen. *Listen*. That thing I told you about with the lady and her kid. Remember that?"

Doctor White nodded. "I remember."

"Yeah, so like … okay, I've never told anybody about that before. I always kept it to myself like … I don't know. Fuck, I don't know, like it was the one thing I could hold on to when shit wasn't going my way. Like, no matter what, I could always say I meant this much to this person once in my life. And that made me feel … Look, here's the thing: Ever since I told you about that, some weird shit has happened to me. Or maybe just happened in my head, and that's why I'm here because isn't that part of what you do? Help people get out of their head when they need to? Because I really need to."

"Let's talk through this," Doctor White said, her voice steady, soothing. This was the right call, Justin already believed. This was where he needed to be. Where he should have been years ago. He'd been "in his head" with the dead bolt locked and doorknob kicked off ever since he was in high school and was only realizing it now. He'd kept it all to himself because, surely, nobody else could understand his experience except him. Not even others ostensibly like him, other star athletes, other people given so much so early, others who saw the path to absolute greatness as more than a journey or even a destination, but a requirement for a decent life. Anything less made them a failure, another example of unfulfilled potential. Joke fodder for those who'd say, *Man, if I was six foot seven, strong and fast, born with all of his gifts, I would have been the best of all time. I would have done more than he did. What a waste.*

"What specifically has happened to you?" Doctor White asked.

"Okay, this is gonna sound … I don't know how this is gonna sound, but I saw—"

Commotion from the front of the office—the waiting room—interrupted him. Shouts. Screams, furniture moving, something falling over, hitting the floor. Doctor White held up a finger, excused herself, and the word *Don't* got caught in Justin's throat as she left her office. Because this sounded somewhat familiar to him. It sounded a bit like the struggle and panic he'd heard over the phone while talking to Trae earlier that day. The man who thought of Justin as a friend. Who Justin had thought of as an adversary even moments before Trae had been … attacked? Altered? What exactly had happened to him? Justin couldn't say, because he'd driven away in the aftermath instead of even trying to think of a way to help his teammate.

Now he heard the doctor screaming louder than the three other voices that sounded like they were pretending to enjoy a bad joke.

Something cut Doctor White's scream short, and seconds later she joined in the laughter. Her voice grew as it came closer, back down the hall that led from her lobby to her office. Justin hadn't moved since she'd left. The door was still open.

He saw the black mark hovering in front of her face a microsecond before he saw her come into view, come into the room. Her smile was like a marble statue that would survive for a thousand years.

She entered the room, came close enough to him to lean in for a kiss, and then whispered without moving her lips, "You really think you're 'the one'? *Who do you think are, Justin Bless?*"

He ran past her, past the three other blacked-out faces in the lobby, and to his car outside.

"I'm sorry. I'm sorry. I'm sorry."

The house was too dark. It was barely dusk, but midnight occupied the home. The same way it was every night when he arrived late after staying hours after practice, or after a game, even one that wrapped in the afternoon. He was used to coming home to darkness in most rooms, save for whichever one Cindy and Aurelia were in, if his daughter was still awake, watching a movie, playing games, coloring or drawing. Even when Aurelia was asleep, Cindy usually waited up for him, and he would find her watching one of her true crime shows or reading a book by lamplight in the bedroom.

No isolated, lit sanctuary was there to guide him today. The house felt as empty as it was dark. Maybe Cindy had left to look for him, dropping Aurelia off with her parents. Maybe they were both at his in-laws, with Cindy finally reevaluating what she had signed up for. What a marriage to a man as obsessed with success as Justin was truly meant, and whether it was worth it.

No, not just obsessed. Selfish.

The One. It was even his jersey number. *One.* The loneliest number, so the song went, but that had been okay with him. He'd once read about a player in China, a guy who had been a legend in college but had flamed out in the pros. In China, though, he had returned to dominance, so much so that the locals gave him a nickname that translated to "the Lonely God." That had sounded marvelous to Justin. He'd pictured a figure atop a steep, windswept, snow-covered mountain, surveying all beneath him, loving that he alone could be above it all. A figure with no family or friends.

The player in question, the actual "Lonely God," had not relished the idea of being revered for having no one in his atmosphere breathing the same air, helping him endure.

Justin felt more like "the One" now than he ever had. A man apart from anything or anyone else, even in the home he shared with his wife and daughter. He could see things no one else saw, hear things no one else heard. He was truly one of one. It was a nightmare he couldn't scream loud enough to wake from.

"I'm sorry! Cindy! Please, can you hear me? *I'm sorry!* I'm sorry I wasn't … I'm sorry I didn't do better. I'm sorry for everything. Please come out! *Please!*"

He had searched the upstairs and downstairs twice. All twelve rooms. There was no sign of clothes hastily packed. None of Aurelia's toys were missing from her toybox. None of her books were missing from the small shelves in her room. Maybe they hadn't left with the intent of never returning. Maybe he should just call again and hope Cindy would answer this time instead of letting it go straight to voicemail. Maybe her phone was dead. Or maybe she was blocking his calls and waiting to come back and pack everything up at a later time.

He was coming downstairs from his third run through the house when he heard laughter. A voice he knew, a tone that was alien. Cindy. Her natural laugh was weightless and soft. This sounded like she was trying to imitate hatchets splitting wood.

Justin descended the stairs slowly. All that moved him forward was the knowledge that he'd failed to do anything for Trae, that he'd run from Doctor White, and that Cindy and Aurelia deserved more.

The hooded man stood in the foyer with Cindy, holding her hand while she held Aurelia with her free arm. Aurelia smiled a smile that wasn't her own. Her warm, patient eyes obscured behind the dark, inkblot mask.

"I'm sorry," Justin said, as if this would wipe the darkness away, restore Cindy to who she was. The words he'd denied himself for years. No, that was a self-centered way of looking at it. Goddammit, he was still doing it. Thinking of himself as "the One." The only. He had withheld apologies from his wife and daughter when they had deserved to hear them a hundred times. From Cindy specifically, he'd withheld even more. He never even gave her a chance to understand. To *listen.* God, he'd give part of his soul to be more honest and open with her now, give her a chance to listen.

Aurelia sucked her thumb and looked at him anxiously. She had broken her thumb-sucking habit a year ago, which told him everything about how scared she was, even though she was working hard to appear brave.

His brave kid. Goddamn. He'd never really noticed it before, much less appreciated it. She grew more agitated and frightened the longer she stared at him, and he realized he was failing her, failing to instill any confidence that he would make all of this right, save her and her mother.

He turned to the hooded man. "Leave my family alone, please. I'll do whatever you want. Just tell me what you want."

The man smiled and laughed and told Justin nothing.

"Tell me what you want! *Tell me!* What do you want?"

"To be what you think you are, Justin Bless," the hooded man said. He removed his other hand from his pocket, let go of Cindy's. Darkness surrounded his hands, swirling, painted clouds. The hooded man took down his hood and revealed that there was nothing above his grin. Not even blackness. Only empty space.

Justin felt panic building deep within him.

"I want to be the one," the hooded man said. "The only one. Alone and on high. Unencumbered. Unobstructed."

Cindy gave Aurelia to the hooded man as Justin's scream ripped out of him and carried his soul with it. He tried to run toward his daughter but felt himself fade, unable to move, dissipating as the empty half of the hooded man's head filled in.

Justin's scream became vapor, and his desperation dissolved along with his physical form. The hooded man put his hands to Aurelia's head like a faith healer. She smiled, her mother cried, and the thing that replaced Justin Bless felt free to become what Justin had thought he was.

XII
יב
١٢
十二
12

THE MERGE MONSTER INCIDENT
ONE YEAR LATER

"I gave up my spot to the couple behind me who wanted to ride together. It was actually my second time through. I had a skip pass, so I was able to jump right back near the front of the line, and I felt bad for taking a space they would have had if I didn't have the pass, so I let them cut ahead of me. I wouldn't be here if I hadn't done that." The man in front of me pauses, his voice doesn't break, it collapses, and I give him time to rebuild his capacity to speak. His paleness makes his hair look darker than it is and makes the bags under his eyes more pronounced. I know that Ian Mullen would not object to me saying he resembles a living corpse more than a survivor because he has already described himself that way more than once during our conversation.

Nearly a minute passes before he speaks again. "I dream about it all the time. I mean *all the time*. Not just every night. Not even just when I'm sleeping. Sometimes I'm wide awake, and I'm in my room where I should feel safe, but at the same time, I'm out there, wherever that thing is. Wherever it took the Singletons and the rest. I'm out there, and I can feel the safety harness over my shoulders, pressing me into the seat, never letting me go, and when I snap back to where my body is, I feel this guilt that's barely like … like *this* far away from my fear."

He brings his fingers close enough to pinch a leaf.

"That's all there is between it, and it doesn't really matter, because it's not like it makes a difference one way or the other. Not like I could really do anything about it if the guilt matched the fear, or was bigger. I can't go out and find them or take their place. But it still matters to me. It means everything to me, because I'll always know I could be there instead of them, and part of me thinks I should be. But I let them go ahead. So I'm here, and they're … they're wherever they are."

Throughout our interview, Meredith Singleton holds a framed picture of her tall, tanned, and toned son, his arm draped over his lovely wife, who looks up at him, chin high like she's watching him accept an award onstage. They're standing on a beach, beautiful waves moving toward them and away from a stunning sunrise. Their sunglasses hide their eyes, but it's impossible not to feel their happiness. Two days after this photo was taken, the two of them, Vince and Tracy, would be among the twenty-eight people still unaccounted for after the Merge Monster incident.

This photograph, taken by Meredith, is now world-famous, seen by hundreds of millions—if not billions—of people online. Some of those people continue to scrutinize the picture, and the couple in it, as much today as they did the days immediately after the massive steel roller coaster reportedly wrenched itself from the grounds of eastern Kentucky's EscapeLand theme park and, for lack of a better term, walked away.

The ardent skeptics find their ranks dwindling, which seems to just embolden the ones clinging to their accusations that the Singletons are "crisis actors" whose likenesses they claim to have matched with others found in archived actor databases. They insist that the Merge Monster incident was a hoax, an elaborate, unbelievable stunt pulled for publicity or propaganda purposes, maybe both. To call this a "theory" would be a disservice to the word, much less the people who were lost—both figuratively and literally—as well as their relatives who are revictimized by these obsessive, irrational inquisitors who aren't above stalking friends and family members of the injured, deceased, and missing.

"To hell with them all," Meredith says. "I don't want to talk about them. No one ought to give a damn what they think."

Indeed, I agree with her, and I've given them too much time on the page already, but I feel it's important to point out that all the evidence (*evidence*, imagine that?) shows that this group is actually losing members. For decades, if not longer, it's felt as though no tragedy in the world was immune to the corrosiveness of instant and insistent denialism. Here, at last, is something so horrific—not in its number of casualties or its global impact, but in its impossibility, and the shift in reality it represents—that its truth feels inescapable.

I think it's this impossibility that also makes it more difficult than it otherwise might be for Meredith Singleton to say much about her son and daughter-in-law. I am amazed that she even agreed to sit with me. Tracy's parents, understandably, declined through a family spokesperson.

Now that she is in front of me, I can't help but think Meredith made a mistake, although it's not my place to make that call for her, and she repeatedly tells me she wants to talk about what happened that day. She wants to talk about the remote hope she still has for finding Vince and Tracy alive ("Why can't that be possible?"). She wants to tell people to keep looking, to never give up the search. When I give her space to find the words to expand on these thoughts—minutes of space that add up to over an hour—she can hardly pull together a few sentences at a time.

"It was just so much," she says. "Just chaos and panic and madness. It didn't even feel real until I remembered I'd left Vince and Tracy in line there, about half an hour before it happened."

I know that she wants to say more, but I can also predict that she will trail off, shake her head, clutch the picture closer to her, and shut her eyes to mutter a sort of aimless prayer. I don't feel I have the right to print what she prays for. It's between her, whatever higher power she hopes is listening, and the two people in the photograph, who are almost like saints to her. Maybe this reflects my failure to remain impartial, and certain inadequacies I have as an interviewer and journalist, at least regarding this story, but as much as I'm driven to keep this prayer private for Meredith Singleton's sake, I'm also wary of putting anything out into the world that could be used to call upon forces we've never been farther from understanding.

So I think it best that Meredith's prayer remains her own. I tell her as much before I leave, and she shakes her head. "What if you're wrong? What if it's not working because I'm the only one saying it?"

I encourage her to share it online if she thinks that's likely, or even just likely enough to be worth the risk of it having a different effect than the one intended. As of the time of this writing, two weeks removed from my sit-down with her, Meredith Singleton's social media accounts are as quiet as they've been since last summer, and a search for the most unique stanzas in her prayer doesn't pull up anything.

I'd never been the praying type prior to any of this, but since meeting with Meredith, I have asked whoever or whatever could be looking over us to help her maintain her faith. I hate to think I contributed to taking anything away from someone who's already lost more than anyone should.

However, in those few moments before bed, when I make this request to an entity I can't name or envision, that might not be listening even if it exists, I do my best to clear my mind of

Meredith's prayer. I don't even want to be thinking the same words, in case an extra mind amplifying her desires is all that's needed to make the Monster return, or for something somehow worse to happen.

Although the area has been cordoned off since the incident last June, anyone with a drone can fly a camera over the scene and see for themselves the damaged, vacant ground where the coaster once was, and would be hard-pressed to explain how it might have been discreetly dismantled in the middle of the busy season, with the park operating daily. Were it a smaller, carnival coaster designed to be disassembled, a "rational" explanation would be easier to come by. But the Merge Monster was seven thousand feet long, twenty stories tall, and estimated to weigh over six hundred tons. While major theme park ride designers and constructors have gone on record to state the obvious, no one should need these experts to tell them that the idea of breaking down and transporting this behemoth surreptitiously was, in a way, harder to believe than its spontaneous animation.

What's more valuable, in my opinion, is the insight some of them can provide about the mastermind behind the Monster. Though most are unwilling to officially implicate, much less outright impugn, a man who, if the note he left behind is to be entirely believed, killed himself not long after the Monster's construction was completed, I spoke to a few who were willing to discuss, and even confirm, certain rumors. Stories that would have sounded outlandish a little over a year ago.

"Sometimes you kind of store information without really remembering it," Horace Locke, creator of the Texas Twister, the main attraction at Cowboy Grande Park in Dallas, tells me. "What I mean is, you don't think of it the next day, or a week later, or however long later. It just doesn't cross your mind until something makes you think of it. You basically forget it, and then you don't. That's how it was for me, when what Lawrence said came back to me after the Monster woke up."

The Lawrence he speaks of probably doesn't need a reintroduction, but I suppose I wouldn't be doing my job well if I didn't give him a space, even though many understandably want his name erased.

Lawrence Coleman, the man behind the Monster. The man who went missing. The man whose name produces interesting and unsettling search results online.

Mad scientist.

Cult leader.

Satan worshipper.

That last one is particularly offensive to those claiming to be his most devout followers. Visit one of their message boards and declare that their beloved Lawrence was one of Satan's apostles, I dare you. See how quickly they swarm to say, "Satan? *Satan?* You think LC, genius that he was, was the follower of a myth so ordinary? So *understood?* You think he was that *simple?*"

Oddly enough, I understand why they see it as an insult. The actual concept of Satan is a little more complex when you dive into original scripture, but as "understood" by the average person, the fallen angel is, indeed, comparatively simple. And nothing about Lawrence or his Monster fits neatly into a description so comprehendible.

"After it happened, it came back to me like it had always been on my mind," Horace Locke says, referring to a conversation he'd had with Lawrence Coleman. I ask him to recall as much of it as he can, explain it to us as though it's among the most important conversations in world history, which it may well be.

"I don't know," he says, shaking his head like he's one of the deniers, ready to disbelieve his own memory. "It was late. We'd had some drinks. Most of the others from the [Global Attractions] Expo had left. It was me, him, [Hideki] Natusuki, and "Rich" Raymond [Lafleur]. The drinkers. We stuck around for another hour after everyone else, and that's when Lawrence started talking about accidents. How there was what he called a 'Dead Ride Graveyard' where the parts of old, decommissioned rides that had killed someone were kept. Mostly from traveling carnivals, because carnies were more superstitious, and more liable to replace a ride that killed someone than the big parks were. He started breaking down numbers and history, and honestly, I was too drunk to pay that much attention at the time, but I will say he sounded convincing. *He* believed it, at least. And then he started talking about visions he had of building something made of all these ... he called them 'graveyard parts.' Like a Frankenstein's monster for roller coasters."

While Raymond Lafleur wouldn't sit down with me, Natsuki, the designer of Tokyo Terror Tower!!! (the triple exclamation points are officially part of the name) was almost too happy to speak with me. I've only made slight adjustments, with his blessing, to his English—which is less "broken" than "barely dented"—to ensure he's clearly understood.

"Frankenstein's monster coaster! I was so excited when Lawrence told us. The others laughed like he couldn't be serious, but I thought it was amazing. I *still* think it's amazing. I think he did it! He just went a little farther than he should have."

You think it's amazing, I ask him, despite the loss of life?

"Many more have died for lesser causes," he told me. "And few of us die in the name of giving something else life. Lawrence, and anyone he might have sacrificed, made a machine *live*. It uprooted itself. It walked. It *walks*. The true tragedy of this is that he left us with such a cryptic letter, instead of proper, detailed instructions for how to replicate his achievement. He changed the world. You're American, aren't you? Your scientists once altered the world by doing something the stars already do. There is no precedent in the known universe for what Lawrence has done. It is uniquely and *most* human."

While my discussions with Ian, Meredith, and Horace saddened me—even weakened me—my talk with Natsuki *troubled* me, because his passion was so infectious, and his argument, simple as it was, made just enough sense to make me question my compassion and humanity. After speaking with him, I had a terrible dream of steel tracks and high speeds, moving darkness that blurred my vision, mouths without faces or bodies in my periphery doomed to endless screaming, and a preacher-like voice reminding me repeatedly that, "People died. *People* died."

Why aren't there any clear pictures or videos?

This is what the remaining deniers cling to. Everyone walks around with a camera in their pocket these days. Every catastrophe is filmed from a thousand different angles. Even the rare, fleeting sight of a meteor exploding in Earth's atmosphere was captured in 2013 by hundreds of cameras in a country where the media isn't nearly as free as it is in the United States. Mass shootings, tornadoes, tsunamis, bombings, all these things have been captured on camera in the moment. But the Merge Monster incident only has shaky, unfocused, or poorly shot footage to corroborate it.

"Oh my God, first of all, you're talking about something never ever *ever* seen before compared to shit people know is real. So it's really *no* comparison." These are the words of Yesenia Silva, one of many who were present, not directly impacted, and eager to talk about what they saw.

I feel it's important to clarify that when I say "not directly impacted," I mean that she wasn't physically injured and didn't have a family member or friend among the casualties. Anyone present that day was, of course, impacted in their own way. I've talked to so many parents who've told me their children still struggle to sleep and flinch at the most innocuous noise that I'm almost numb to it. I'm not dismissive of the post-traumatic stress suffered by those who witnessed the Monster come to life, I'm just moved more by those who lost a life, limb, or loved one to the Monster's awakening.

This is on my mind even as I hear Yesenia speak, but the force of her words, the disdain in her tone for anyone who wasn't there and can't begin to understand, brings me back to the moment with her.

"I see dumbasses online talking about this and that. Stupid. You don't *know*. You weren't *there*. You know, it's amazing that any of us can even talk about it. Like … like, imagine if this house we're in right now, or even the one across the street there," and she points through a window, "picture if that just got up and started moving on its own. Do you think you'd hold on to your mind, or nah?"

The professional, somewhat egotistical side of me wants to believe that, yes, I would keep a grip on my sanity. I'd not only "hold on" to my mind, I'd grab my digital camera, take snapshots, flip to video mode and start recording, go back and forth between the two settings as needed for the best shots.

The realist in me remembers ducking under a table during the first earthquake I ever experienced, not long after a briefing warning me that these things weren't uncommon in California, and nonetheless feeling like I was going to die, and like the planet was violating a pact it had with humankind—that the ground *doesn't MOVE*. Then I think of how earthquakes are a known natural phenomenon. How even meteor strikes have been observed and documented in the past. These things really can't compare to a huge, man-made, metal superstructure coming to life as though its evil or incredibly stupid fairy godmother granted it a wish, then loping past onlookers on its way to the high hills it could hide within.

I'm looking back over what I've just written, and although I've had a year to process the Monster's awakening, and months to plan this article and these interviews, it suddenly strikes me as an absurd dream. A roller coaster came to life, killed dozens as it stomped and dropped debris over crowds at a popular amusement park, and then went *missing*.

It's been sighted multiple times, allegedly, but hasn't been found. Somehow that's more ludicrous than anything else.

"You know, most people don't actually grab their phones, then open the camera app, then press record, then lock on to the best shot when they're seeing something horrible," Yesenia says. "And they definitely don't do any of that when it's something nobody would have thought was possible before. We were all running for our lives, or running to check on somebody we cared about, okay? You know, I feel like most of these assholes talking shit behind a keyboard about how this is fake, that's fake, whatever, they're also the type to barely go outside, and when they do they only go around people who already believe in what they believe, so they wouldn't understand. They don't even understand what the world is normally like, so how are they going to say shit about what people do when the world goes wrong?"

She runs a hand through her hair in frustration, looks at it, then shows me the strands clinging to her palm and fingers. "I'm fucking twenty-eight. This never happened before that day."

For the first time, I notice that her hair isn't as full as I would have thought it to be had someone only described her to me. She's not balding, won't need a wig anytime soon, but she's lost enough for it to be noticeable when you're looking for it.

I ask her a stupid question, because sometimes that's part of my job. You know a dumb question will get a strong response, and that's ultimately what will get you closer to the heart of the story.

"So you never thought to pull your phone out to get a picture?"

"Are you listening?" she says, gesturing toward me like she wants to choke me, like she thinks breathing is the last distraction keeping me from understanding her. "You know what, I saw way more dropped phones than I saw anybody trying to play cameraman, okay? And even those trying to film it were running and weren't looking. I ran past at least twenty or thirty people who'd frozen up, they were so scared. They looked like they were dead on their feet. Is that so hard for people to understand? Really?"

I don't think it is. When you actually look at the footage of certain catastrophes, the Tohoku tsunami, for instance, nearly all the video comes from people safely observing the situation from afar, or from surviving security camera footage. I haven't seen any video captured by anyone on the verge of being swallowed by the wave. And regarding the Chelyabinsk meteor, which I referenced earlier, the surplus of video captured is a direct product of so many Russians having dashcams to combat car-accident insurance fraud. No such unique circumstance applied to EscapeLand, or its patrons, and none of the park's security cameras have any reason to be pointed skyward, where they would have captured the Monster in all its horrifying glory, its cars and riders still winding through its skeleton.

These are easy conclusions and explanations to come to, for those who want to *think*, but some only want to *believe*, or disbelieve, as they please. Others want to disengage completely, move on, passively accept what has happened without contemplating what it means for the future, for the world.

The fact is, even those of us who weren't present that day are still "directly impacted," because, as Natsuki pointed out, this is something without precedent, just as momentous and disruptive as the revelation that there was an entire second half of the world that neither side knew about. Except we're all on the side that got landed on. But many of us, a year later, are trying our damnedest not to think about that.

The planet is getting hotter, wars we know of take headlines while others we haven't heard of rage on, novel viruses lie in wait to cripple civilization, and now … *now* …

How could I blame you, reading this, for deciding now to put this article down and read something else? Something more uplifting, or at least less downbeat. How could I blame the person who opted out after reading the title for doing so?

Didn't the world have more than enough to deal with without previously unimagined abominations emerging and then, worse, disappearing in Appalachia?

It did. It still does. But none of that changes what happened, and what's still out there.

Flight 1414 has become part of the Merge Monster "lore," if you're more accepting of that term than I am. Having spoken to some people on the east-facing side of the plane who allegedly spotted the Monster in the Appalachian Mountains, and even to others on the opposite side who are convinced of what the others saw simply because of how they reacted to it, I'm less inclined to use a word that I feel implies unreality or unbelievability, although, to be fair, neither of those adjectives, nor anything like them, are part of lore's official definition.

In another way, I suppose it's more fitting than words like *history* or *record*. It also inherently suggests the fantastical, and how could something associated with the Merge Monster incident be anything but?

"I heard this kid shout first, 'There it is!'" says Wayne Ford, a bank manager from Minneapolis who was flying to Charlotte on a business trip. He says he was asleep when the shouting started and had the shade down over his window.

"All these people were talking over each other, saying they could see something, some saying they couldn't, and then the other half of the plane was talking over them trying to get an answer on if this was some kind of emergency or what, and then you had the flight attendants trying to settle people down. There was a lot going on, is what I'm saying, so I wasn't exactly clearheaded when I lifted the shade up. I don't think anybody was, so, you know, maybe it was all hysteria."

It's remarkable to me how reluctant we remain to admit this thing has happened, how embarrassed some of us sound when discussing it, like we're the last of our classmates to still believe in Santa Claus.

I ask if he really thinks it was mass hysteria, and he shakes his head almost immediately.

"I looked out the window, and it was down there. It was in the mountains; you could see it above the trees. Walking, but more kind of ... what's the word? Lurching, I think. Or lunging? I don't know. It moved like it was too heavy to stay balanced, just barely keeping from tipping over, and ... and you could still see the cars on it, still moving. It was just so strange and wrong. You ever see something so wrong that you know it has to be real? It's too wrong for your brain to make it up? That's probably a stupid question. I'm sorry, it's just hard to explain.

"I think I get one thing now, though. I was always one of those people kind of leaning toward believing it might be a hoax or something, because there's video of everything these days, right? So it was weird to me that nobody at the park seemed to get a good shot of this giant thing that came to life right in front of them. But there's a difference—a *big* one—between seeing something horrible and something unimaginable."

Few scientists I reached out to returned my messages, and fewer of the ones who did wanted to be named in this piece, just as they've been reluctant to commit to any public statements on the matter through any recognized institutions. It must be on all their minds. I'd wager there are certain fields and pursuits suffering neglect due to the surplus of attention the Monster's receiving. Every researcher who can cook up a reason for studying every bit of data available on the incident has to be doing so, whether it's in their area of study or not, unless they're borderline berserk about whatever they were previously committed to.

Many would rather save their official statements and hypotheses on the subject for academic articles or peer-to-peer discussions. Some of these are worthy reads, but even these stubbornly refuse to mention Lawrence Coleman's interests in mysticism without being pithy and dismissive, if not outright derisive. Most postulate the use of advanced robotics while presuming the actual event as described by witnesses must be at least somewhat exaggerated. They are not deniers, but they are skeptics. To some extent, this is defensible. Science has certain standards of proof that must be met. Extraordinary claims require extraordinary evidence, as they say. But there should be some malleability to that rule when faced with extraordinary circumstances. The ardent commitment to what is understood to be "scientific" over what is considered "paranormal" in the face of what happened feels almost arbitrary.

There is, obviously, one voice in the scientific community that must be recognized in this piece and placed above others. The man who left his laboratory to do field research, made a terrible discovery, and lost two of his partners in the process.

Dr. Paresh Patel is not happy to revisit and recount his excursion into the woods, but he knows how important it is to do so, even if it's for the dozenth time. I apologize for having to do my job, and he says he understands even though his tone belies this.

"Can you tell me what happened?" I say.

He sighs through his nostrils, a long display of exasperation. I, of course, know the story already, and he's aware of this. I understand his frustration with being asked yet again to repeat it, especially considering the amount of scrutiny and outright doubt he's faced, to say nothing of the misplaced blame and ludicrous accusations. It's possible he thinks I'm looking to trip him up, catch him changing his account in a way that no one else has, but that's not my intention. I mostly want to see for myself how it affects him to tell the story, which is selfish and a little cruel but important enough to warrant it.

"We were in the camp and heard a rumbling and loud metal creaking," Patel says, skipping past the parts about interviews they had conducted with locals who had warned them that they had heard strange, booming, grating sounds bouncing between the peaks and hollows of the area. His eyes are flat, and it seems to me his lips are barely moving. I've read before that he felt like he died out there with his colleagues, despite coming home, which was clichéd, and seen by people looking to chastise him as insensitive to the actual dead. Seeing him in person, however, gives substance to his sentiment. What he said might have been indelicate and unoriginal, but that didn't mean it was insincere. Just compare any picture of him from before and after his encounter with the Monster. He looks like he's losing a long battle with a voracious illness.

"It was night. No moon. Limited visibility. The ... I guess you would call it a leg. The appendage. However you would refer to it, it stepped into our camp and crushed poor Cooper in his tent when he went back for his camera. I told Lindsay to run, and I heard her go for a few seconds before something carried her voice into the air until it was gone. Then I was alone. That's what happened."

A couple of omissions surprise me. First, he makes no mention of hearing not just his colleague Lindsay McIntyre's screams in the sky, but the weaker, strained screams and groans of somewhere between a half dozen to a dozen other voices that moved in tandem with the whir and clack of carts on a metal track.

He also left out information he'd picked up from suspicious, "superstitious" locals. He'd heard from at least two different people that there had been recent rumors of a body dropping from the sky. A father and son whom no one would identify found the body of a young woman. Supposedly, she was wearing an orange-and-white wristband on her left wrist. The black lettering on the band was starting to fade, but still plainly read "SKIP PASS." The color scheme matched EscapeLand's, and while they were hardly the only theme park to use some version of a skip pass, or even those exact words, the combination of the term, along with the colors, and, hardly least of all, the presence of the band on a battered, desiccated corpse inexplicably deposited somewhere in eastern Kentucky made the arithmetic undeniable.

This was a body that had fallen or was flung from the Merge Monster.

I try to ask Dr. Patel if he'd been looking for where those two men allegedly buried the woman's body, as had been initially reported. I know he'll be defensive about this, although I don't think he needs to be, just as I don't think any finger-pointing at him for pursuing said body, as if he were in the wrong, is justified. The body of that young lady would be important to acquire and study. For those claiming Dr. Patel and his team were aspirant graverobbers, I would counter that wherever she's buried isn't the final resting place her relatives would have chosen for her. Realistically, of course, an opportunity for her family to find some added closure would not have come quickly, if the greater good was prioritized. She would have to be autopsied and studied at some length to ensure we knew when she died, and how. If she genuinely was the dried husk some alleged her to be, then how had she come to that state? Dehydration and exposure? Or something else?

Could the Merge Monster have done something to physically drain her?

I can't get to those questions before asking if he was there for the body, however, and when I do, Dr. Patel shakes his head, leaves his chair, and walks to the exit of the café where we've met. This isn't the first time this has happened to me. I'm sympathetic. Sometimes, someone agrees to a discussion that they are not actually prepared to have. When the day comes, their mood is different, or when they hear the questions they realize how difficult it will be for them to give answers to the stranger in front of them.

I knew this was a possibility. Even so, I had hoped it would go better, and it's difficult for me to just let him leave because I haven't been able to ask him the most important question. Maybe I should have led with it, foregoing any professional pretense that I needed to hear him explain what happened that night. He wouldn't have been happy to hear the question I had for him, but he would have had to respond to it. I didn't want to blindside him with a supposition so awful right away, however. I didn't want to come across as a ghoul.

The question that I, and others, have, is whether Paresh's colleague Lindsay wasn't just killed by the Monster but swept up into it to fill a recently emptied seat.

I was, I thought, almost finished with what I had planned for this piece a couple of months ago, before the alleged sighting and circumstances at West Virginia's Mercer County Fair.

No one associated with this incident has been willing to sit down and speak with me, or even conduct an email or text exchange. Not the people who were stuck upside down for half an hour on the middle loop of the Tripleta roller coaster, initially scared because they were concerned about the safety harnesses failing, then terrified because they thought they saw something large and metallic peeking over and then hiding behind the trees in the tall hills beneath the moonlight.

Not the ones who had been in the front cars of the coaster who allegedly, through unconfirmed reports, saw a phantom, hooded figure appear at the crest of the track before the first big drop.

Not the ones in the Ferris wheel that came to such an abrupt stop that its open cabins swung back and forth violently enough to nearly spill people from their seats. These people as well nearly screamed because they were afraid to fall, and then, later, because they thought they saw something huge in the distance, moving toward the park.

Supposedly, some of these folks, as well as others throughout the park, heard and even felt some of the rides, including the Tripleta and the Big Wheel, twisting and straining to free themselves from whatever fastened them to the ground. Video seems to corroborate this, with the sounds of metal groaning and hard plastics cracking, screws, bars, and other parts dropping to the ground.

None of these machines repeated the Monster's accomplishment. Perhaps they weren't made from enough parts taken from the Dead Ride Graveyard. Unless we discover a hidden letter written by Lawrence Coleman, fully explaining himself and his process, or we track down any of the people he might have partnered with, we can never be sure.

There's little question, however, as to why the people who were so shaken by what happened at the Mercer County Fair aren't willing to talk about their experience.

I can't speak for any other journalists, but I've reached out to dozens of these people, and I have offered to give them aliases to keep their identities undisclosed, and I've received rejection after rejection. I think I understand why. The rhetoric surrounding what may or may not be happening—the worst fears that people have—is shifting. I have come across a disturbing amount of victim blaming online. Not all the fringe, lunatic theorists who initially doubted that the Merge Monster incident actually occurred have simply let go of their denialism. They instead remolded it to start attacking people who survived, who were there, who have been willing to go on record in interviews. These poor, innocent people who've already suffered through something previously unimaginable are now being accused of being conspirators, not as part of an extraordinary hoax, but participants in an evil ritual designed to let demons possess objects and run amok.

Since the men who are most likely responsible—including the one who claimed responsibility—are either dead or have made themselves inaccessible, and, for many, because it would take more than two minutes to look up the names of the people they should actually be wary of, the mob has turned to the people who are easier to find. The grifters who base their entire business model and seemingly entire lives on whipping people into a frenzy in between shilling for cryptocurrency and energy drinks have gotten to work targeting the Meredith Singletons and Wayne Fords of the world. I want to believe this wasn't inevitable, but I'm probably wrong, and what's scarier is that I can't decide which I think is worse—that we're incapable of avoiding this kind of behavior, or that we just refused to avoid it.

It's ridiculous that anyone even has to expend energy fearing such things when there is a much clearer potential threat out there.

An investigation into the incident at the fair quickly revealed that Lawrence Coleman had not been involved in the construction of any of the rides present, but his colleague Raymond Lafleur had. Lafleur was nicknamed "Rich" by his fellow ride designers and engineers, in part to distinguish him from another notable Raymond in his field, but also because he is the son of not-quite-billionaire Diedrich Lafleur, owner of LFM Parts, Inc., one of the largest automotive parts suppliers in the world.

Not only did Raymond apparently go into hiding to avoid questioning following the incident at the Mercer County Fair, but his father did as well. So have, allegedly, a handful of people rumored to have been close to the Lafleurs, and Coleman by extension. Most notably, two well-known architects, and the head of one of the world's largest manufacturers of building materials. Their names are being withheld from this article to comply with a cease and desist and lawsuit threat sent in response to requests for interviews or comments from these individuals.

If your concern or curiosity is getting the best of you, however, I've found that an internet search of "Lafleur Coleman architect friends" and "Lafleur Coleman construction" produces reliable results.

In the meantime, I think we'd all be much wiser to ignore and depower the unconscionable harassment campaigns directed at victims and work on sifting through the rumors about newer, possibly related incidents that are emerging. I know it's difficult, and can be overwhelming, and I wish I had better, more comforting advice to give than "stay vigilant." But it's all I can think to write at this time.

I don't want to believe it's a warning that three runaway 18-wheelers inexplicably careered through traffic on a slight incline in Arkansas, with each driver claiming that they couldn't keep their trucks from accelerating, but I've never heard of something like that happening before, and the reports of all three vehicles being serviced at the same location with parts supplied by LFM seem legitimate.

I don't want to believe it's a warning that a recently constructed high-rise tower full of condos in downtown Austin shook so hard one morning that over a hundred of its windows cracked, and most of its residents evacuated under the assumption that the city was experiencing an earthquake, which would be incredibly rare for the region. But no other building in the vicinity felt the same rumbling, and according to some accounts, the building is now measurably, if not visibly, *twisted.* It was, of course, designed by the aforementioned missing architect, and comprised of parts from the material supply company.

I don't want to believe that necessarily means anything, but not believing in something doesn't make it less true.

I CAUGHT A GHOST IN MY EYE

I caught a ghost in my right eye a week ago at the haunted house Shadows of Grier Street.

I say *caught* in the sense of catching a cold, something that happens to you. Not like I intentionally snared it.

Right away, I was sure it wasn't an eye floater, because that's what I wanted it to be, and I couldn't convince myself of it being that. There's a significant difference between a speck, line, or even small web that isn't really there, and the shape of a man dressed in black formals sitting or standing to your right at all times, not quite out of sight. Even at a size that suggests considerable distance, I could make out these details. This was a man, he wore black, and on the first day he appeared to be resting in a chair, then on the second he was standing, and on the third he was coming forward, getting slightly larger.

Still, I told my doctor about it during the visit I had scheduled already, because I could have been wrong. He recommended a visit to an optometrist when he couldn't spot anything. I made an appointment with the one closest to me who could also work me in on the same day. He couldn't find anything either but still tried to sell me a prescription and glasses that might correct the issue he couldn't identify. I declined the offer, of course. For all I knew, glasses would just upset the ghost I'd caught for some damn reason.

About the house, Shadows of Grier Street has been around since well before haunted house attractions popped up so commonly every October. It was one of Biloxi's lesser-known haunted houses. A place that had been someone's homestead, then a family-owned bed-and-breakfast that developed a reputation for inexplicable disturbances in the night. Supposedly, more than one murder-suicide had been enacted inside the building. That it had survived both of Biloxi's big hurricanes—Camille and Katrina—enhanced its mythos. Its website even boasted of this.

Mother Nature has tried to kill it, but she can't. The house is too evil to die.

I had gone with friends for the unique experience, quite unlike any other haunted house in the area, in the state, possibly in any neighboring state. It was neither a ghost tour nor the amusement park funhouse more typically associated with Halloween attractions. It was a dinner party among friends and strangers.

To summarize the lore told to us over the courses of dinner, the first deadly incident at the house happened at such a party. At least thirty guests had been seated at the lengthy table of the dining hall, the homeowner's two marrying-age daughters among them. They were both beautiful, but the older sister, twenty-four, was being presented at this party to a banker in his fifties, which wizened beyond his years, while the younger sister, twenty-two, was showcased to a handsome military hero who wouldn't be thirty for a few months.

During the second course of the meal, that military man who'd won a Medal of Honor and seen considerable bloodshed on battlefields abroad bolted up from his seat, rushed out of the room and house, and tried to flee into the night. The master of the house, a military veteran himself, and still hearty, ran after the man, thinking something must have triggered a bad reminiscence for him. He managed to catch up to him and asked if the younger man had gone mad.

No, the young man said. No, no, no. I just saw it and heard it and I couldn't stand it anymore. Why didn't you say something to it? Do something about it? Couldn't you see it too?

What in the devil are you talking about, man, the master of the house asked.

The devil. Yes, *the devil.* Or *a* devil. One was standing behind your older daughter. Didn't you notice how quiet she was? She was listening to it. It was telling her over and over again to … to do something horrible!

The master worked to quiet and calm the man for a while, long enough for his servants to find him in the nearby woods. He started to tell them that there was nothing to be concerned over anymore, that the young soldier's nerves had temporarily bested him, but the older veteran's stoicism and wisdom had soothed the younger hero, but the servants uncharacteristically interrupted to tell him he was needed back at the manor right away. Something terrible had happened.

His older daughter had smashed her drinking glass against the table, then used its jagged edges to stab the banker in his neck, then slash her sister's face and gouge out one of her eyes.

This is accounted for in official records. At the dinner I attended, the hosts of the event passed around newspaper clippings supporting portions of the story. The older sister did indeed kill the man her father wanted her to marry, and in some unspecified way maimed her sister. Nothing in the articles mentioned, much less confirmed, the part about the younger man fleeing the house and talking about some demon that influenced the sister, though. I just took that aspect for the frivolous fun and embellishment anyone would believe it to be.

These people—the daughters, the banker, and the father—had names. They were listed in the article passed around to me and my friends at the table. I ought to remember those names, but I don't. I could probably look them up, but I can't be bothered to care. I'm only concerned with myself, because I have a goddamned ghost in my goddamned eye.

After dinner, we went on a short tour of the house where there were assorted other stories. A diaphanous woman who allegedly appears by the window of one room during a certain hour of the night. Another room where the faucets are heard running in the bathroom late into the night, even though there's no sign of water in the sink or tubs when you check. A room where a man can be heard weeping and a woman can be heard screeching at him, "It was your fault!"

None of these rooms were the source of my trouble. The locked room was where I caught the ghost.

I can admit that I wasn't as reverent or respectful of the specters as I should have been. In my defense, *I didn't think ghosts were real.* I was there to have fun in the spirit of the season, on Halloween night. I was invited by friends to something I normally wouldn't have attended, and yes, I accepted because of a young lady I was interested in. I made a mistake based on a relatively common belief, and I was in that position for defensible reasons, so pardon me if I come across as defensive, but I don't think I'm to blame. And even if I do share some degree of blame, I don't think I *deserved* this. Killers and abusers deserve this. I'm neither. I'm just ... me.

A man who caught a ghost in his eye.

Our host guided us through the upstairs rooms, told us every story, and then brought us to the locked room, the last room, which no one was allowed to enter. A man had slaughtered his wife and two young sons in that room, the host said. A happy man with a happy family, according to the proprietors of the bed-and-breakfast at the time. A man who, for no reason anyone could discern, cut and slashed his family to death. He'd used the bits of a porcelain lamp he'd smashed against the wall. The largest shard was still embedded in his throat when they found his body.

But there were also teeth marks on his wife in a dozen different places, and slivers of the porcelain also embedded in his teeth and gums. He'd bitten her after shredding her with the sharp but fragile weapon that cut his own hand while he wielded it. He'd gone entirely mad.

It was said he still inhabited the room, tortured by what he'd done, and no one was allowed to enter. Of all the rooms in the house, this one was supremely evil. The most haunted.

All anyone was allowed to do was look through the keyhole, to see if they spotted a glowing figure seated at the edge of the bed, with his back turned to the door. But any who did had to be careful. You were not allowed to look for longer than five seconds, or else the ghost might realize it was being watched, and the man, ashamed of what he'd done, ashamed to be seen, might come for the person watching him.

I can't recall what I'd said that was so offensive, but I can recall seeing the host's face change when I challenged the veracity of the house's hauntings. Not only that, I recall the faces of some of my friends, and particularly that of the young lady with whom I'd been hoping to get more acquainted. They all appeared upset or disappointed with me. Apparently I had crossed a line. Again, I can't remember what I said, but I know it must have only been a joke. Nothing close to a truly objectionable insult.

I did *not* do or say anything to deserve this.

The host invited anyone in our party to look through the keyhole into the locked room, but he stared at me when he made the invitation, and the others around me looked as well. He was daring me. He challenged me. Yes, I was a fool to fall for this challenge, but he is worse for knowing what would happen to me.

He must have known, just as knew he could face no repercussion for his action. I was still the one who accepted the unspoken dare, after all. Even if he'd spoken it, I was still at fault for agreeing to look through the keyhole. How could anyone prove he knew what would happen? Even if you could, were there any laws about luring an unsuspecting fool into catching an ocular, spectral infection? Probably not.

I still think he should hold the brunt of the blame, although he probably doesn't care, probably sleeps well, and knows I can't find him, at least until next year when Shadows of Grier reopens. He might think I won't be around by then, and honestly, if I am, and raving mad because of my ordeal, that would only benefit his business. What better publicity could there be than, *This man claims he saw a ghost here and it drove him insane. Do you dare … ?*

I dared. Fool. Stupid goddamned moron. I dared. I looked.

He counted. One. Two. Three. Four. Five.

Six.

Seven.

Eight.

I started to chuckle before he got to nine, waiting for him to give up counting and admit to how silly this was, which would redeem me in the eyes of my friends, I thought.

Before he said nine, however, a shot of air, like someone blowing smoke through a straw, struck my eye. I jumped back, I cursed, I accused him of having someone on the other side of the keyhole waiting for just the right moment, and when I described what had hit my eye as just air—just cold, *cold* air—my friends laughed. After I calmed down, I laughed with them and admitted to the host that it was a clever trick.

He smiled weakly at me, and thinking back on it, I believe there was regret in his eyes.

That night I went to sleep with my eye still oddly cool, like every blink birthed a snowflake I couldn't cry out.

The next morning, I woke to a ghost dressed in black in the corner of the same eye.

The first day it sat.

The second day it stood.

The third day it walked, and my eye grew colder.

The fourth day, it raised its right arm toward me.

The fifth day, its mouth dropped open, and it felt like I had a ball of ice in my skull.

You can understand why I asked my doctor about what was happening to me. Obviously I didn't say that there was a ghost in my eye, reaching toward me and shouting at me. I just said there was something there that I couldn't get rid of. When he asked me to describe it, I told him it was a dark speck.

I didn't say it was a gray-faced man in a coat and dark pants with flecks of something reddish staining the hand he raised toward me.

The sixth day it came closer.

The seventh day it came closer, and half of my face felt frozen.

The eighth day I could see its teeth. Stone colored. A mouthful of old, makeshift grave markers placed by people who didn't have access to a chisel and hammer.

On the ninth day, the dimness of his eyes was evident. This was a spirit in eternal agony. As well he should be. He'd killed his wife and his children, if the story was to be believed. Maybe it should be doubted, though. That might have been the source of its despair. It reached toward me because I was one more person apt to spread lies about what it had done, when it had been innocent. Someone else had invaded the man's room, killed his family, cut his throat, then escaped unsuspected, and now, decades later, people accused him of the crime. That would make any spirit restless, wouldn't it?

I spent the next two days telling myself that the man was innocent and apologizing for ever thinking he could have done something so heinous.

On the tenth day, he was larger, closer. Still reaching.

On the eleventh day, his jaw distended farther, as if he was preparing to bite something bigger than his own head.

I went online to share what had happened to me and to clear the man's name. I know *his* name because of this. I stumbled across the name of the man who originally built and owned the house as part of my research but deliberately forgot it as a sort of offering to the ghost in my eye.

Do you see? I see, I am forced *to see, but do* you *see? Mr. Alexander, do you see? I am forcing the thought and remembrance of anyone else in the house out of my mind so that only you and your poor family members exist to me. Your poor wife. Your poor sons. If I knew the name of the bastard who really killed them and framed you, I would remember that, too, so I could scream it to the world for you. The way you want to scream it at me.*

Your mouth is so wide because your scream will be so loud, right? Not because you plan to do anything else, right?

Right?

On the twelfth day, I realized that I might have been too focused on his eyes and teeth. The weathered, unkempt-corpse color of his skin.

Skin? A ghost didn't have skin. What it had was a strange cover that it projected because it couldn't think of itself as healthy and alive again but also couldn't fully accept that it was, by now, dusty bones at best.

Still, I paid too much attention to this part of its image, as well as its clothes. God, why did I know so much about its clothes? The white of its shirt and dark of its tie under the black of its coat that matched the black of its cloak and pants. These were unimportant things, but I saw them, I fixated on them, and something about them unsettled me. Its size disturbed me as well.

By the sixth day it was occupying at least a quarter of the vision in my right eye, and it was encroaching on a quarter of my vision every ensuing day. How long before it took up half? How long before it occupied all of it?

Would I be alive by then? If alive, sane?

These things dominated my thoughts day after day, as I called in sick to my work and declined first my friends' invitations to spend time with them out somewhere, then their offers to come spend time with me at my home, and then finally any calls and text messages they tried to place.

I didn't want to see any of them. I didn't want to talk to any of them. None of them could help me. None knew what it was like to catch a ghost in your eye.

Even I didn't understand what it was truly like. I was suffering through it, but I didn't comprehend what was happening. I was like a newborn pushed out of one comfortable existence and into a foreign one, only there was no one there to help me, so I instinctually knew that there was no point in crying over it because no one would answer that cry.

I might not be alone here in a strictly factual sense, but only in the way that the last survivor of a catastrophe on an unknown island might not be the last man alive on the planet.

Don't you know that there are others like you on other unknown islands at this very moment? Is this knowledge any good to you? No, but it is the truth. It is accurate, so … that's all.

It occurred to me early, by the fifth night, that I couldn't be the first person to have caught a ghost in their eye. It would be egotistical to think I'm so unique. So I tried to look online for others who were going through what I was going through, and found nothing. Maybe it was because internet searches aren't as useful today as they'd been ten years ago. Maybe there were others but none of them had thought to share their stories online, much less create the support group I was desperately hoping to find.

I was all alone in this. If not the first, then the one, right now. The one for years in either direction, past and future.

It didn't really matter which hypothesis was accurate. Two plus two equaled two times two equaled the square root of sixteen equaled I was alone. I only had myself to trust and rely on to save me, and I had misread what the spirit was doing.

I thought I had offended it. Him. I thought I could placate him with prayers and apologies, but those were useless because I didn't understand. I was too afraid of his reaching hand to truly see what he was doing, afraid more of his widening, cavernous mouth and the teeth residing within.

They weren't even sharp, or large. That might not have mattered had he intended to do what I thought he meant to do, but as I think back now, it's something that stands out. I should have recognized how innocuous they were and realized I should put my attention elsewhere. Back to his reaching hand.

Which wasn't *reaching*, actually, although I wouldn't have noticed that initially. I wonder how soon I might have seen it had I been paying proper attention.

On the thirteenth day, I saw that the index finger on the hand of his outstretched arm was *pointing*. I realized that his eyes were looking past me, to my left.

His mouth was open for a scream that was a warning to me. There was despair in his face deep enough to pierce the planet's core. It almost melted his jowls into his jaw and gave him rolls in his neck despite how gaunt he appeared.

I fell asleep wondering what he was pointing at.

In my dreams, I remembered the story of the war hero who ran from the house because he could no longer stand seeing and hearing the demon behind the older daughter, telling her to kill.

I awoke on the fourteenth day to an uncomfortable warmth in my left eye, like someone was holding a hot needle close to it, and I could feel the burn and puncture before it even touched.

The ghost in my right eye was larger still, and lurching forward, pointing with its entire body. Its eyes almost stole the entire top half of its skull. The tip of its index finger was bone. It was pulling itself through its skin to point toward the burning.

Something red was in the corner of my left eye. It had horns under the blood-colored flames that wrapped it. Not just on its head, but all over its body, like pocks from a skin disease. Although it was small now, I could still see these features.

Although it was small, I could still hear its voice, however faint.

It told me to do horrible things.

XII
יב
١٢
十二
12

HE USED TO SCARE ME BY ACCIDENT

Our first real date was a horror movie. A ghost story called *The Others*, which he was excited to show me when he found out I hadn't seen it. It was playing for one night only at a theater on the northside, and I was keen to get some time alone with him after talking and laughing with him at a couple of parties thrown by mutual friends, so I lied and said that I was into scary movies.

I don't remember very much of the film because I spent most of it with my eyes cast down, or to the side, when I wasn't burying my face in Stephen's shoulder. I held his hand so tight through certain scenes he joked that my handshake would impress his grandfather.

Afterward, I asked him to come home with me, mostly because his cologne was so alluring—pine, citrus, leather, and something else that was sort of tenderly masculine. It made me think of a photograph I'd seen of a World War II soldier feeding a kitten, which apparently earned the man thousands of unsolicited marriage proposals. The way Stephen patted and squeezed my thigh to comfort me wasn't the same, but it showed at least an ounce of the strength and sensitivity that I was attracted to.

Besides, I had been daydreaming of my hands on him and his lips on me since we'd agreed to the date. As long as he wasn't terrible to me, my plan was to invite him over.

A small part of me, however, wanted him to spend the night because I didn't think my nerves could take being alone, listening to my upstairs neighbors thump across the floor of their unit at some ungodly hour. After the movie, I wouldn't have been able to convince myself it was just their third bathroom trip in the middle of the night or another march to the kitchen for a glass of water that would make them get out of bed yet again in an hour or two. So I asked him to come back to my place, and he said yes.

A few hours later, after we were finished, I was startled awake in my bed by what I thought was a clacking or cracking sound, or both, one right after the other. It came from inside my bedroom. I bolted upright and saw a figure standing in a doorway. I made this strange little scared noise like the warm-up to a real scream, and I reached for Stephen beside me, to wake him up and tell him I heard something. His side of the bed was empty, though, and it only took another couple of seconds for me to realize what I'd heard and who I was looking at.

The *clack crack* I thought I'd heard was just the doorknob turning the latch in the master bathroom, followed by the door itself opening. Stephen stood there a moment, probably waiting to be sure I didn't scream. It would have been nice to hear him reassure me that it was really him and that I should relax, but instead, he asked, "Did I scare you?"

I came clean about my general dislike of horror movies the next day, when he tried to recommend another one for a second date. I think he did that on purpose to test me. He wasn't upset about my lie and took it as a compliment that I would subject myself to something I didn't enjoy just to be around him, so I couldn't hold it against him if he was indeed testing me.

Anyway, we took one of those little cooking classes together for our second date instead, which is where I found out he couldn't chop a carrot to save his life and had considerably more enthusiasm than talent for cooking. Not that I was a culinary wizard, but even the instructor asked me to take the knife from him before he hurt himself. I was so happy to see him be able to laugh at himself. I won't go as far as saying I knew then that I wanted to marry him, but I can say it's when I first thought there might be a chance.

Things moved quickly enough that it divided my friends, half of them thinking I should slow down, the other half encouraging me. Two of them who were already married fell into the latter camp and confessed to me over brunch one day that they envied the chemistry they saw between Stephen and me. A couple of weeks after that conversation—two and a half months into our relationship—I took up his offer to move in with him.

He had a nice one-bedroom condo that was still fairly spacious and open, which didn't leave too many blind spots for him to be inadvertently hiding behind. Nonetheless, he made me jump a couple of times. Once when he just happened to be passing right by the bathroom door as I was coming out. The second was shortly after he left to go grab a drink with a friend. I wasn't feeling up to it—allergies and sinus issues—so I just went back to the bedroom to lie down. I think my head being so stuffy and ears feeling plugged are to blame for why I didn't hear the door open. I was also medicated and a little drowsy, though I hadn't been planning to fall asleep, just to rest for a little while. I must have faded out of consciousness for a moment, however, because I swear I'd been facing the bedroom doorway, looking past it into the living room one moment, and then, without a blink—at least not one that I registered—Stephen was there, walking around to his side of the bed.

I felt my blood racing, felt my body somehow sinking in place, not actually moving but finding a place underneath itself nonetheless. It was a tremendous fear that persisted even after I understood that this wasn't a phantom or an intruder. Stephen finally noticed this after he'd already retrieved his wallet, which he'd come back for, from the nightstand where he'd forgotten it. He looked at me with considerable concern.

"Babe, are you—?" he started before my scream cut him off. It came and went like a twitch I'd been trying to fend off, and it was a small relief to have it escape me, but embarrassment quickly filled the vacancy. The way Stephen stared at me made me wonder if he was going to ask me to leave, tell me that we'd rushed into living together, and he didn't see this working after all. I was preparing to defend myself, citing the sinus congestion and antihistamines, when he said, "Should I be wearing a bell?"

Whatever tension might have been in the room—if there had ever been any on his part—was ushered out with that little joke. I laughed, mostly to see if he would follow suit, and when he did I laughed harder. After a moment he told me, "Seriously, though, maybe I should announce myself so you know where I'm at. I don't want to keep scaring you like this."

Yes, I did jump when he proposed to me, but in fairness he set me up that time, having one of my friends distract me so he could approach with my back turned while I thought he was still out of town for work. I hit him on the arm after I turned and saw him, hard enough to almost make him drop the ring. Everyone found it pretty funny.

Each time he scared me after was considerably worse.

He followed through on his idea of announcing his whereabouts in the house that we moved into any time either he was on the move, or he heard that I was.

"I'm in the living room."

"I'm coming up the stairs."

"I'm right outside the door."

I had set up a small workstation in the spare bedroom where I could craft some homemade jewelry I sold to friends, coworkers at the office, and, sparingly, online. I would put in my earbuds to listen to some jazz or classical instrumentals, lock into what I was doing, and find some peace. And then my wonderful, strong, somewhat hirsute husband's mountain-man voice would bellow, "I'm right down the hall," and my heart would nearly pop. Either that or I would be on my way downstairs, and a strong, unseen voice would declare, "I'm in the kitchen." As if I couldn't already tell by the smell. It almost startled me into missing a step more than once.

I didn't have it in me to tell him that his solution wasn't any better, though. Instead, I told myself I would get used to it eventually, while also trying to desensitize myself to the suddenness of his voice barreling through my soothing music. I traded out listening to instrumentals for audiobooks and podcasts, thinking that if I was already listening to someone talking, it would soften the impact of Stephen's voice. Yes, they were true crime stories, almost exclusively, and yes, they did sometimes give me chills, and no, I can't explain why I found them practically addicting while still having such an aversion for scary movies, and even horror-fiction audiobooks, which I tried a couple of times and shut off before the first fake person could get killed.

In hindsight, maybe if I had been listening to some romance instead, or catching up on classics I missed or hadn't read since tenth grade like *The Count of Monte Cristo*, things could have been different. I've had a couple of years to think about it now and still can't decide whether it's better to believe I could have made a choice that changed things or believe what happened was inevitable. Either way, I'm still blaming myself, it's just either for a bad decision or for my naturally nervous disposition.

I wasn't entirely wrong about the switch to audiobooks and podcasts helping me withstand his declarations. After about two months, it proved fairly effective. He was so loud I could hear him shout, "I'm in the garage," from the kitchen, where I was spending a little more time, to make sure I was "doing my part" with regard to cooking, I had told him, but really to make sure the majority of our weekly meals were something to look forward to, as opposed to power through.

Anyway, my birthday was coming up—my first since we'd gotten married—and he was working on something special for me in a section of the garage he'd tarped off. I never took a peek, tempted as I was, and I swear he would sometimes use tools completely unrelated to whatever he was making for me to try to throw me off. I would find out later he was building me a new workstation with storage spaces for all my materials, and convenient outlets for my glue gun and soldering iron. While I understand why he needed the sander for it, I still don't think he actually needed the chainsaw, or to hammer metal like he was trying to kill a robot.

I'd gotten as used to that racket as I could, as well as to his pronouncement when he heard me pulling pans from the cupboard through the thin shared wall between the garage and kitchen. I don't think I jumped at all when I heard his voice the day it happened. I was practically spellbound by the story I was listening to about a man who snapped and dismembered his elderly parents.

I was so caught up in that, and in chopping the peppers on the cutting board in front of me, that I didn't hear the door open. I didn't hear him coming toward me. I just heard a woman describing a disturbed man using every implement in his shed to butcher the bodies of the people who'd raised him. Then I sensed someone large behind me and saw their shadow cover me. And I knew it was him, I must have, most of me must have at least, but something else in me told me not to trust that it was only him. That was how people in all these stories I was listening to died. By being too comfortable, too unaware, too sure that it could never happen to them.

Next, there was a heavy hand on my shoulder, and as I turned, I saw the hammer in Stephen's hand before I saw his face. I saw the stains on his smock that weren't really red but in that weird, yellowish light of the kitchen—because we kept procrastinating on changing the bulbs out for the whiter, "natural daylight" style we preferred—I don't know ... when I think back on them, I think they could have been reddish? Sort of a rust color?

It doesn't matter. I knew it was him. Who else could it be? And I knew his smell. I knew his hand. I knew. But I also knew his voice and shape and face, and I still jumped at those when I didn't expect them, didn't I?

I turned around too fast, I jumped, and I still had the damn chef's knife in my hand.

The knife was part of an expensive, high-quality set Stephen purchased after our cooking class, because the instructor said sharp knives are safer than duller ones due to less force being needed, lowering the chance of them slipping, and what-the-hell-ever, screw her, she was wrong. The sharper knife was worse.

The tip slipped right through the meat on the underside of the arm he had placed on my shoulder. That actually didn't seem so bad at first. I was almost relieved, after realizing what I'd done, to see that I at least hadn't gotten him in the neck or the chest. But then considerably more blood than I was prepared to see started streaming down the knife. Enough that it completely covered my hand before I thought to pull it away. I took the knife out when I did, which I know now probably made things worse, but I wasn't thinking about that at the time. I don't even know if I was aware of it, and if I was, it was just from some movie or TV show, which, for all I knew, was just spreading a lie.

I also didn't know, at the time, about brachial arteries.

I didn't know about tying a tourniquet.

I didn't know how much longer it would take for paramedics to arrive, because we'd gotten a good deal on our starter house in a new neighborhood that gave us the illusion of living more in the countryside, as opposed to the congestion of the city, which felt like a blessing right up until the moment you needed an ambulance to arrive just a few minutes earlier.

Just a few minutes earlier. I think that would have made the difference. Hell, if I'd gotten started a few minutes earlier, I'd have been done by the time he surprised me, and he might have only gotten a face full of salt or a chicken breast thrown at him or something. Had he walked in a few minutes earlier I might not have started yet, and things would have been fine. If I had been listening to "Clair de lune" instead of a podcast, I might have heard him coming inside.

If, if, if.

What a worthless word.

My sister, Emelia, stayed with me the night I slept at my house, not at my parents' place, a week after Stephen's funeral. Knowing what I know now, I should have never come home. Even then I knew I wouldn't be able to stand living there without him, but I wanted to be in our bed again. I don't know why. I knew it would be painful to be there, but I also couldn't stop thinking about it. I wondered if the sheets would still smell like him. I wondered if it would feel good to wake up in the middle of the night and forget, just for a second, that he wasn't beside me, and never would be again. The realization to follow would be hell, but I wouldn't know if the seconds preceding it would be worth it until I experienced them. I never had that experience, though.

Emelia and I shared the bed, and while I was having as much difficulty sleeping as I'd had since Stephen's death, I think she was able to nod off relatively quickly. I turned away from her, listened to her breathing, and sort of lulled myself into nearly falling asleep after about an hour of fighting with my thoughts, fighting with that stupid word *if* and the equally useless question of *Why?*

And then I heard him.

"Olivia … I'm in the living room … Olivia … I'm coming up the stairs … Olivia … I'm in the hallway."

His voice was weaker, but it was his. There was no mistaking it. I felt a tingling cold rush through me. It was like that first night when I had invited him back to my apartment, only magnified by an amount I can't even put a number to. When I sat up in bed, I thought my spirit was leaving my body, and I hated the feeling as much as the pins-and-needles sensation when you have a body part on the verge of being numb.

I stared at the open doorway of my bedroom—our bedroom—and didn't have a desire to see him there. Something felt terribly wrong about hearing his voice. It should have struck me as a miracle, a mercy. I should have spoken up and answered him and either told him to come in and hold me again, or told him again that I was sorry, the way I'd said it on the day I accidentally killed him. Instead, I stayed quiet as if I was too scared to answer him.

Not *as if.* I *was* scared. Terrified.

Something in the corner of my eye elevated that terror even though I had thought it was at its peak. I looked to my left and saw Emelia also sitting up in bed, her widened eyes a mirror of my own.

I found the strength to turn to her even though I felt too stiff to move, and before I could ask, she said, "Did you hear that?"

That.

I would have said nearly the same thing, except I think I would have said, "Him," and maybe that would have made a difference.

Maybe I should have told her, "I heard *him,*" instead of just nodding, as though not only affirming what we'd heard but her designation of Stephen as no longer being a person. A man she had loved like a newfound sibling and whom I had been in love with. A man instead reduced to *that.*

I have to think that upset him. It's the only reason I can think of for why he is determined to torment me.

Well, besides the fact that I killed … that I was responsible for his death.

If that wasn't bad enough, now I had confirmation that his spirit still lingered. My sister had heard his ghost speaking to me.

Then she called him *that*, and I didn't correct her.

If … *if* I were in his place, I think that would have upset me too.

I didn't sleep in the house again. I sold it. I moved into an apartment.

He followed me.

Olivia … I'm at the front door. Olivia … I've come inside. Olivia … I'm at the bedroom door.

At first, I only heard him at night, near sleep, and that was awful enough, but then he started to speak to me during the day.

Olivia … I'm in the living room.

I would jump up and look around, trying to place which part of the room the voice had come from.

Olivia … I'm in the bedroom.

Olivia … I'm in the shower.

The people I sold the house to reached out to me once and asked if I had ever heard strange noises when I'd been there. I asked them to elaborate, but they had been coy, as if they didn't want to sound stupid. I told them that I heard something that sounded like a voice once but couldn't explain it, hoping that would invite them to give me details.

Was part of him still in the house, looking for me, while the remainder of him had followed me to the new apartment?

The new homeowners wouldn't say more, and I was too afraid to go back to the house to find out any more for myself. It wasn't like they'd let me spend the night to hear if he would call to me again there, anyway.

Olivia … I'm in the kitchen.

Olivia … I'm in the bed.

Every time I heard him it didn't just frighten me, it tightened my heart until I thought it would calcify. It constricted my breathing while evaporating my mind.

It gave me the strangest agony. Every damn time.

I tried to escape. I moved apartments, but he followed me. I stayed in a hotel for a few nights, and on the second night, he found me there.

Olivia, I'm in the elevator.

I'm on the second floor.

I'm on the ninth floor.

I'm on your floor.

I'm in the hallway.

I'm at your door.

Emelia invited me to go camping with her. We traveled one state over and slept under the stars for a week. On the last day, I heard him.

I'm under the moon.

Olivia, I'm in the dark.

Olivia, I'm by the creek.

I'm in the clearing.

I'm near your tent.

My primary care doctor has warned me that my blood pressure is too high. She has prescribed hypertension medication that has done nothing for me. She's prescribed sleep aids that barely get me through the night. The anxiety pills aren't helpful either.

I still hear him, at various hours. If I knew it would only ever come at night, I could be somewhat prepared for it, but he sometimes announces himself in the morning, sometimes in the middle of the day. Even when I'm not at home. Even when I'm at work, or out at lunch with friends who have been trying their hardest to get me back to my "old self" as if that was an option.

Olivia, I'm at the door.

Olivia, I'm in the chair beside you.

I'm right behind you.

Turn around. I'm right behind you.

I am in therapy. I have been to a medium. I have visited one of my elderly cousins, who is a curandero. Emelia invited me to come to her church, and I've been going steadily for a year now. I joined her for Bible studies on Wednesdays and have consulted with the preacher. People in the congregation have noticed my health issues, commented on deterioration in that politely blunt way church folk have mastered.

"Honey, you're not getting enough rest."

I know.

"We're having a cookout. You should come by. We've got to get you eating more."

I know.

"Olivia, I'm gonna keep praying for you."

Thank you.

It won't help.

He won't stop.

He knows how sorry I am. Not just for what I did, but for not answering him that first night he spoke to me. I've told him how sorry I am. I've begged him to forgive me. He acts like he can't hear me. The way I acted the night I came back home after …

After I killed him.

I'm so, so sorry, but it doesn't matter.

I can't get away from him. He won't leave me alone.

I'll always hear him telling me where he is.

Olivia, I'm at the foot of the stairs.

I'm at the top of the stairs.

I'm down the hall.

I'm in your room.

Olivia, turn around, I'm right behind you.

He's been gone for two years, but he's still with me. He still scares me.

It used to be by accident.

WHATEVER HAPPENED TO CRASH TEST CHRIS?

I've always had poor impulse control, which has done me plenty of harm but is also how I found out about my ability.

I was twelve years old, scrawny, tall, and mixed with three different races. My skin tone and hair were 100 percent "What are you?" A dream target for bullies.

There was this kid Rocky whose favorite pastime was kicking my ass. I used to dream of knocking him out, but I knew I didn't have it in me.

One day, in the middle of a beating, this crazy thought jumped into my head. What if he really hurt me? Took it so far that all the other kids would think he crossed the line from wannabe tough to full-on psycho?

What could he do that would be so overboard everyone would turn on him, though? A weird little voice popped into my head and said, "Let him break your jaw." And I understood that that voice meant let him *really* break it so that it's hard to look at afterward. Sure enough, the next time his hand landed on one side of my face, my jawbone tried to exit out the other side.

It didn't hurt; it was just uncomfortable. Not nearly as bad as a broken and dislocated jaw should feel. I knew right away how messed up it looked, though, because I heard a bunch of kids gasp like they were trying to suck every drop of oxygen out of the air. Rocky's eyes were bugging out to get a closer look at the damage, while the rest of him was pulling away. I can't describe what I looked like because obviously I couldn't see my own face, but I saw my jaw bulging in my peripheral vision, and I remember the bulge having some points and edges to it, so just try to picture that as best as you can.

Although it didn't hurt, the sound of it made my legs weak. It had sounded like I'd taken a hard bite out of something that had teeth of its own, and it took a harder bite back. I was rightly freaked out. I've been nice and high plenty of times since then, mostly to cope with my condition. I've taken shit that left me half out of my head, but the first time I used my little power is still the most unique mind-screw of my life, partly because I realized I made it happen. Rocky was my age, and not freakishly strong or anything. No way could he smack my face into oblivion like that. That was all me.

I tried to shout, "What did you do!" but it came out garbled. Bet you can guess why. Still, Rocky didn't have to understand what I said to understand me. He ran off the way idiots do when they know they've gone too far. It's one thing to bloody a lip or blacken an eye, a whole other thing to disfigure somebody.

My crazy idea worked for the most part. Rocky got suspended, and when he came back to school, he never screwed with me again. Neither did anybody else. I was out of school for a while too, and when I came back, I was way more of an outcast than Rocky, but being left alone was fine by me. It's important to say, though, that I wasn't out of school because I needed time to heal.

The principal or teachers should have called an ambulance for me, but they kept me in the nurse's office with ice on my jaw and called my parents to come get me instead. Either they were too freaked out or too dumb to know the right thing to do. When my folks saw me, they were livid. Never heard anyone before or since say the things my mother said to those people, and I've been around some profound profaners since then.

On the way to the hospital, in the back of my parents' car, I started getting nervous about what might happen if a doctor got a look at my jaw. My dad was talking about surgery. It got my heart thumping and my brain working in overdrive, and I felt like I had to try something, so I started to push things around on my face, work parts back into place. It goes back to that lack of impulse control I mentioned earlier.

Fixing my jaw was surprisingly easy. It was like I was working off a diagram. By the time we got to the hospital, I was shouting at my folks that I was fine, and I was. They could see it, but they were in a frenzy already. My inexplicable healing didn't help. I opened and closed my mouth over and over to show how unbroken my jaw was, but that didn't matter to them. They dragged me into the ER and demanded someone see me right away. We must've looked like all the stupid in the world crammed into the shape of a small family.

Back home, my folks doted on me like I was either the most fragile boy who ever lived or some trickster god they didn't want to upset. They kept me out of school while they tried to make sense of what had happened, and eventually settled on pretending it wasn't that big of a deal. Meanwhile, whenever I was by myself, I started breaking and unbreaking things. First my left pinky. Then the ring finger. Then my wrist and forearm. Then I fully hyperextended my elbow and popped it right back into place like it was nothing. It was pretty exciting. I couldn't see how useless the skill was at the time. I just felt powerful. I could do something that I assumed nobody else could do, and that had to be worth something, didn't it?

It took longer than I like to admit for me to realize it wasn't worth much. Maybe I just lacked the imagination to make the most of it. Oh well. Things turned out as they did. Eventually, the best use of my ability that I could think of was to carve out a place for myself in the pro wrestling business.

After I got over my delusions of becoming a superhero, and then supervillain, and then ordinary villain, I thought about joining a carnival sideshow. See the Boy Who Can Wreck and Rebuild Himself. By the time I graduated high school, I snapped out of that funk and planned to be a movie stuntman. Mind you, this was the early eighties, before the computer effects got any good. I thought I could rent myself out to get injured in pictures, either the ones made on the cheap that couldn't afford good effects or ones made by hardcore directors who were desperate for authenticity. Need a guy's arm to snap in half? I can do it live on camera, no cutaway. Same goes for the legs, the fingers, the face. I can do dislocations, broken noses, and dented chins. I can even do compound fractures, the broken skin mends as easily as the bone with a little massaging. Whatever you need.

I took a bus out to Hollywood where I found out most people didn't take me seriously. The one guy who gave me a chance to audition was too disturbed by my demonstration to call me back.

It occurred to me afterward that I ought to be more careful about who I showed off my ability to. Wouldn't it be my luck to snap my shin and reset it in front of a guy who knows a guy who works for some secret government agency? Next thing I know, I'm in an operating lab with a bunch of old German doctors crushing bones that *I'm* not focused on breaking, and I'm screaming at them that it doesn't work that way. "I have to be in on it before it happens or else it's just a regular injury, assholes! Also, this fucking hurts!"

So I was living the reality of almost everyone who goes to LA to live their dream. I waited tables in diners, delivered food in shabby neighborhoods, did some other stuff I'm going to plead the fifth about. One day, after a shift, a buddy of mine invited me to a wrestling show.

I'd never been into wrestling, and being a daft know-it-all the first thing I said was, "You know that stuff isn't real, right?"

He said, "No shit, neither is *Star Wars*, but you talk about that like it really happened." I stood there in my *Empire Strikes Back* T-shirt, unable to think of a comeback. So I agreed to go with him, and that's how I ended up near the front row of a sparsely attended show at the old Grand Olympic Auditorium.

It wasn't much of a show. The guys and gals on the card tried hard, but I learned later the local wrestling landscape had changed, and the energy wasn't the same as it had been a few years earlier. Attendance for the weekly events was shrinking. The writing was on the wall and underlined twice.

I don't think I would've got my shot if the local scene had been healthier. It also helped that this was in the last decade or so of people inside the wrestling world still doing what they could to "protect the business," present everything as though it's a legit sport, even if most fans over ten years old knew it was scripted. That helped me make my case for how I could be useful. What could look more legit than an actual broken bone?

It also gave me more faith in the people I ended up working with than I expected to have, even the crooks and liars. They'd all built their careers and sometimes their lives around keeping secrets and keeping up appearances. Pro wrestling has some roots in the old carny days and that was still a pretty big influence on what the ethics were back then. I was basically applying for the role of freak show performer, and as long as I could make some money for some people, nobody was going to tell the outside world about me. It would violate the code.

I asked my buddy if there was a wrestler he could introduce me to, being the superfan that he was, and he knew someone on the low end of the card. Doc Payne, whose real name was Jim Peyton, but I still think of him as Doc. We caught up with Doc at a bar after midnight. My buddy introduced me, and instead of asking him, "How do I become a wrestler?" I said, "Can I show you something pretty cool?" He had just put his beer to his lips, so I went ahead and showed him before he could answer. Grabbed my left forearm with my right hand and cranked it down and around until it was very clearly pointed the wrong way. Audibly snapped and dislocated my elbow.

Doc spit his beer across the bar, which, thankfully, was a mostly empty dive. I flipped the arm back into place before the bartender could turn and see what I'd done. I glanced at my buddy, who stared at me with his mouth wide, and I just shrugged. "Double-jointed," I said, then looked at Doc again and saw that he was already thinking what I hoped he would be.

"You can do that at will?" he said, and when I said yeah, he told me to meet him the next day at a private gym just outside of town.

When I got there, Doc introduced me to "Wild" Bill Hill, whose wildness seemed limited to his puffy-ass beard. He was tall and tree-trunk thick, and was a bruiser in his day, but was long retired from the ring when I met him. He had these deep, relaxed eyes that looked like they'd seen too much to be stunned by anything ever again. When I showed him the arm trick, he didn't flinch, just grinned a little and nodded.

"Just the arm?" he said. "Anything else?"

I broke a couple of fingers for him and would have shown him everything on the menu if needed, but he held up his hands to show he'd seen enough.

"That doesn't hurt?" he asked.

I shook my head, too nervous to speak, worried that my bright ideas about how I could be useful would get shot down by this man who looked underwhelmed by my demonstration.

"You'll still need to learn some basics before we get you in the ring," he said. "Otherwise you could get injured for real, presuming that's possible."

I told him it was.

He said, "Okay then. We'll put you through a crash course. Gonna be tough. I'm warning you now, so don't claim I didn't later on. But with your trick there, I don't much mind rushing you into a squash or two. Pull a chair up. Let's go over some details."

There are a lot of shady people in the wrestling industry, or at least there were back then. I hear it's better now, but when I was working, man, some of the shitbags I dealt with would tell you a lie that contradicted a different lie they'd just told you ten seconds earlier. Bill wasn't one of those. He told me that I had value as a stunt for a promotion that needed a quick boost. But what I was worth was a little limited because you could only use my trick once, twice at the most, for a few different reasons.

For one, if you're trying to maintain the illusion that it's legit, you can't have somebody snap my arm in half one week and then two weeks or even a month later have me come back like nothing happened. Second, even if I'm on the shelf for a while, you can't just bring me back to do the exact same thing again. You're killing the shock value if you do that. And finally, on a more personal note, if I do the same trick too often in the same territory, I'm liable to be found out by people outside of the business, which brings me back to my earlier concern about ending up on some government scientist's operating table.

Funny how now I don't really mind that idea, which is probably obvious since I agreed to sit down and talk with you. Maybe some of those boys who specialize in surgical war crimes would fuck around and fix me on their way to finding out what makes me like this.

Anyway, back to Bill, the man didn't short me on pay. Not only that, he told me how I'd be of the best use in the business, going from territory to territory, putting over any big bad heels they really wanted the audience to hate. He told me to remember the value I had. I could do one or two shows and effectively still be the story for weeks or even months after my part was done, so I should be paid for what I was worth long-term, not just the one or two appearances. Bill was a good guy. Had a heart attack a few months after I left LA. Was really sad to hear about him passing.

Anyway, after a few months at the gym, where one of the guys gave me the nickname "Crash Test," I made my first appearance at the Olympic. Bill had a good mind for the business. He booked me for two shows. The first, I twist up my ankle on a "bad landing" from a dive from the post. Roll it over nasty enough to where it's clear that my foot's not quite on right, but not so bad that the kids in attendance throw up in their popcorn bags. I was fighting Bruce Dozer that night. Big man, tattooed all over, had a shaved head before it was mainstream. Had a good scowl, gravelly voice. He looked the part of the monster who gets off on injuring people. He'd gone undefeated for three months prior to our match. That night, per the script, the ref sees my ankle twisted up and calls off the match, then waves for the medical staff to help me.

Dozer gets pissed that the match is called a "no-contest" because of my injury, killing his winning streak. He throws the ref and medics out of the ring to get to me. Throws me around a little more and stomps my ankle when I'm down on the mat. The whole time I'm yelling like this man is about to take my foot clean off. Bill, Doc, and the rest of the boys and girls in back told me later how well I sold it. Dozer even said that, for a second, he almost thought I was hurt for real. To cap it off he got the classic metal folding chair and started whaling away on my ankle. By then the fans were booing so loud it sounded like there were five times as many people in attendance as there were. When the top face in the company—Ricky Angel—showed up to save me, those people cheered like an actual angel had come down through the ceiling.

Dozer and Angel had a face-off at the next show—which had about a 20 percent increase in attendance. They said the expected stuff. Dozer said Angel should've stayed out of his business, Angel said he was going to stop Dozer's reign of terror, you know the story. There's only so many stories to tell. Anyway, the week after that, I return in a cast and on crutches. I get a lot of cheers and I cut a promo to tell everyone I appreciate their support, and that I won't let a man like Dozer keep me from living my dream as a pro wrestler.

Of course, Dozer interrupts my interview, blindsides me and goes right for my injured leg. Gives me some more chair shots and stomps, then positions the chair over my cast while I'm laid out on the mat, and delivers a knee drop through the chair that snaps my lower shin. Everyone can see my shin's broken even though the cast hides the worst of it. Bill thought people would freak out if they saw my naked, broken leg. Still, even through the cast it must've looked ugly, because people screamed like they'd seen a man get shot. Some people booed and cussed and shouted, but most of them just hollered like it was an emergency.

I got a great payday, and the Olympic shows saw a boost in attendance for a few months. Dozer beat Angel for the championship, which built up anticipation for a rematch, but unfortunately, Dozer got hurt in a car accident before that second match and was out for the rest of the year. That pretty much killed the story. I was up in Portland by then, getting ready to do my thing up there.

That was my role for the next couple years. The territories were struggling, but they were trying to hold on and were also still pretty isolated, so my gimmick was fresh everywhere I went. To play it safe, each place would either throw a mask on me, or paint my face, or dye my hair, anything to change up my look, just in case. And, of course, I used a different ring name everywhere I went. My role was always the same. Show up and get broken in some graphic and brutal manner that made the local bad guy look like the *worst* guy. Never failed to whip the fans into a frenzy. Sometimes the promoters set it up to keep my injury a little concealed, like Bill did, and other times they just said screw it, show it all.

In Memphis, I let their superheavyweight, Japanese heel do his "sumo drop" on my gut to break my ribs so that they kind of fanned outward. That one was probably a little too far. They stretchered me out and people legit thought I was dying. I had to show up two weeks later to tell the all-American, white-meat hero to make sure he took the title off that "foreign bastard" who'd injured me, even though I looked like I could be the Japanese guy's darker half brother. Really, I was just there to reassure the fans that they hadn't seen a man get murdered two weeks ago.

I had a good run doing what I did. Some of the boys were jealous because I was doing a fraction of the actual wrestling they were doing, but getting paid like I was one of the mid-card guys at worst, and even like the top of the card guys in a couple of territories. Maybe I got a little full of myself, too, but I knew my worth and I wasn't going to let anyone short me. Still, it got to a point where I was making more enemies than friends, so I guess what happened in my last match shouldn't have surprised me.

There was some practical thought behind my demand to finally win a match. It wasn't just ego. I saw the way the tides were turning. The territories were being bought up. Pretty soon the good money would only go to wrestlers who signed with one of the few big promotions left standing. My whole career was built on going from one region to the next, and so on. What was I going to do when there were no regions left? At least none that could pay well.

I needed a home. I wasn't dumb enough to think I could jump on with one of the big promotions right away, but I thought that if I established myself as a real draw in one of the stronger holdouts, I could build up a following and show that I had some value when the buyout came.

I'd had more downtime than the average guy, and I used it to work out and train. I still didn't quite have the physique that was popular at the time—steroids were in, but I didn't trust injecting anything that might not mix well with whatever was going on with me, biologically speaking. I got pretty buff, though, and I learned a decent enough set of moves. Hell, there were champs in some areas whose entire move set was five or six words long, depending on whether or not you hyphenate *body slam*. I didn't think it was crazy for me to be considered a legit wrestler by then.

I had to start getting some victories if I was ever going to be more than a one-off, traveling gimmick, and then a has-been before I even hit thirty. I thought I had enough leverage to politic my way into being booked to go over. Nothing humiliating for my opponent, mind you. Surprise roll-up, one-two-three, I get the win, and then the other guy attacks me to get his heat back. Give me another win in a rematch so that it's not a complete fluke, then have the guy really go ape over losing to me twice. Then we can do a broken limb spot, but by that time I've shown that I can get wins, and when I make a surprise, early return from my injury, showing off some good old guts and gumption, I'll instantly be one of the more popular faces in the promotion.

That's the pitch I made to Teddy Garrett, who ran TCW out of Fort Worth. Teddy was a snuff-chewing, boot-wearing Connecticut native who fancied himself a born-again Texan. The guy he wanted me up against was Blackheart Buckhorn, formerly Big Hank Buckhorn, a lower-card wrestler who had just discovered his dark side on his way to becoming TCW's top bad guy. Teddy was rushing Buckhorn into main-event status, in my opinion, which I know sounds arrogant coming from a guy who hadn't been in the business long, but I stand by that opinion. Buckhorn and Teddy were cousins, though, and that explained the abrupt push toward the top, even though fans were barely reacting to him. Teddy wanted me to come in and do what I do, but I played hardball. I knew just as well as Teddy that I was the surest way to make Buckhorn the top heel in the company. I could make him one of the most hated men in Texas, but they were going to have to do it my way.

We didn't plan or practice much of the match besides the ending. It wouldn't be a very long match, so there wouldn't be much to call in the ring. Some slams, maybe a clothesline, some taunting, a cheap shot from Buckhorn to get the crowd going, and then some surprise offense from me. I was getting good height on my dropkick, and I was looking forward to busting that out. Then Buckhorn would get overeager during his comeback, I'd sneak a roll-up, barely get the pin, and that would be that.

That's mostly how it went, except he kicked out at two on the roll-up.

Obviously I'm biased, but based on what I remember of how hot the crowd was for my offense and my pin attempt, I had the money idea. Those people would've gone crazy for me getting the upset, and they would have despised Buckhorn for attacking me afterward. He'd have been set. Everybody wins. Apparently, he and Teddy didn't see it that way.

I know Teddy was in on it because Buckhorn wouldn't have gone off-script without getting permission. The ref didn't seem confused either. Maybe the guy was just the biggest professional in the business—the show has to go on, after all—but it seemed to me like he knew the kick-out was coming too.

There I was, stuck in the ring with no ally, with a grinning Buckhorn walking toward me, and all I could think of was how Blackheart Buckhorn's real name was Dewey McClendon, and how Dewey had once been an All-District high school wrestler and had spent a few years in the army before being dishonorably discharged. I knew that because he told me so during our brief meetings before the match. "This is a hell of a job I'm doing for you," he'd also said. "You know how this would go in a shoot fight?"

I had no actual combat training. I'd built all my aspirations around being breakable. What I should have done at that moment was slide out of the ring and head for the exit. But I was still in denial. I hoped that Dewey, who wasn't playing "Buckhorn" anymore, had just screwed up the finish of the match and would call a spot to make it right.

He put me in a "sleeper hold" that was really a legit rear-naked choke, which I'm guessing he learned in the service. He whispered, "You're gonna wake up in a world of hurt," and that's when I understood that choking me out wasn't going to be the end of it. If he just wanted to shoot pin me or kick my ass, he wouldn't need me unconscious for that. I guess he wouldn't need me unconscious to break some bones either, but it would make it a lot easier.

I thought, *You stupid fuck, I have to be in on it for it to work*, but I was still fooling myself even up to that last second. Dewey and Teddy didn't care about how I did what I did or what the aftermath would be for me. They were putting me in my place, on behalf of themselves and anyone else who wasn't happy with my pay and recent demands.

Now, had I been thinking clearly, I probably would have told myself that being choked out and dealing with broken bones that I couldn't self-heal might not be so bad compared to what I was about to do. But I was starting to black out a bit, and I was feeling betrayed and emotional and overwhelmed by the situation.

There's also that lack of impulse control I mentioned before.

I twisted my body around, breaking my own neck in the process, so that my head was on backward. The sound of it was crazy. One of those really loud, bright snaps of thunder you hear when the lightning is too close. The ref screamed right away. I pushed away from Dewey, and he yelped and pushed me down. I fell on my front, and an arena full of people got a clear look at my upturned, should-be-face-down face. They got to screaming in pretty good earnest, but they found out how loud they could really scream when I started to get up.

I was pretty scared. I'd never broken my neck before. Fixing myself was a manual process, and if I had just fucked myself up to the point of not being able to use my arms again, then I'd just fucked myself up permanently. So pushing myself up was just me trying to make sure I could still do it. I wasn't thinking about how it would look to everyone who had every reason to think I should be paralyzed at the minimum.

About halfway up I was already getting dizzy, and I soon realized that walking around with my head on backward was going to present a challenge. Man was not meant to be looking in reverse while going forward.

I settled on crawling on all fours and sort of leaning my head down, upside down, hair sliding across the mat as I put one hand in front of the other, then followed with my feet. I moved toward Dewey, who had backed into a corner like an idiot in a horror movie, which is behavior based more on reality than people understand. A certain level of fear can short-circuit anyone's ability to make good decisions. I, for example, had just broken my damn neck out of panic. Now Dewey was standing by the turnbuckles with his arms out, telling me not to come closer, instead of just making an easy escape through the ring ropes.

All of his bravado had vanished. It's one thing to be ready to see a man's limbs broken. It's something else to see a man who should be dead—or at least paralyzed—crawling toward you with a smile on his upside-down face.

The sound of the crowd screaming sort of turned into a song to me. I might have been a bit out of my mind at the moment, but I swear I heard this weird harmony in the way they screamed. The noise rose and fell and rose, people cutting loose, catching their breaths, then cutting loose again. Some were yelling for somebody to help me, others yelled for someone to stop me. Some called out to Jesus and others cried out that I must be the devil.

The best part of it was seeing Dewey unable to make a sound. When I got too close, he finally tried to get away. His legs failed him as if he were a giant toddler, and he fell on his ass. I had a good laugh at that and came even closer to him now that we were about at eye level, and it was clear as day that his heart might burst if I managed to touch him. He managed to roll out of the ring under the bottom rope before I got to him. I didn't go after him. I turned around to find the ref, who I presumed had been behind me the whole time, but I was alone in the ring. He must've fled right away. No other refs or medics came down to check on me the way they normally would for a shoot injury.

I figured this would probably be the only time I'd get a moment to myself in the ring to bask in the roar of a packed house. I got to my feet very carefully, stood tall, spread my arms wide, closed my eyes, and soaked it in. The noise they made is still the loudest thing I've ever heard.

This being the eighties it was possible for footage to get lost, and that footage was probably tossed into a fire before the last fan left the arena. I guess all you can do is take my word for what happened. Teddy's passed. I know Dewey and that ref wouldn't want to discuss it, and nobody else could give you the inside details of what happened. But it shouldn't be too hard to take me at my word, given what you see of me here.

Maybe I should have spent more time trying to understand my ability, rather than just experimenting with it, but looking back I don't know where I'd even begin with that. Hell, I'm still not sure if getting stuck this way was a result of something I accidentally shut off when I broke my neck or the result of me not having the nerve to fix myself. On the one hand, I'm not any kind of paralyzed, so it's not a conventional break. On the other hand, any time I try to right myself I feel a real bad pain that I hadn't ever felt before when I put my parts back in order. When I feel that pain, I get scared that I'm not going to do it right.

Lucky for me, I hadn't burned every bridge I crossed in the business. Dozer still liked me and felt like he owed me for getting him over back in LA. Maybe he also thought Wild Bill would've wanted somebody to help me out. Once he heard about what happened, he came to Texas, brought me back to LA, and let me crash at his place while he made some calls.

Back when he was touring Japan, he met a horror movie director named Hiroshi who was making some grimy stuff at the time. That guy loved me at first sight. Cast me as the title creature in this movie series called *Trap of the Devastated Man*, which had a pretty good run overseas. The remake in the States didn't do well. They went with computer effects when I didn't answer their attempts to contact me, but since Hiroshi looked out for me and got me a small percentage to go along with my salary from the first movie, I still got paid. That's evergreen income right there. Every time some channel or streaming service picks up the rights or renews them, I get a deposit. It's not a king's ransom, but it's good enough money that I don't have to go find work if I keep living humbly, which is good for me. I like being outdoors, getting outside on my little bit of property up here, but I'm not always good on a jobsite, for obvious reasons.

Anyway, I knew the time to tell my story would come. I'm surprised it took this long for someone like you to track me down. People stopped protecting the business and pretending there wasn't a script a long time ago. I figured folks would drop some clues about me here and there. Maybe not even people who worked with me directly, but ones who had been in the business at the time and heard all the rumors about Crash Test Chris. Hard story to believe, but a harder one to keep to yourself.

I want your audience to know I'm in good spirits. I don't want people thinking I'm sour about any of it. I've adjusted to my condition pretty well, I'd say, and I think I've got at least as many good memories from my time in the business as I do bad ones. Hell, depending on how well this is received, I might see if anyone wants to book me for a convention. Pose for some photos, tell a few more stories if people are interested. Maybe even see if I could get booked for one last match in one of these new promotions. Finally get that win that Dewey and Teddy stole from me.

That would be something.

THE HAPPY PEOPLE

Laugh through the pain. No matter how immense, how pure, how total, you must find a way to laugh through it. Summon every joy you've ever known as if it's your final defense, because it is, and laugh. Don't just make the sound. Laugh like you mean it. That's what the doctor had taught her and Tate, through two years of meticulous, literally torturous trials.

The man who'd taken her from her car after she left the bar late, the one time—the *one* damn time—she turned down the offer from one of the bouncers to walk her out. The man who'd taken Tate from who knew where, and who knew how, because Tate never told her, because it probably embarrassed him, the male ego being what it is. But that man, the doctor, the do-gooder, the believer, dreamer, torturer, and murderer, that man had taught them the secret to nigh-invulnerability. Virtual immortality.

Laugh through the pain.

Tate had failed at this, ultimately, and fell to pieces crying in her arms, countless cuts, gouges, contusions, and more catching up to him all at once. Four years of damage in total, counting the two they'd spent as the doctor's subjects and the next two that they'd spent on the road, trying to find someone else to partner with them. Help them survive. He'd been shot through the chest, drilled through the lungs, battered with a hammer, slashed across the eyes, burned over half of his body, and had not only survived it all but had healed himself simply by doing what the doctor had taught them. Until he couldn't anymore.

A twinge of guilt, for not being able to pull him from his despair in time, slipped past her happiness, and she felt an old, deep injury reforming within her. She managed to choke up a chuckle before the damage reached her heart, and the ticklishness of the wound's reversal made her laugh harder, hastening the healing process.

The police sirens that had sounded distant seconds earlier were concerningly close now. Concern and curative happiness didn't naturally cohabit well, but she'd found a way to make them work together. Both, in her case, operated in service of self-preservation. The concern motivated her to get moving. She couldn't just sit here in the bloody, unseamed mess that had been Tate.

The girls who had escaped had given authorities the exact location of the house, the cops had made their way this far out, into the countryside and up the hill to one of the doctor's old houses, and all the while Farrah had just sat there. Her clothes soaking in Tate's blood, her mind adrift in the good times they'd had. And there *were* good times. Enough to balance out the considerable challenges, such as the forced nature of their pairing, and the need for them to sleep in shifts, in case one slipped into a nightmare that threatened to make all their old wounds resurface and reopen. The inability to resume a normal life, the realization that they had to stay by each other's side to keep their spirits up, and the darker revelation they came to on their own that to better ensure their survival, and make sure all their suffering hadn't been for nothing, they needed to recruit others.

They spent a lot of time and energy searching for someone through trial and error—like the doctor did—who had the right genetics, disposition, and pain tolerance, and just the right reaction to his drug cocktail. Someone who wouldn't have a choice but to join them and help share and ease the responsibility of positivity, especially as they helped them find others to join their group.

That process had been the worst of it. Laughing through her own pain wasn't easy. Laughing through the cutting, bludgeoning, and burning she had to administer to others was several degrees more difficult. Particularly because she and Tate never found someone else like them. Someone who responded to the "treatment" well. That only amplified the nightmares, and made it harder to persist, which in turn only fed the urgency of the situation and demanded that they try more frequently, leading to more dead people, and on it went. When the screams of others started overwhelming her own in her dreams, she knew she and Tate had both gone too far and also couldn't stop going. Quite the contrary, they had to speed up.

Still, in spite of the toll this took on them, they'd made the most of their situation and condition. They'd found time each day to sing some, dance some, trade corny jokes, enjoy life. They weren't a couple, but they were a pair. They were closer than siblings. Tate was the only person in the world who understood what she was and why she had to do what she did, and now he was gone. Practically disassembled. Split, pierced, and broken in dozens of places.

The time for reminiscing about him was over, and should have been over several minutes ago at least. Farrah had to go on.

She stood, grabbed the knife on the floor that Tate had been carving up one of the girls with. Then she removed the surgical drill embedded in his cheekbone, just under his right eye.

Farrah couldn't admit to herself now that she wasn't sure whether she wanted to live or die anymore. How long would she make it without a partner to wake her up at the first sign of her skin fissuring while she twisted and groaned through another hideous dream? Maybe she'd figure that out, somehow, or maybe it wasn't worth waiting to see if she could. She couldn't think on that now, but she could let the police on the scene effectively decide if she was going to have a chance.

A bullet in the brain, at a high enough caliber or placed well enough, would shut her off. Hard to summon happy thoughts when one's thinker has a hole in it.

She wasn't just going to turn herself over to them, though, much less give them an easy target. She might not have been sure of how she could continue, and whether it was worth trying, but that didn't mean she was ready to give up. If that were the case, she'd be a pile of rent remains resting beside Tate's.

Two stories below, she heard the front door creak as it was pushed fully open, then heard one of the officers announce himself.

She could have left the house through the back and run into the surrounding woods and had a decent chance of escaping, especially if she had taken off when she should have, but now she planned to take advantage of this moment. Either prove how much of a survivor she was or see all of her own pain and all of the killing she was responsible for go to waste with a shot to her skull.

The officers on the scene might take her down, but she was going to make them earn it.

I got her, didn't I?

He was sure that he had, and he hadn't been the first. Richards and Sampson had put rounds through the Black woman in the blood-caked white dress. She had waved to them with a knife in her hand at the top of the house's main staircase. It was a justified use of force given her condition and refusal to drop the weapon as ordered. And what had been in her other hand? Some kind of drill? That last question wasn't as important to Officer Lake right now. The only question that mattered was one he was trying to answer in the affirmative just by asking.

I got her, didn't I?

After Sampson and Richards flooded her with shots, aiming at center mass, the largest target that would stop an assailant, as they were trained to do, the woman had wheezed out a giggle at them, then quickly backed up through a darkened doorway into a room with no windows. They couldn't spot her after she got a few feet inside, and they were slow to react because she should have dropped and fell forward down the stairs, but instead she'd laughed and stepped away.

She had to be on something, but what? Lake had heard a couple of stories, even before enrolling in the academy, about people who absorbed bullets and kept moving because they were on coke or PCP or something. He'd even seen a video online once of a man marching through four point-blank shots to his torso while shouting wildly, along with a link to the news story that verified this was a legitimate incident. He knew this was possible, but somehow this felt unreal to him. A step beyond that, actually. He felt like he'd awakened to a world where physics and biology had warped.

There was an old short story in a faded, torn paperback that his dad loved, a story called "Something Passed Through" that he read when he was young because he wondered why his dad reread this book to the point of it coming apart. The pages occupied by that story had the most folds and stains and were the most worn, so he started there, and then couldn't read anything else because the story was too strange to him. It talked about a version of Earth where, as the title said, some unknown, cosmic disturbance had passed through the planet and upended the laws of nature. Water was combustible; gasoline was drinkable; invisible, giant fists made of pure gravity could pulverize a city block without notice; miniature vortices that sucked all of the atmosphere out of an area could appear out of nowhere in a room in your house. So on and so forth. Lake felt like he was living in that reality now.

Ten to twelve .357 rounds from a peace officer's sidearm could tear chunks out of a woman standing about thirty feet away, at most, and not incapacitate her. Not drop her. Not keep her from laughing it off. What the hell was going on?

They should have waited for backup to arrive then. They could easily explain that after she went into the room, they had no way of knowing what kind of arsenal she might have in there. Yes, the emergency call they'd received described the assailant as being armed only with knives, but that was only what the survivors saw. Maybe this sicko was waiting to use the rifles and semiautomatic pistols on law enforcement. Maybe they were more interested in carving up their captives but wouldn't hesitate to break out the firepower when they got raided.

Whether or not that was the case was a moot point now. Sampson and Richards had rushed ahead, probably thinking the woman had barely made it through the doorway before collapsing, even though the sound of her body hitting the hardwood would have echoed through the large house. Lake knew this but couldn't find the words to articulate it in time to stop his colleagues from going ahead. You can get trained for any number of situations, you can psych yourself up, you can try to be prepared, but you can't really know what you might do until the moment comes.

In the moment, Sampson and Richards made a mistake. Some cops make a mistake that gets somebody else killed, and others make one that will be their last. This was a case of the latter.

When Richards made it to the doorway, he thought to stop for a moment, try to wait on one side of the opening, against the wall, so his colleagues could catch up. This made a certain amount of sense, factoring in that he shouldn't have gone up the stairs in the first place. The woman's arm whipped around the doorframe almost like it was boneless, the long knife she brandished landing in Richards's neck with shocking precision, pinning him to the wall like decoration. He got one more shot off at nothing, then dropped the gun to try to pull the knife free but lost most of his strength before his hand even got to the handle.

Sampson rushed up to help him, screaming Richards's name, then screaming for Lake to help without looking back, just knowing that the younger officer wasn't moving, even though Lake was about three-quarters up the stairway.

The woman emerged from the room as Sampson got to Richards, holding something that looked for a moment like a gun, to Lake, but not an ordinary one. It was silver and smooth and looked like something from a future imagined by a 1950s science-fiction writer. Then he remembered she'd been holding a drill. Not one that would be used by a carpenter or handyman, but one that looked like it should be in a scientist's hand. Were there scientist-specific drills? How did his head have space right now for a question like that?

Because time moves strangely in a situation like this. Things happen quickly, but your mind finds a way to slow it down just enough for the odd thought to come across, sometimes one that's helpful, sometimes one that's just random. When he'd been younger, and considerably dumber, Lake found himself fighting with another man holding a knife, wrestling in the parking lot of his apartment complex, all over a girl that didn't really like either of them that much. Lake managed to hold the man off and get the fight back to standing while another car crept by slowly, the driver's-side window down like they were just gawking at a roadside accident. Lake had told the driver, "Call the cops, this guy's trying to kill me!"

His attacker had shouted back, "No, I'm not. I'm just defending myself. He's got a gun!"

"Look, just call the cops either way, it's like a Solomon and the baby thing," Lake had said. Which hadn't been an apt comparison, but his mind had slowed the situation down enough for him to at least try to explain the situation in a way that he hoped would make sense to the driver.

The cops did show up shortly after, so maybe his comparison had been effective, or maybe one of the other people in the apartment complex heard the commotion and dialed 9-1-1 instead. Whatever the case, that moment had stuck with him, and it flashed through his mind again here, for perspective, alongside the oddball thought of whether scientists had their own, specially made drills, because he thought both things were about equal or somewhat related. Just random things he'd have never considered outside of specific, arduous circumstances.

The sound of the drill bit chewing skin, pulverizing bone, and shredding tissue pushed any other thoughts out of Lake's mind as the woman pushed the drill through Sampson's temple. Sampson screamed for a second as he fired one last shot, pumping a bullet through the woman's hip, which she barely flinched at. As the bit went deeper into his skull and started pulping part of his brain, Sampson's scream transformed into a weird "uh-uh-uh-uh" noise, like he was trying to mimic a dumb kid who couldn't answer the teacher's question and a stuttering motor at the same time.

Lake lifted his gun at the woman and fired. Four shots, each higher than the last. One near her waist, one through her ribs, one through her armpit, the last through her shoulder and into her mouth, blowing several of her teeth out.

Had he been thinking clearly, maybe he would have remembered every zombie movie he'd ever seen, every comic book about the walking dead he'd ever read, and thought, *The brain, go for the brain, shoot her in the goddamn brain!* But he wasn't thinking clearly. He was thinking, *I got her, didn't I?*

Keep firing, another part of him screamed, but he couldn't reconcile that with what he knew ought to be true. She ought to be down. She ought to be dead.

I got her I know I got her I got her didn't I? I got her I got her I—

The woman leaped down the stairs like she wasn't concerned with what might happen to her. She tackled Lake as he got two more shots off. He didn't see where they landed, but—

I got her, didn't I? I got her, didn't I?

He heard a crack that made him think one of the wooden boards he landed on at the bottom of the stairs had snapped in half, then he tried to shove the woman away from him and found himself unable to move. The immediate disconnection from his body was bizarre because up until this moment he'd been able to gauge his fear by how hard and quickly his heart was beating, but now he couldn't feel that. In his mind, his heart must be racing, but so far as he could tell right now, he had no heart. He had no arms or legs. He had eyes to blink and lips that could open and close, and that seemed to be about it. He must have still been breathing because it didn't feel like he was suffocating, but he couldn't feel his lungs inflate. He couldn't tell he had anything below his neck.

The woman hovered over him. Not literally, but it seemed like it, since he couldn't feel any pressure from her body on him.

She floated there, and she grinned through her broken mouth, and the strangest, most maddening thing yet happened. The teeth he'd just shot out started growing back before his eyes. A steady flow of her blood spilled onto his face, into his mouth, and down his throat against his will, until her facial injury healed with unnatural speed.

A burbling chuckle replaced the blood flow that had spilled out of her mouth. This grew into heartier, louder laughter that went on for somewhere between several seconds and seven hundred years, he couldn't tell, but it made him want to laugh with her, at the absurdity of all of this if nothing else. Fear felt more tethered to his central nervous system than mirth. Fear was associated with a pulse rate, gooseflesh, hairs standing up, but amusement? That was just in your head.

The corners of Lake's lips turned up into a smile almost against his will, and what followed finally broke his mind.

He heard something in his neck snap, like a magnetic puzzle piece finding its place, and almost immediately after, he could feel his heartbeat again. He felt himself breathing. He thought to move his fingers and thought he could, although he was still pinned in too awkward a position to see it. Sensing it was enough, though. It made him deliriously giddy. He'd just been coming to grips with being paralyzed while a woman who should have been dead twelve times over magically, inexplicably healed right in front of him, and now, now there was at least a *tingling* in his toes and fingertips again.

He never could have understood how good it was to feel that again until after he'd been severed from it.

It made him laugh a little. Just a little. But then the woman's laughter got that much louder at the sound of his laughter. A different level of delight flooded her eyes, to the point they became watery, and what was that about? He would have asked her if his mind had been functioning properly. His brain was fully operational, but his *mind*, the thing governed by consciousness, not strict biology, was still a long way from where it had been before he'd gotten the call to come to this house to find the person who'd attempted to murder those girls. The killer who had survived, who lay atop him now, laughing herself to tears.

The happy lady.

Why are you so happy? he wanted to ask her.

How are you still alive? he wanted to ask her.

What's so funny?

He didn't ask any of these things, because even as he recovered now, he was still stuck on the last question he'd had before the woman launched herself at him, knocked him down the stairs and broke his neck.

"I got you, didn't I?" he said.

"You did," she answered, then raised the drill she still held and pressed it to the center of his forehead.

The tingling in his toes and fingers was spreading through the rest of the muscles in his legs and arms, but not quickly enough for him to do anything about the drill going into his head.

I'm sorry, but I don't know you.

She wasn't just apologizing to the officer, but to herself as well, because this was what she'd been waiting for. This was what she and Tate had been working for. To find someone like them. Someone who could laugh through the pain and heal from almost anything.

Someone she could trust. That was the problem.

She didn't know this man. She hadn't spent any time with him. The doctor had kept her and Tate locked up for months before his experiment proved effective, and then several months afterward as well, just to be sure. Just to win them over, and on the day he set them free they had butchered him to repay all the pain he'd caused.

This cop could do the same to her the moment she shut her eyes or just turned her head from him. Payback for making him this way, and for killing his partners. Or he might be grateful and understanding after she explained everything to him, but she couldn't risk that.

I'm sorry, I'm so sorry, but I don't know you.

What she did know now, though, was that the selection process could be so much simpler than it had been before. It was a shame she and Tate hadn't thought of it. So many deaths and nightmares could have been avoided.

They were trying to find someone who would respond well to the doctor's drug, someone with the right genetics. Well, the drug was in her blood, and, obviously, so was her DNA. She didn't understand how this worked. She wasn't a doctor, and right now, not for the first time, she wished she and Tate hadn't impulsively killed the man, but at least she had an idea of what to do now. She and Tate had tried to replicate the doctor's trial-and-error process, but the idea of giving someone else their blood hadn't occurred to them. But here she'd spilled her DNA into this officer's mouth and had seen the effect in less than a minute.

Now she knew the way. She could do this again, just with someone she could take her time with. Build trust with.

"I'm sor—"

She started to apologize to him as the drill dug into his head, but that sentiment wasn't very happy, was it? No, she could tell by the way her teeth started to crack again, remembering the gunshot that shattered them, that this wasn't what she should be thinking, much less saying.

The officer tried to buck his hips to thrust her off him, like a mechanical bull running on 1 percent of its power. This helped her see the humor in things again. Life was full of strange, funny, happy moments, no matter what was going on, if you knew where to look, and the right perspective to look from.

Farrah laughed and pressed the drill down and was looking forward to finding someone new, someone she could trust as much as she'd trusted Tate, well before the man beneath her stopped squirming and lay dead.

DEAD BASTARD REVIVAL SERVICES

Twenty-five people had gathered in the small church to witness the resurrection of Lyle Lee Everly and partake in his reckoning. The oldest among them was seventy-five. The youngest sixteen. Seven women, eighteen men. All present had held a weapon.

Blunt instruments mostly. Baseball bats, hammers, crowbars. One large, industrious man had used rolls of duct tape to bind five rebars, then had hammered one end of the cluster into a slimmer shaft, forming the handle for a crude club.

Tomas and Dina had forbidden anyone from bringing a firearm and had discouraged using anything sharp. "Cut too deep, or cut something off, and there's a chance you might release him," Dina had said, although her actual concern was with people hurting each other in a frenzy once things commenced. It was a hell of a lot easier—and generally more harmful—to accidentally cut someone than it was to mistakenly hit them. A nicked vein could let a lot more blood than the average person might suspect, to say nothing of an artery, and such an accident would be bad for business.

The man who brought a large bowie knife swore he only wanted to "take it to his eyes. Maybe skin him a little bit." But he promised no hacking or slashing, no wild swooping motions. Dina supposed she could live with that.

Truth was, there was no chance that any of the people in the church could do anything to release Lyle Everly back into the After. The electrical network that would soon bind him to the humanoid, robotic vessel was too sturdy and intricate to be undone, even by cutting the power cord. Once he entered the vessel, Lyle Everly would be stuck there until the programming ran its course in three days, the expiration date for the vessel's rental. The program would then automatically run the commands to set him free.

The twenty-five parishioners of the Old Rugged Cross Baptist Church gathered around the inanimate machine, which spent most of its days resting in a storage locker labeled "DB-One." It was shackled at the wrists, forearms, calves, and ankles to a large metal armchair near the altar of the church.

At ten minutes to midnight, the heat of the day lingered. Such was the South in the summer. Dina was sweating like she'd run a marathon. How people down here could stand these temperatures was a mystery to her. She was looking forward to getting back to Seattle after this was over.

For the third time in five minutes, a member of the congregation approached her and asked, "Where is he?"

"He'll be here soon," she said.

There is always money in breaking the law. No matter how much a civilization might evolve, how advanced and enlightened it might become, how grand its discoveries, there are always laws—natural and man-made—and always profit waiting for violators of those laws. Those with the means and privilege to do this on a grand scale, and for an extended time period, could make a fortune.

Tomas contemplated this while holding a man's soul between his thumb and forefinger.

The drive containing Lyle Lee Everly's ghost looked like a small, opaque vial, four inches long, two inches wide. A USB plug stuck out from one end. Through the clear plastic covering, Tomas watched a dense mist swirl and rush in search of an exit. He held it closer, squinted, tried to make out a face, a mouth, any identifiable feature. He listened for a scream.

Spirits looked human—or rather like sentient smoke impersonating a human—out in their element, in the After. They had voices there too. Here, confined to the illicit technology developed to imprison them, the spirits had no form and no means of expression. They could not plead or beg. They could not rage. Not in a way that would reach anyone, at least.

It all comes back to this, Tomas thought. The detection of souls, the discovery of an afterlife, and the realization that death is a form of liberation. These discoveries had redefined the meaning of life and existence, even as they produced a thousand new questions to go along with a handful of answers. The unveiling of the After had changed everything. Science, religion, politics, business, ecology, and economy. And yet, for all of that, it all came down to this. Law and crime. Opportunity and profit.

How large could he and Dina grow this enterprise to be? There were certain logistic limitations. Upkeep of machinery, the tools necessary to both breach the wall dividing the living world from the After and to rip a ghost away from its new natural habitat, as well as the worn and torn robots used to temporarily cage a captive spirit when the time came to deliver the service they provided.

Then there was the matter of finding clientele. Their operation wasn't designed to have "repeat customers," although one person, a grieving father, had recently reached back out to them about getting a chance to do it over again. Still, he was the only one. The others, Tomas thought, felt either enough satisfaction or too much shame to even want to think about what they'd done, much less repeat it. The extreme illegality of their operation also made it difficult for people to find them, as well as for him and Dina to find buyers.

At least their "product" would never be in short supply. The After had a surplus of dead, deserving bastards.

When he and Dina died one day, would the spirits on the other side know them? Would they be able to do anything to them? Would most of them even consider what they did wrong?

On this side, that matter was settled. Without a proper license, afforded to fewer than five hundred researchers worldwide, any deliberate interaction with a spirit was illegal. Actually, trying to contain one was a "Class X" felony—the only one of its kind—recognized by the majority of the world's governments, and punishable by life imprisonment at an undisclosed facility rumored to be uniquely unpleasant by design.

In a way, it felt as though witch hunts had returned, except this new, modern "witchcraft" had scientific roots, and many of the old occultist tools and tactics, like Ouija boards and séances, were seen as quaint. Technically against the law, yes, but not nearly as concerning as the methods that employed technology. That had proven results.

That let you hold a dead murderer's ghost in what amounted to a digital vial.

Tomas looked at his watch. Close to midnight. He got out of his car and walked to the church.

Pastor Jackson—"Pastor Junior" to his congregation—stood in the foyer of Old Rugged Cross Baptist looking at a portrait of his father. "Pastor Senior" smiled forever through the oil painting, his hair a grandfatherly gray, his eyes full and sparkling despite being painted dark on a flat canvas. Jackson Junior had been his father's mirror image through much of his adult life. In the six years since the Discovery, and the two years following Lyle Everly's rampage, stress and insomnia had ravaged him. He was a hollow, narrow shade of his former self, and of his father. Bald and feeble. Weary.

His people had lost faith in the wake of Lyle Everly's attack. Maybe they could have coped with Lyle Everly's attack in a more "Christian" manner if they knew that the nine children he had gunned down on the playground were resting in the everlasting arms of the Lord and that Everly would burn in a molten lake for eternity. But all they heard on the news about this "After" seemed to indicate that spirits just roamed Earth. If scientists had proof of an afterlife, then where was the proof of heaven? Where was hell? Why couldn't they find that? Why had Lyle Everly's spirit been allowed to roam the woods he'd fled to after the shooting? The place where he'd eaten the last bullet in his gun, allegedly with a smile on his face, though no one was present to verify that last detail.

People claimed to have heard him snickering out in those woods, however. They heard him taunt them about the murdered children, brag about how he'd been "brave" enough to end things on his own terms, to set himself "free," and chide them for not having the courage to do the same when this life had no meaning.

A congregation that had been two hundred strong six years ago was down to thirty-nine true believers. Thirty-nine who had faith that their Lord lived inside of them. They believed that the After must be a waiting room; that heaven was a place still too luminous and splendid for living men to observe, even with their science and instruments. But even within the small group of thirty-nine, there had been a schism. Only twenty-five believed they had the right to exact God's retribution.

To Me belongeth vengeance. Deuteronomy.

Echoed in Romans and Hebrews: *It is Mine to avenge; I will repay*.

Passages in the New Testament warned to never render evil unto evil. The word of the Lord was clear.

And yet, if God lived within them all, then surely His vengeance could be exacted through His followers.

Sister Beulah, effectively the matriarch of the church at seventy-seven years old, had called upon Pastor Jackson to explain 1 Samuel 16:14. *An evil spirit from the Lord tormented him.*

"Pastor, you say don't pay evil back with evil—"

"I don't say it, Sister, the *Lord* says—"

"God Himself sent an evil spirit to torment Saul. God Himself created and has domain over all, and that includes evil, and He may be calling upon us to do it. Have you thought of that?"

Junior lacked the conviction to argue with the older woman, especially when she had the backing of the majority of the congregation. The twenty-five in the church tonight believed that if what they were doing was wrong, it was still justified in the eyes of God, and to hold what remained of his church together, heaven forgive him, Pastor Jackson Jr. let them believe it. Not only that, he gave them permission to use the church as the site for their vengeance. He wondered if his father would have done the same.

Behind him, the front doors opened. In stepped Tomas. He was a stout man who looked like he could stomp his feet through concrete and root himself deep enough to stand upright through a hurricane. He had a closely shaved beard, small eyes, black hair. There was a primal brutality in the way he carried himself. It made him look like the living counterargument to the axiom "Violence never solves anything."

In short, to Pastor Junior, he looked more like a man who made a living beating debts out of gambling addicts than one who used code and circuits to trap apparitions. The pastor supposed he shouldn't judge the man like that but told himself it was fine because Tomas was surely judging him.

"Are they inside?" Tomas asked.

The pastor swallowed and nodded.

"And everything is ready?"

Another nod. "Yes, I think so. Your partner said it's all set up."

Tomas said no more, leaving the foyer and opening the double doors to enter the church hall. Numbness overtook Pastor Junior. This was happening. This madness was the world he lived in now. He turned back to the portrait of his father and tried to remember the last time he'd said a prayer when no one was watching.

"How the hell can they afford this?" Tomas whispered, looking around the interior of the church, which lived up to the first two words of its name: *old* and *rugged*.

The town of Myersville, Mississippi, didn't make much of an impression, even in passing. Every building near the church was a husk that jobs and commerce had left long ago. Most of the houses around town—the ones that weren't boarded up and empty—were presentable, at least, but not enough to make up for the evidence elsewhere that Myersville was on its deathbed.

"The people in here pitched in to raise enough for the deposit," Dina said. "But the rest was donated by somebody with money a couple of towns over."

"Did this donor understand what we do?"

"Oh yes," Dina said. "He made sure he knew. Get this—it was the guy's own uncle."

Dina pointed at the flash drive. Tomas looked at it, exhaled a low, breathy whistle. "Shit. If your own people think you've got it coming …"

"Yeah. Let's get started."

Tomas handed Dina the flash drive, and she plugged it into a port in the lowest cervical vertebrae of the vessel's spine.

The man with the makeshift rebar club stepped from the crowd, which kept its distance to let Dina and Tomas work. The man asked, "Hey, are you about to … Is it time?"

"Just give us another second," Dina said. "Step back, please."

Dina turned the flash drive in the port like a key, locking it into place. The mist inside was vacuumed into the machine. After a final spot-check of the cords connected to her tablet, Dina walked to the laptop placed on the altar behind her. A few more members of the congregation tentatively approached the vessel. Tomas held out a hand, and they stopped like he was a traffic guard. "Just another moment, please."

The indicator light at the base of the machine's spine ebbed blue, indicating it was awaiting final input. With a few taps on the tablet, and subsequent password entries, Dina executed her homemade program, "DBRez.exe."

The vessel's fingers twitched.

The congregation murmured, curious at first, then excited as the DB-One's skeletal hands opened wide and vibrated. Its chest heaved, its back arched. The head turned left, right, fell back, looked straight. The entire body settled in and rested for a moment, then suffered a violent spasm. A strange wailing emanated from the mouthless metal face, traveled around the church, surrounded everyone. The wailing carried disparate words spoken by multiple, overlapping voices that belonged to the same person.

Where …

Trapped!

I can't see!

Where did everything go!

I can't move!

I was free!

I'm trapped!

For the few present who had either known Lyle Lee Everly when he was alive, or who had heard his spirit in the woods, his voice was unmistakable.

"It's him," a woman said. "They really did it. It really is him."

"It really *is*," another man said.

The sixteen-year-old started to back away toward the door, but Sister Beulah reached out and took his hand, squeezed it to infuse him with the strength to stay.

Dina calmly entered another command into her tablet, which had an easier user interface than the laptop. The command made Everly's multiple voices congeal into one. He stuttered at first. His spirit was unused to having a physical form again, particularly one made of metal and plastic, and crafted with the facsimile of a central nervous system. A network of optical fibers transmitted mixed messages to the CPU acting as the spirit's "brain."

Breathe, the brain commanded, then reminded Everly that he had no lungs.

Look around. But he was eyeless.

Can you hear? it asked, knowing he could not.

Then the CPU compensated for these missing parts, artificially replicating enough of Everly's senses to let him perceive his surroundings. It burdened him with the illusion of sensation. Lyle Lee Everly could see—through the optical receptors in DB-One's head—the translucent hologram of his skin covering his new, artificial body. He felt the cold shackles on his wrists when he should not have been able to do so. And though he had no heart, he felt his pulse race.

"Let me go," Everly said. "This can't be … I can't be here! I was *free*! Let me go!"

The congregation stood in awe. Tomas and Dina stepped away. They were both seasoned enough to know what came next.

The man with the knife—Damon MacArthur, a mechanic and father of a twelve-year-old boy who had survived the attack with permanent brain damage—stepped forward. "You ain't going nowhere, you son of a bitch."

The body thrashed and struggled, but its bindings were secure, and the spirit had no hope of successfully operating this crude form anyway. Where once there had been awe and curiosity among the crowd of twenty-five, now there was intensifying anger.

"You killed my little sister," said the teenage boy still holding Sister Beulah's hand.

The heavy man with the rebar club, Brother Mathis, spoke up next. "You *thought* you got away. You thought you could escape judgment. But the Lord has seen you back to us, boy! And we *are* His vengeance! 'If any mischief follow, then thou shalt give life for life, eye for eye, tooth for tooth, hand for hand ...'"

"Amen!"

"Tell him!"

"'... foot for foot. *Burning for burning!*'" Tears streaked his face. He trembled and could not finish, so Beulah did for him.

"Wound for wound! *STRIPE FOR STRIPE!*"

Lyle Everly, his voice stretched thin and needle sharp, pleaded, "Let me go!"

Damon MacArthur came forward and jabbed his knife into the recessed eye sockets. The blade didn't penetrate the Plexiglas ocular lens, but Everly's spirit screamed nonetheless. A pain beyond anything a living person could experience enveloped Lyle Everly, a pain never meant to exist. Damon pressed the tip forward as hard as he could, twisted it, and smiled, a mad display of gratification. The congregation cheered. Then they closed in. Tomas and Dina quietly exited.

The sound of it broke him. Pastor Jackson Jr. knew that this was the last defeat he could stand. He'd failed to bolster the faith of those who'd left the church six years ago, but he'd done a greater disservice to the ones who had stayed. Here in the house of God they whooped and howled with glee and fury as they did the unthinkable and violated the sacrosanct.

Lyle Everly was excrement who deserved to suffer in hell. But the members of Rugged Cross weren't meant for such deeds. They were not meant to be evil spirits from the Lord. But here they were, tearing apart a human *soul*. This was beyond criminal. Beyond sin. And it was his fault for entertaining the notion, much less permitting them to take it this far.

"Pastor?"

He turned. It was the woman, Dina. "We'll be back in three days to pick it up. If anything goes wrong in the meantime, particularly if anyone comes asking around, call us *immediately*. You have the number?"

Pastor Jackson wanted to hurl something at her and Tomas. Demand that they leave and take that God-forsaken thing they'd brought into his church along with them. But it was too late for that. And what was he anymore? Certainly no one with the strength to stand up for what he believed was right.

"Yes," he said, "I do."

Dina and Tomas offered him polite parting nods, then left.

Two days later, Pastor Jackson Templeton Jr. woke up, dressed in the Sunday best stretched out on his bed, held his Bible clutched to his chest, and waited for the half bottle of sleeping pills he had swallowed to usher him into the After.

Before he passed, he prayed, "Please, please, *please* let me stay dead."

XII
১২
יב
ΔII
12
١٢
十二

ABOUT THE AUTHOR

Johnny Compton is the author of the Bram Stoker® Award-nominated *The Spite House*. His short stories have appeared in *PseudoPod*, *Strange Horizons*, *The NoSleep Podcast*, and many other outlets. He is a Horror Writers Association member and creator and host of the podcast *Healthy Fears*.

XII
יב
١٢
十二
12